A Beth-Hill Novel: Wild Hunt Series, Book 5: All that Glitters

By Jennifer St. Clair

Writers Exchange E-Publishing
http://www.writers-exchange.com

A Beth-Hill Novel: Wild Hunt Series, Book 5: All that Glitters

Writers Exchange E-Publishing
PO Box 372
ATHERTON QLD 4883

Cover Art by: Germancreative

Published by Writers Exchange E-Publishing
http://www.writers-exchange.com

To Grey, with love.

Arthur

Arthur met Iris the year they both turned twelve. She was a cousin; a Morgan, yes, but her status in the household would never amount to anything because of her parents, who had left to raise their daughter away from the household, only for her mother to return with her tails tucked between their legs (he didn't quite understand this analogy, since they were vampires, not werewolves, but his grandmother had said it, so it must be true.) Iris' father had died in a Hunter attack. Arthur never wondered about the truth of that story, because it seemed to happen quite frequently to vampires who had left the household to live on their own.

Iris was small and dainty and blonde, and when Arthur first met her, wore a frilly pink dress and pigtails, which he pulled. And she'd burst into tears and run away from him, and he'd expected not to see her again, because she was obviously a coward and unsuited for life in the Morgan household. But she had appeared the next day during class time, when the children of the household gathered to learn (certain, specific, *approved* things) and where Arthur knew he could do whatever he wanted, because he would not get into trouble.

Not by anyone important, at least.

So, the second time he met Iris, he took a pair of scissors from the teacher's desk and he cut off one of her braids.

She had two of them, after all. And he was honestly quite confused when Iris burst into tears again and when the teacher, who wouldn't go so far as to actually discipline the son of the head of the household, confiscated the scissors.

Arthur placed the braid in the room his father had given him for his trophies, which was where Iris found him a few hours later, minus the other braid now. Short, her hair curled in ringlets around her elfin face.

No one had ever followed him to the trophy room before. No one important, at least. And Iris was absolutely not supposed to be there, but being so new, Arthur had to wonder if anyone had told her the rules yet.

"I've come for my braid," Iris said, and held out one small hand. "Please."

Arthur stared at her solemnly. "It's mine," he said. "By right of conquest."

"I would like it back, please," Iris said, equally solemn, and strangely unafraid.

She should have been afraid.

"Do you know who I am?" Arthur asked haughtily, but she wasn't listening to him now; she'd seen past him and into his trophy room, and her eyes grew wide.

With awe, Arthur thought at first. He *was,* after all, very proud of his trophies. And, in turn, his father was very proud of him *because* of his trophies.

"Would you like to see them?" he asked, and picked up the nearest one; not yet mounted; a tiny fairy no larger than his hand with beautiful butterfly wings he'd been careful not to damage.

Iris gasped. Reached out to touch the fairy; Arthur moved it out of her reach, wary that she would inadvertently destroy it.

"You are Arthur Morgan," she said, answering his previous question. "Only son of Ichabod Morgan, who is the head of this household." She paused. "And not a nice person."

Arthur stared at her. No one had ever said that to him before, and he wasn't quite certain how to respond. "What is a 'nice person'?" he asked eventually.

The look she gave him was rather akin to the look his father gave those who'd displeased him, right before their executions.

"A nice person doesn't cut off other people's hair, or kill fairies," Iris said.

Arthur nodded, on firmer ground now. "Then you're right," he said. "I'm not a nice person."

Iris gave him another look, but he couldn't interpret this one as easily. To cover his ignorance, he said, "You shouldn't be here."

"I came for my braid," Iris reminded him, unconcerned by her trespass. She folded her arms. "And I'm not leaving until you give it back."

"Then I'll call the guards," Arthur told her smugly. "And they'll drag you away and throw you in a cell, and you will die." Nearly all of those who argued with his father died in the cells; Arthur had watched the executions. He wasn't quite certain--exactly--if Iris *would* be dragged away (probably screaming and crying) if he called for the guards; he'd never actually had to call for the guards before.

Would they even come for him?

"My braid," Iris said ominously, and stuck out her hand.

"I won't give it to you," Arthur decided.

"Then I'll scream," Iris threatened. "And if anyone comes, I will say that you tried to kill me for your trophy room."

"But that would be a lie," Arthur said, puzzled. "I'm only supposed to trap and kill the small folk for my trophies."

"Then why won't you give me back my braid?" Iris asked.

Arthur looked at her curiously. "Because I like it."

Iris sighed. "Wouldn't it have looked better still attached?"

"I don't think so," Arthur said. "You could have changed it. You cut off the other one--but the one I have will look the same, forever."

Iris frowned at him. "Nothing is the same forever," she said.

Arthur showed her the fairy again. "They are," he said simply.

"What do you do with them?" Iris asked, staring past him at the trophies that hung on the walls.

The only people who had ever shown an interest in Arthur's trophies were his father and grandmother, the latter who had closely inspected his delicate work at preserving them, and, eventually, had grudgingly declared that Arthur was really doing the household a service by ridding the forest of vermin.

His father had responded by encouraging him with books on taxidermy and bottles of poisons and weapons that were useless against the small folk if he wanted to preserve them. The poisons had come in handy, however, and so had the books, even if they were more on preserving animals and not fairies. He had never accidentally poisoned himself, or anyone else. Arthur was too careful for mistakes.

And he wasn't about to complain. He'd seen what happened to those who dared complain to his father, and had no doubt he would suffer the same fate if he dared to do so himself.

And no one, until now, had ever asked him to explain himself.

"They're my trophies," he said, and wondered if that was enough of an explanation for Iris. He suspected not.

His father had never forbidden him from showing his trophy room to anyone, but Arthur couldn't imagine that he'd be pleased by Iris' presence.

Perhaps he didn't need to know.

"I can show you," he offered, then immediately wanted to take back his words, because he knew someone would have seen her come here, and he knew he would be punished if his father--or grandmother--found out what he had done.

But no one had ever dared to ask to see his trophies. And Arthur suddenly found that he truly wanted her to say yes.

"Okay," Iris said uncertainly, as if she sensed some of his unease. And she made a little sound when he grabbed her hand and pulled her inside; only a small sound, but a sound, nonetheless. And Arthur slowly closed the door behind her, tense for the shout of discovery.

He heard nothing beyond the door.

When he turned to face Iris, she stood near his workbench, staring down at his current project, wide-eyed at the tiny pile of bones beside the carefully preserved skin of the fairy he'd been working on. The wings were already completed; they graced the wire armature that would become the basis of the trophy's skeleton once the skin finished curing.

"Don't touch anything!" He tried not to shout, but the words came out sharper than he intended.

"I wasn't," Iris said. She sounded a bit annoyed that he wouldn't trust her, although he wouldn't have put it past her to take something away from him in retaliation for her braid. He wondered if he should just give it to her, then realized she would probably just discard it, because it was of no use to her now.

At least if *he* kept it, he could keep it safe.

Without speaking, Iris moved away from the workbench to look at the trophies Arthur had hung on the wall. They were more recent; his earlier attempts at preservation had not worked out so well, although his father had never said a word against them, Arthur had been a bit embarrassed to leave them up, now that he knew more about preservation. He'd buried the early mistakes in the forest, with no thought for the creatures he had killed. The trophies were all that mattered, especially since his father approved.

And his father's approval was--and would remain--a very important thing.

"You've killed all of these fairies," Iris said sadly, and reached up to gently stroke the edge of an iridescent wing.

"Yes," Arthur said. "What *else* would I do with them?"

Iris' frown deepened. "You could let them go," she said. "Leave them in peace to live out their lives."

"But then how would I get my trophies?" Arthur asked, because she clearly did not understand. And he didn't think he would be able to make her do so.

She sniffed, frowned again, then said, "I'm leaving."

"I won't stop you," Arthur said. "But--" he hesitated, then, not wanting to owe her anything for her silence.

"I won't tell anyone what you do here," Iris said quickly, then added, "Do you think you could--maybe--let the next one go?"

Arthur didn't answer. He *couldn't* answer, because he knew he couldn't do that; his father approved of his trophies and expected him to bring at least one back each time. He'd perfected a way to kill the fairies quickly, at least, without harming a hair on their heads. They did not suffer, but he could not let them go.

Perhaps Iris saw some of his thoughts in the expression on his face. Perhaps she'd given up on him as a lost cause. Either way, she nodded and let herself out without another word.

Only later did he realize that she'd taken back her braid when he'd opened the drawer he'd stored it in and found it gone.

He did not pursue her or demand it back. Secretly, he admired her courage, and wished he could be so brave. Secretly, he wondered what would happen if he returned without a trophy, for whatever reason.

His father's temper was a volatile, unpredictable thing, and something Arthur had--of yet--avoided.

Later, after sunset, he left his workroom and walked down the hall, speaking to no one, although no one ever tried to speak to him at all, except for Iris. And perhaps it was Iris that made him realize how the others fell silent as he approached; how they would not meet his gaze; how they tried their best to pretend he wasn't among them, as if they thought that Arthur, by extension, would treat them like his father for any imagined--or real--transgression.

He'd set his traps the day before, out in the forest. Arthur did not have to ask permission to leave the house and grounds like everyone else; he did not have to notify his father or grandmother of his whereabouts, or what he intended to do, because he left the house for only one reason: to bring back trophies.

He *did* stop in the kitchen for a handful of sugar cubes; the fairies could not resist sugar cubes, and the bell jars he used as traps had proved to be quite efficient.

In fact, Arthur had lost all sense of challenge long ago, now that he had perfected both his traps and his method to dispatch his prey. And as he approached his first trap, he saw a small form inside the jar. This was not unexpected. Nor was the fact that the fairy had eaten all the sugar cubes he'd left inside, and now, presumably, had fallen asleep, curled up on its side.

Or dead, Arthur thought, seeing what looked like a smear of blood on the glass.

He crouched down in front of it and gently tapped on the jar. The fairy's wings were in tatters, and it was much thinner and dirtier than the others he'd caught, although the dirt could have been due to the fact that it apparently had tried to escape by digging a tunnel to freedom. It hadn't gotten very far since the ground was rocky and hard here, which was one of the reasons why Arthur had set the trap in this spot and not another.

The fairy did not respond to his tap, so he eased up the edge of the jar and slipped a thin mat underneath, gently easing the fairy's body onto the mat. It would seal once he inverted it, and then his captive would be trapped until he dispatched it with the gas.

But this fairy seemed to be dead already. At least, it made no peep; no move to attempt to fly; its limbs flopped carelessly as Arthur inverted the glass and sealed its fate. Its eyes were open; blankly staring; its mouth hung loose; its tongue stuck out grotesquely.

It wasn't even worth his time to bother with, considering his other traps were likely occupied.

He unsealed the jar and removed its occupant by dumping it out onto a nearby fallen tree trunk. The fairy lay sprawled every-which-way, unmoving. Not breathing, either, as far as Arthur could tell.

He did not leave it lying there, but took a square of cloth out of his pocket and transferred the fairy's body onto it. And then, he carefully wrapped the corpse, dug a shallow grave, and laid the fairy to rest. After that, he cleaned off the bell jar, reset the trap, and gathered his supplies to move on to the next trap.

And then, abruptly, he sensed that he was no longer alone.

His first thought was that Iris had followed him somehow; his next that the fairy had returned to life, even though the grave seemed to be undisturbed. And he doubted that Iris could hide from him so thoroughly, which meant it was likely another fairy or one of the small folk.

Unconcerned, he made his way to the second trap, which was empty and untriggered. The sugar cubes had melted into an unpalatable mess, however, so he replaced them and moved on.

The last trap was beside a nearly dry creekbed that tended to flood when it rained. This one was occupied by a specimen with wings flecked with green and gold and purple; a riot of color that managed not to become overwhelming at all, considering its hair was fluffy like a dandelion gone to seed and nearly the same color. It was standing as he approached, its hands pressed against the glass, just staring at him, unafraid.

What if he *did* let this one go? What if he took Iris' advice and let it fly free? What if he returned home and informed his father that the traps had been empty? Would his father kill him right away like he had some of the others? Or would he give Arthur a second chance to prove himself?

"I'm sorry," Arthur said, feeling awkward, because he had no idea if the fairy could understand him, much less sympathize with his plight, especially since he intended to kill it. Still, it *was* legal prey, despite what Iris believed. And she was just a silly girl anyway, wasn't she?

He avoided the fairy's gaze and prepared the mat to slip under it, feeling dull now, hopeless that he could safely attempt Iris' suggestion that he let one of the fairies go free without losing his life in the process.

What would the rest of his life be like? An endless circle of trophies as he grew older? And perhaps his father would eventually give him orders to kill those who betrayed him; perhaps he would be groomed to become his father's executioner, destined to have blood on his hands for the rest of his life.

All of a sudden, Arthur realized that he didn't *want* to become his father's executioner. He did not want any more innocent blood on his hands.

He drew in his breath sharply. Knelt there on the ground with his supplies around him; supplies enough to kill a dozen fairies, and likely enough to kill one young vampire as well, or, at the very least, knock him unconscious so that the sun could do its job come dawn.

Or he could slit his wrists and let the blood loss weaken him enough to prevent him from returning home.

He realized his hands were shaking now; he felt a bit dizzy and short of breath. But even then, realizing he was frightened--terrified, really--did not weaken his resolve.

Before he could stop himself, he pushed the bell jar over--the fairy crouched down as if it expected him to try to grab it, but Arthur let the jar roll away, where it shattered against a nearby rock as he turned his back on the fairy.

How should he do it? Would the poisons in his bag even *affect* a vampire? He had syringes for injection, but would drinking it work better? Or both?

He heard something rustle behind him as he inserted the needle into a bottle of poison and pulled the plunger up to fill the syringe, but he did not look around; the fairies couldn't stop him, after all, and no one would have followed him out of the house. Perhaps they'd find a pile of ash when they realized he was gone; he doubted anyone would notice his absence before dawn, and he thought he was far away from the house that they would have trouble tracking him down, especially since there weren't any werewolves to sniff out his trail.

Some of the households hired werewolves, but the Morgans did not.

Keeping his mind carefully blank, Arthur squirted a bit of the poison out of the needle (although it didn't matter, really, if there was any air trapped inside, since he intended to die from this) and then rolled up his sleeve.

For a moment, he wished Iris was there so that he could tell her that she'd been correct; that he wasn't a nice person, and likely would never be a nice person, and that was why he'd decided to do this, but he had no way to tell her this, and he didn't want to leave her a note, so he inserted the needle into a vein in his arm and pressed the plunger down--

It was cold; searingly cold; with numb fingers, he removed the lid from another bottle and drank it down for good measure, and then he realized he'd fallen forward into the dirt and leaves and that his muscles seemed to be moving on their own; jerking his arms and legs as if attempting to throw off the effects of the poison, and there was no pain, at least; just searing cold and numbness, just that, nothing more.

And then, dimly, he heard a voice above him. And the voice asked, "Do you suppose he knows he's past the Veil?"

And another voice answered with a question, "Why would he do this to himself?"

The second voice was a small voice, soft like he imagined the fairy's hair would be. Arthur tried to open his eyes to identify the speakers, but he had no control over his body now; no control at all, and he couldn't do anything but slip further and further into darkness, until there was nothing left of himself at all.

He awoke with the warmth of the sun on his face, but he had no strength for panic because his stomach seemed to be trying to turn itself inside out. Vampires did not get sick unless they were poisoned and Arthur had, very effectively, poisoned himself. He couldn't open his eyes; couldn't feel anything except the warmth of sun on his face.

The warmth of the sun--

He heard a noise; a moan, and realized the noise came from his own lips. Feeling slowly returned, not that he particularly wanted it to, considering he hadn't expected to wake up at all.

He heard something else, then; the faint crackle of flames, but they were off to his left, not the result of his body burning in the sun. And he felt something scratchy on his bare skin--a blanket?

No one from the Morgan household would have given him a blanket. Except maybe Iris, and she wouldn't have known how to start a fire.

When he tried to open his eyes, the light was so bright; so terrifyingly bright that he heard himself cry out; his body twisted sideways, trying to escape the searing light.

"Does he know?" a voice asked very close to his ear.

"Likely not," another voice commented; a quietly powerful voice that sent chills up Arthur's spine. A moment later, something fell across his head; another blanket. Darkness, blessed darkness reigned, but he still couldn't see; orange and yellow sunbursts dazzled his sight from his brief glimpse of the sun. He drew in a breath. Coughed, then ventured, "I'm not dead."

"But I bet you wish you were," the first voice commented.

Arthur couldn't answer that. "Please let me die."

"I'm sorry," the second voice said. Both were female, but this one sounded bossier than the first. "That would entail dragging you past the Veil, because I doubt you can walk right now, and neither of us are inclined to do that."

"Then I'll crawl," Arthur managed to say, but nothing happened when he tried to move. Presently, knowing they were probably laughing at him, even though he heard nothing, he asked, "Why *past* the Veil?"

"Because the sunlight in Faerie won't harm you," the first voice said quietly. "You didn't know? They didn't tell you?"

Arthur thought about lying to protect what fragile dignity he had left, but then he remembered that he lay at their mercy, covered with blankets against the sun, but not, apparently, to protect him from its rays. No, they'd given him the blankets for *comfort,* and word completely alien in the Morgan household.

"I imagine my father knows," he finally said. "But I also imagine he would never think to share that information with anyone."

"And who is your father?" the second voice asked.

"His name is Ichabod Morgan," Arthur murmured, hoping that they'd realize his importance now and kill him; they had to, didn't they? Especially if they thought his father would care? "The head of the Morgan household," he added, just in case they didn't know.

"Ah," the second voice said in a sort of tone that made Arthur suspect she'd already known this. "Your name is Arthur, then."

"Yes," Arthur said, seeing no reason to lie.

"And why do you want to die so badly, Arthur Morgan?" the first voice asked.

Arthur felt something hot and wet slide across his face and dribble down his cheeks. "Will I die?" he asked mournfully.

"From this?" the second voice asked. "No. The poison you took will only make you feel wretched for a little while, and we've already explained about the sunlight."

"I do feel very wretched," Arthur admitted, which was true, because the pain in his stomach had not subsided, and he felt horribly dizzy and weak.

The first voice, he thought, stifled a laugh. Or, really, more of a giggle, which awoke anger, which pushed away some of the pain. But anger was useless here; he knew that instinctively, because he had no true status outside the household; not one that mattered, anyway. And anyway, a vampire lying on the ground covered with blankets was probably an amusing sight. They would probably laugh at him long after he was gone.

"Blossom," the second voice said sharply; a rebuke.

"I apologize for laughing at you," the first voice said quietly.

"I'd probably laugh at me too," Arthur murmured, and closed his eyes.

"Why do you wish to die so badly?" the second voice asked.

In a monotone, Arthur told them how he had come to his failed decision. He didn't mention Iris or how he had come to even consider releasing one of the fairies. And he wasn't entirely certain what would happen to him now; or if he could, perhaps, find another way to end his life. It was, after all, past dawn now. There was a slim possibility that no one would miss him for a little while, at least, so he still had time. Only, he wasn't certain how long it would take him to crawl to the edge of the Veil.

To be honest, he wasn't quite sure of anything at all, including which direction to crawl. Or *how* to crawl, for that matter, since his arms and legs seemed to be on revolt.

"I see," the second voice said, entirely neutral. "That is quite a dilemma."

"Not really," Arthur told her. "The simplest solution is for me to die. Don't you see?" He managed to raise his head--just a little, and opened his eyes. Light leaked in from under the edge of the blanket now; it made his eyes water even more.

"What if there's an alternative?" the second voice asked.

"There is no alternative," Arthur whispered, and lowered his head again. He didn't want to hear alternatives or platitudes or anything at all, because none of that mattered, since his father would likely kill him if he returned home without a trophy.

And death by his father's hands would be much more painful than death by his own.

"How old are you?" the second voice asked curiously.

"Why does it matter?" Arthur asked, despondent now; he truly could not see a way out of this, not without more pain, and he was in enough pain as it was. He closed his eyes. Maybe if he stayed silent, they would leave him alone.

Probably not, but he could hope.

"Because you're awfully young to want to throw away your life," the second voice said quietly. "And you not wanting to become your father's executioner tells *me* that there's something in that heart of yours worth saving."

Forgetting he'd decided to ignore them, Arthur said, "My father would not agree." And then, "Nor would my grandmother."

"Your grandmother raised your father," the second voice said. "Remember that."

Arthur had never thought about it that way before, not that it helped anything at all, of course. Had his grandmother molded his father into what he had become? And, in turn, his father had molded him? Was it too late for Arthur to do anything about it? He'd been killing the small folk for years already; what sort of sacrifice would it take for him to set his sights on larger prey? He remembered what Iris had threatened; to tell the guards that he had intended to kill her for his trophy room. Would they have believed her?

He felt sick at the thought. Small folk were--they were one thing. Easily captured; easily dispatched. But other vampires? Humans, even? Where would it end?

"Your thoughts are very dark," the first voice--Blossom, he remembered--said, loudly enough for him to think that she crouched right beside his ear, close enough for him to reach out and touch.

He didn't try to reach out and touch her, though. He'd already decided that she was the fairy he'd released. The other voice, the older one, was more difficult to classify. "You can read my thoughts?" Arthur asked, horrified.

"I can feel them," Blossom said. "Like a tsunami of despair, enveloping everything else in your mind."

"What's a tsunami?" Arthur asked.

"A very big wave that destroys everything in its path," the second voice said.

That sounded about right. And Arthur was just about to sink back into the tsunami when Blossom asked, "Who is Iris?"

The waves of pain were lessening, but left him weak and dizzy and nauseous. Perhaps he'd said Iris' name aloud; perhaps Blossom could really read his thoughts. He hadn't intended to tell them about her, but he found himself telling them about her anyway, and what he had done, and what she had suggested he do.

"I'm surprised you spoke to her at all, considering she had no status in the household," the second voice said after he was finished.

"She spoke to *me,"* Arthur whispered. "No one does that." And then, he realized that if he never returned; if he did manage to die out here in the forest, Iris would be the first one questioned; the first one killed by his father's wrath. By deciding to commit suicide, he had effectively killed her anyway, because someone would have seen her on her way to Arthur's trophy room, and that someone would not hesitate to turn her in for a favor from Arthur's father when he tried to determine what had happened to his son.

That's how things worked in the Morgan household.

"What do you mean, 'you've become what your father wanted anyway'?" the second voice asked.

Arthur hadn't realized he'd spoken aloud. "Iris will be killed when my father tries to find out what happened to me," he said. "And it will be my fault." From somewhere deep inside, he found the strength to push himself upright, although he did not remove the blankets. Sitting up, however, made the dizziness increase, and the sunlight piercing through the edges of the blanket didn't help, because it made the nausea increase, and so he huddled there for a moment with his arms wrapped around his stomach, trying desperately not to be sick.

"I have to go back."

"I don't think you're in any condition to go anywhere just yet," the second voice said. "And anyway, what will your father think if you come crawling back to the household without a trophy?"

"Maybe Iris won't be blamed, then," Arthur whispered. "And he'll just kill me instead." He shuddered at the thought, because he'd *watched* the executions; he knew exactly what to expect.

"What if--" the second voice began, and Arthur's temper exploded.

"There are no 'what ifs'!" He shouted the words, or, rather, raised his voice as much as he possibly could. "There are no alternatives! There are no other choices!"

And then, he fell over, because that had taken the last of his strength. And he closed his eyes and let himself fall into darkness.

This time, when he awoke, he felt something cool draped across his face, and sensed that he no longer lay in the forest beside a campfire in full sunlight. Water dripped somewhere in the distance, echoing faintly; he opened his eyes and saw fading sunbursts at first; it seemed to take ages for his eyes to adjust. But when they adjusted, he saw stone walls around him, and sand beneath him, damp and cool, and realized he either lay in a cave or a dungeon, deep down underground.

Instead of feeling panicked, he felt--calm. It was so quiet and peaceful away from the sunlight that he found himself starting to drift off again; he curled up under the blanket and dislodged a wet washcloth from his forehead. He had no idea how much time had passed, and wouldn't have cared if he hadn't remembered Iris and what might happen to her if he did not return.

That was the only thing that propelled him to an upright position. The only thing that made him even remotely curious about his surroundings, which were too natural to be a dungeon. No human--or vampire--hand had carved these walls.

So, a cave, although he supposed a cave could double as a dungeon, nonetheless.

He stood on shaky legs and wrapped the blanket around him, because the air here was cool and damp, and while he'd welcomed the coolness while lying under the blanket, his clothes were also damp and that made it feel even colder. And perhaps the poison's effects were still coursing through his body, because he found it difficult to close his hand tightly around the blanket to keep it in place; it was as if his fingers had decided to stop working, although he saw nothing obvious wrong with them.

He seemed to be alone in this quiet place; they'd left him to recover or to die or just to get him away from the sunlight. He wondered where they were; Blossom and the other person. Had they left him in disgust? In frustration? In anger?

He turned around in the middle of the narrow space so that he could see his entire surroundings. There were two openings--a continuation of the space he'd been left in. Saw a cloth bag sitting against the wall near one of the openings. Crouched to open it, and found two stoppered and sealed bottles.

He'd seen those bottles before, even though the Morgan household's official position on bottled blood was to pretend it didn't exist. It just wasn't feasible to feed every single vampire in a household fresh blood from human veins. The care and feeding of the humans involved was much more costly than buying bottled blood and allowing the vampires to believe they were drinking fresh blood. Those humans kept for feeding only fed the elite of the household, and were not well cared for. Arthur wasn't allowed to go into the human section of the household. Or, at least, he'd never asked, and his father had never offered to show him. He had only rumors to go on, and those rumors weren't kind to the humans involved.

With difficulty, Arthur turned his mind away from those thoughts and studied the two bottles. He supposed he should drink one of them if he'd decided to return, because he would need his strength for a little while, at least, until he could find a way to die that would not mean Iris' death as well.

But then again, if he died out here and then Iris died because of him, he would never know, since he would be dead.

That thought did not cheer him as much as it should have.

In the end, exhausted from walking only a few feet, he sat down beside the bag and drank one of the bottles. And then he fell asleep again, curled up against the wall.

When he opened his eyes, the fairy was watching him from atop an outcropping of rocks. She sat with her legs crossed, leaning forward with her chin on her fists, just watching him, although she straightened up when she saw that he was awake.

"You drank," she said, approvingly.

"You're Blossom," he whispered in response. He hadn't vomited up anything, but his stomach still didn't feel right, and the dizziness had returned while he slept.

"I am," the fairy said, and launched herself from the rocks, fluttering close enough to touch, although he didn't bother to try. She peered into the bag. "You should drink the other one."

"I don't think I can right now," Arthur said, and closed his eyes.

"What if I helped you?" Blossom asked.

No one had ever offered to help Arthur before, at least, not without some ulterior motive. Arthur opened his eyes and looked at her closely. He saw nothing false in her gaze. "It's not that--that I don't want to drink it," he finally said. "I'm afraid that if I drink it, I'll just throw it up again." And then, he said, "I didn't know fairies could talk." Somehow, the fact that they could made it so much worse that he had killed so many of them. He felt something hot and wet slip down the sides of his face and covered his head with the blanket so that she wouldn't see his tears.

"There's a lot you don't know about fairies," Blossom said after a moment. "And the small folk, as well."

"It doesn't matter now," Arthur whispered, and didn't even try to stop the tears. "Nothing matters now."

"Except for Iris," Blossom reminded him, but that only made him cry harder; he curled up in a ball and sobbed because he had no other recourse. He had done terrible, terrible, *terrible* things. The small folk and the fairies should have been lining up to kill him, not giving him bottled blood to drink and patting him on the shoulder through the blanket with a hand barely bigger than his thumb.

"Why didn't you leave me there?" he asked, his voice rough with tears. "Why?"

"Because you were hurt," Blossom said. "Because you let me go." She hesitated. "Because Maya said you didn't deserve to die."

"Maya is the other voice," Arthur said after a moment. "The one who sounds as if she expects to be obeyed."

"She does, doesn't she?" Blossom asked, and giggled. "Yes, her name is Maya. She should be back soon."

Cautiously, Arthur lowered the blanket and wiped away the remnants of his tears. "Where did she go?" Would it be smart to express any interest in her whereabouts? Should he just accept the fact that she'd left him here with Blossom as a nursemaid and not ask any questions?

Blossom glanced towards the doorway, or opening, presumably the one that led outside. "She went to ask someone she trusts about your options, without naming any names or identifying you in any way." She said the latter part as if she expected him to protest, but he no longer cared.

"I have no options," Arthur said woodenly. He managed to get to his feet, and, holding onto the wall with one hand and the blanket with the other, lurched towards the doorway that presumably led outside. "Which way is the Veil?"

"It's still day outside," Blossom said. "You can't--" He felt the breeze of her passage ruffle the hair on top of his head, but he ignored her and concentrated on putting one foot in front of the other. And then, when he turned a corner and encountered the searing brightness of sunlight again, she finished, "see. You've never been outside during the day, have you?"

He'd fallen back, eyes streaming, barely able to take a breath. "No." But then, determined, he draped the blanket over his head and walked out of the cave, straight into a tree.

This time, when he fell over, he decided he would not get up, and he did not try to brush the fairy away when she draped the blanket over his face again.

"Maya will be back soon," she said. "I'll be here with you until then."

"Why?"

"Because you were kind to me," Blossom said, and he felt her hand on his shoulder again, trying to comfort him even though no comfort could be found.

"Not on purpose," Arthur said. "I don't know how to be kind, or nice, or anything that Iris thinks is important." He paused. "All I know how to do is kill fairies and small folk, and preserve them for my trophies."

"But you can *learn* to be kind and nice and everything that Iris thinks is important," Blossom said encouragingly. "You can learn to do other things, too."

"Not in the Morgan household," Arthur said hopelessly, and she fell silent, obviously agreeing with him.

But then, she said, "I could show you how to be nice right now. Just a little niceness, nothing too difficult. And then, even if you do die, you'll know what it means, at least."

Arthur thought about this for a moment. "What is it?" he asked. "What do you want me to do?"

"Drink the rest of what Maya brought, and offer me a sugar cube, since I didn't bring anything to eat," Blossom said promptly. "Share a meal with me."

"And how is that being nice?" Arthur asked curiously.

"You're offering me something to eat," Blossom said. "Without any reason."

"Other than I know fairies really like sugar cubes," Arthur pointed out. "And I don't know what happened to my bag."

"It's in the cave," Blossom said. "Maya brought it. She cleaned up everything and brought it with us."

What would it hurt to do this? To venture back into the cave and give her a sugar cube while he finished the first bottle and opened the second? He *knew* he would feel better if he drank more blood. If he didn't throw it up afterwards, at least.

"I'll help you," Blossom said. "Just--follow the sound of my voice. I won't direct you the wrong way."

Arthur supposed he would have to trust her, not that she'd tried to hurt him yet. In fact, she seemed to have plenty of patience, despite the fact that he believed his situation to be hopeless and that he wouldn't live very long once he returned to the household.

Once he could walk without running into trees, at least. Once he could find his way back.

But he took her at her word this time, and crawled back into the cave, and she directed him into the dark coolness without a single wrong turn. And he leaned back against the wall and rested for a little while because his eyes needed to adjust again, and then he managed to walk back into the room where he'd awakened. And he saw his bag sitting against the opposite wall where someone had placed it, and nearly overbalanced when he crouched down in front of it to remove the little bag of sugar cubes.

But he managed. He carried the bag over to the bottles, sat down, and solemnly offered a sugar cube to Blossom, who held it with both hands and took a large bite.

Well, a very *small* bite to Arthur, but it took her a moment of chewing before she could speak again.

"Now you," she said, and he lifted the bottle to his lips and drank.

"This is being nice?" he asked, because it really made no sense; Iris had said nice people didn't cut off braids or kill fairies, but she'd not told him what nice people actually *did.* Just the simple act of sharing a meal was nice?

He'd seen it many times before, even in the household, with mothers and children and husbands and wives.

He supposed Iris' mother had been nice by braiding her hair that first day.

"This is being nice," Blossom confirmed, and Arthur heard a small sound past the doorway. Not a large enough sound to be Maya, but a small enough sound to be another fairy, or one of the small folk.

Blossom's eyes widened. She quickly shoved the rest of the sugar cube in her mouth and flew through the doorway, as if to shoo the other fairy--or fairies--away.

"There's a whole bag," Arthur said. "And unless you planned to eat them all, you could share too."

He felt better now. Not perfect, but better. Not well enough to tackle the sunlight, but well enough to realize that he would likely be able to walk home once the sun set. And, clear-eyed, he realized he would be walking home to his death, but that seemed to be okay now. He wasn't frightened.

Not anymore, at least.

Blossom poked her head back through the doorway. "Um," she said. "They must have smelled the sugar cubes when you opened the bag."

Arthur held it out. "There's plenty. Well, maybe thirty or so left."

"There are ten fairies," Blossom reported. "If you don't mind."

"I won't need them anymore," Arthur said, and removed ten sugar cubes from the bag.

"Hold out your hand, then," Blossom said, and he obeyed. He almost wanted to close his eyes, but he did not, and watched as one fairy after another crept into the narrow room, snatched a sugar cube from his hand, and vanished back the way they'd come.

Only the last one spoke. "Thank you," she said in a very small voice, her eyes wide as if she knew exactly who he was and what he had done.

"You're welcome," Arthur said, because that was probably the correct response. "There's still more left," he said to Blossom once they were gone. "They don't stay fresh very long. Would you like another one?"

"No, thank you," Blossom said, and he found himself oddly annoyed by her refusal. Wouldn't it be *nicer* to say yes, regardless? She must have seen something on his face, because she added, "But if you want to share more, I can find other fairies."

"I'm tired," Arthur said, and retreated to his blanket, unable to explain how he felt, and why. He left the bag of sugar cubes on the floor.

Blossom ignored the bag and followed him. "Why are you angry?" she asked.

"I'm not angry," Arthur said, but he *was* angry; angry and sad at the same time. "I don't know. You--you said you didn't want another sugar cube, even when I offered you one."

"Because I didn't *want* one," Blossom said patiently. "Because I'd eaten one already." When he didn't respond, she continued. "If I'd taken one and then thrown it away, how would you have felt?"

"Angry," Arthur said after a moment. "And confused. I think."

"But you're angry and sad because I told you the truth," Blossom said. "Why is that?"

"Because I offered you something, and you refused," Arthur told her. "What's nice about that?"

"Not everyone will take what you offer," Blossom said quietly. "And that doesn't mean they're being cruel. Sometimes it means they just don't want what you have. And that's okay. It doesn't mean they're not nice."

"I don't understand," Arthur said, and turned his back on her, wrapping himself in the blanket again.

"Why don't you get some rest?" Blossom asked. "I'll stay with you, like I promised."

"You should go," Arthur whispered, and closed his eyes. After a little while, he felt her hand on his shoulder again, and then, gently, she wiped away his tears with a scrap of cloth.

"Sleep," she whispered in his ear. "Sleep."

Arthur slept.

When he awoke, something had changed. Perhaps it was because he had finished the second bottle; perhaps it was because Blossom had curled up on his lap and fallen asleep, resting her head on the crook of his arm. Perhaps it was the faint rustle of paper behind him; apparently someone or something had decided to help themselves to the sugar cubes.

Arthur did not mind, or particularly care.

"You'd best," a familiar voice said quietly, "save some for later."

"They don't last," Arthur murmured, and the sugar cube thief squeaked and the rustling stopped. Arthur raised his head to look at Maya for the first time.

As he'd thought, she wasn't a fairy or one of the small folk, even. She was taller than him, an adult, and wore her hair in long ropes that looked like seaweed. (Not that Arthur had ever seen seaweed before, of course, but he'd seen a picture once, in a book before his father burned it.) Her green tinged skin named her as some sort of water fairy, but Arthur didn't know what kind.

It also didn't seem like she was wearing any clothing, at least at first, but that changed as he stared at her, as if some sort of magical censor had decided he shouldn't see her naked.

"You're Maya," he said, unafraid.

"I am," she agreed. "And you are Arthur Morgan, and in a world of trouble."

"No," Arthur said. "I'll be dead soon, so it won't matter how much trouble I'm in." He couldn't tell if the sun had set, and didn't want to disturb the sleeping fairy, so he stayed where he was, sitting against the wall.

"What if you don't have to die?" Maya asked.

"I have to," Arthur told her. "Otherwise, I'll become what my father wants me to become, and I don't want that to happen." He felt very calm about this now. He'd made his decision; now all he had to do was return home and accept the consequences of his actions.

He wondered if his father would kill him quickly, or if he would linger for days like some of the others.

"You think your father will kill you because you'll return without a trophy," Maya said. "What if I give you a trophy?"

"Then what about next time?" Arthur asked. "And the time after that?" He held himself very still as Blossom awoke, and stretched, and gently patted his arm as if to thank it for being such a nice pillow. "And what happens when my father wants me to--" He couldn't think about that right now, so he stopped talking. "Has the sun set?"

"Nearly," Maya said, and glanced away, towards the entrance of the cave.

"Then I thank you for your hospitality, but it's time for me to go," Arthur said formally, and forced his legs to hold him. Blossom launched herself into the air and hovered in front of him, frowning. Arthur tried his best to ignore her.

"I heard you shared your sugar cubes," Maya said.

"They can have the rest of them," Arthur said. "I don't care." He shed the blanket, too, and stood there in the cool air, shivering. And then, with one hand on the wall, he started to move past Maya from where she sat near the doorway.

She reached out to stop him. "Wait. Please."

"Nothing you do will help," Arthur said quietly. "Even if I bring back a trophy and my father doesn't kill me for being out past dawn, he will still want me to kill for him, eventually. I know this for a fact."

"How old are you?" Maya asked.

Arthur didn't want to answer her. He didn't want to see pity in her gaze. "Twelve."

"If you never went back, they would search for you," Maya said. "And likely kill scores of us before they gave up."

"I know," Arthur told her. "I don't want that to happen either." He met her gaze. "It's better this way."

And perhaps that would have been the end, of Arthur and of trophies and of everything else. Perhaps he would have returned empty-handed, and perhaps his father would have killed him without a single thought.

"I can give you a trophy to bring back with you," Maya said. "This time, and every other time until you are of age and can flee safely."

"It will never be safe for me to flee," Arthur said, but he was wavering now; he didn't really (truly) want to die by his father's hand.

If he had any sort of choice in the matter of his life or death.

"You could save Iris," Maya said, and that decided everything.

"How?" Arthur asked.

"Do you trust her?" Maya asked.

"I think she is trustworthy," Arthur said. "We've really only just met."

"If you take her into your confidence, you wouldn't be alone," Maya said. "And you could visit with us when you come to claim your trophies, and we can teach you what you'll never learn in the Morgan household."

To not be alone seemed more important than anything, especially now. He started to speak, but had to stop and clear his throat. "Like what?"

"Sharing sugar cubes with the fairies was a good start," Maya said. "But we can help you become a better person. A nicer person. A person Iris would want to be her friend."

Her friend. Arthur didn't have any friends.

How would it feel to have one?

"I could be your friend, too," Blossom offered.

"Oh," Arthur said, shocked. "Why--why would you want to do that?"

Blossom smiled. "Because you can bring more sugar cubes," she said.

Arthur could understand this; she wanted something from him, so she offered to be his friend. "I could," he said, but didn't miss Maya's frown. Carefully, he asked, "Why are you frowning? Don't you want her to be my friend?"

"Not because of sugar cubes," Maya said.

Blossom flew up to Arthur's face. "Not just because of sugar cubes," she said. "Because I want to help you become a better person." She glanced at Maya. "But if you want to *bring* sugar cubes with you--"

"I would anyway," Arthur told her. "To bait my traps. *Someone* needs to eat them."

Blossom smiled and clapped her hands together.

Arthur felt something--*twinge*--inside his chest. Something alien; a sharp but not quite uncomfortable pain that made him wonder if he truly was as recovered as he'd thought.

If his father noticed he'd been gone all day. *If* he didn't react angrily to that fact. *If* the trophy Maya offered was special enough for Arthur to miss the dawn curfew. *If* Iris was trustworthy. *If* she would agree to be his confidant. *If*--

There were too many ifs.

But the only way to determine which would become facts was to make the decision--aloud--that he'd already made in his heart. "Okay," he said, his voice rough and unsteady.

"Okay," Maya said quietly.

"It might not work," Arthur warned her. "If you never see me again--"

"Then we'll know we weren't successful," Maya said, and held out a small bundle. "Here is your trophy."

Arthur made no move to take it. Suddenly fearful, he asked, "Did you--did you kill it? For me? I don't want you to do that--"

"No," Maya said. "I did not kill it for you. No one did. It died of natural causes, and the others will have, too. You have my word on that."

Carefully, reverently, Arthur accepted the bundle and cradled it against his chest. He felt--strange, he decided. Different. Odd.

And then, he realized what it was. For this to work, he would have to lie to his father. He would have to tell him what he expected to hear, not the truth of what had really happened.

He had never lied to his father before. He had no idea if he could do it now.

He wasn't afraid. That much was true. Whatever happened, he wasn't afraid. Not anymore, at least. If his father believed him; took him at his word; accepted the trophy for what it was and nothing more, then he would have a secret to protect. And he intended to protect it, or die trying.

"Thank you," he said.

"You're welcome," Maya said gravely.

The walk back to the Veil took no time at all. Blossom rode on his shoulder for most of it; she flew away as he crossed over, and he missed the faint weight of her presence as he walked the familiar path home. He passed both of his traps, untriggered, and almost knocked them over, but left them in place at the last minute, just in case someone came to verify the story he was about to tell.

As dusk deepened to darkness, he slipped into the household by the back door and carried the bundle and his bag into his trophy room. He saw no one, but that wasn't really a surprise. To vampires, it was early morning, after all, and most would still be asleep, if they slept during the day.

Arthur suspected his father never slept, but he'd never summoned up enough courage to ask. Still, he half-expected his father to be waiting for him as he turned to regard his sanctuary, but neither his grandmother nor his father lurked in the shadows.

But Iris did, her slight form huddled against his workbench. She'd fallen asleep, but woke up as soon as he closed the door behind him.

"You've been gone all day!"

Arthur made himself set down his bag and bundle before replying. "Did anyone miss me?" Perhaps this would be easier than he expected.

Iris slowly rose to her feet. "*I* did," she said.

"Did anyone else?" Arthur asked.

"I don't think so," Iris said, then blurted, "What happened? How did you survive the sunlight? Did you go past the Veil?" And then, she saw the bundle Arthur had placed on his workbench. Her eyes widened. "What is that?"

"A trophy," Arthur said, then added, "I didn't kill it. I haven't even looked at it yet." He paused. "I--I took your advice. I let one of them go."

"But you brought one back, too," Iris said sadly.

"So that my father wouldn't kill me for my failure," Arthur said tightly. "And so that he wouldn't kill me for staying out all day long." He hesitated. "Did you know that the sunlight in Faerie won't hurt us?"

"No, I didn't," Iris said. "You walked in sunlight? Why would your father kill you? You're his only son!" She'd clearly been talking to someone, or listening to gossip, because she added, slightly bitterly, "You can do no wrong."

"That's because I haven't done anything against him yet," Arthur said. "My father *or* my grandmother." He took a deep breath. "Can I trust you?"

"I told you I wouldn't say anything," Iris said automatically.

"That's not what I meant," Arthur said. "I--how did you get in here, anyway? I locked the door when I left."

Iris glanced down at her hands, which were balled into fists. "A spell," she finally said. "When you didn't come to class, I got worried."

"I don't always go to class," Arthur said.

"I didn't know that," Iris said quietly. "And since we'd--spoken the day before, I thought that maybe--" She looked at him. "I took back my braid."

"I know," Arthur told her. "You can keep it."

Iris folded her arms. "I wasn't going to give it back!"

"I know," Arthur said, then asked again, "Can I trust you?"

"Yes," Iris said.

"I mean it," Arthur told her. "Like, *really* trust you."

"Yes," Iris repeated. "You can *really* trust me."

Still, Arthur hesitated, because what he wanted to tell her, about what he had done and what had happened afterwards, would not only get him killed but would probably start a war between the Morgan household and the small folk if his father heard any inkling of it. Perhaps it wasn't a good idea, to take her into his confidence. Perhaps--

"You look really terrible," Iris commented. "What happened to you out in the forest?"

"I decided that I didn't want to become the person my father wants me to become," Arthur whispered. "And I--I decided that the only way to succeed in that goal was to die. But I didn't die, and I came back because I knew you would be the first one to die in the event of my disappearance, and I didn't want you to die because of me."

Iris' mouth dropped open. "You--"

The door opened behind Arthur. He spun around, forgetting Iris; forgetting everything but the fact that his father stood in the doorway now, and then, his father stepped into the room.

"Were you gone all day?" he asked. There was no anger in his voice--yet.

"Yes," Arthur said.

"And you brought back a worthy prize?" his father asked, not questioning how he'd survived.

Not caring, Arthur thought. "Yes," he said aloud.

"Show me," his father said, and Arthur turned to his worktable. Unwrapped the bundle, which contained--

Iris gasped.

Arthur ignored her. The bundle contained a fairy so tiny and delicate it would have fit into an eggshell. It lay curled on its side, its silver wings softly glowing in the dim light of the lamp above the worktable. The wings were twice its size, and completely undamaged, despite the bundling.

"Who is this?" Arthur's father asked, frowning at Iris.

"My assistant," Arthur said without thinking.

Arthur's father did not protest. *He did not protest.* That, in itself, was a miracle. Instead, he peered down at the tiny fairy, and said, "I would like to see this mounted, when you're finished. I'm certain you'll do an excellent job." And then he was gone, as quickly as he had come, closing the door behind him.

Arthur waited for one stunned moment before he sat down in his chair, staring at the delicate project before him, forgetting Iris' presence until she asked, curiously, "Your assistant?"

"He saw you," Arthur told her. "I had to have an explanation, and he had no protest."

He wanted to pinch himself, to make sure he hadn't dreamed his father's lack of protest.

"Well, then," Iris said. "If I'm to be your assistant, then what do you usually do next?"

"You don't actually have to be my assistant," Arthur said slowly.

"Then tell me about what you intended to do in the forest," Iris said. "You were going to tell me before your father arrived."

"I think you were the one talking," Arthur said. She'd only gotten out the one word, but he knew what she'd intended to say.

"You said you decided to die," Iris said quietly.

"Yes," Arthur said, not meeting her gaze.

"How?" Her voice was very soft.

"The poison I use to dispatch the fairies," Arthur said. "I--injected it and drank a bottle of it for good measure." He rubbed his arm; it still hurt a bit, although his stomach had settled down.

"Let me see," Iris said, and inspected his arm when he held it out and rolled up his sleeve. It was mottled with bruises. She gently touched the red mark of the needle. "You'll want to keep this covered, or someone will ask questions you won't want to answer."

"I will," Arthur whispered.

"Does it hurt?" Iris asked.

"Not now," Arthur said, and then, "A little. Not like before, though."

"Why did you do it?" Iris asked.

In a monotone, Arthur told her what he had determined his future would become. "I don't want that to happen," he finished. "I still don't." He told her about Maya, and Blossom, and what they had offered him. And what he had decided.

"That's why you wanted to know if you could trust me," Iris said, nodded. "I understand now." She hesitated. "I think I would like to meet Blossom, someday."

"I think she would like to meet you," Arthur told her. "I'll--We'll have to go into the forest together, someday. Someday soon, I think, if you want to go with me."

"Assistants should probably go with their Masters," Iris said solemnly.

Arthur stared at her. "I'm not your Master," he protested, not liking that word.

"But your father thinks you are," Iris said, which was likely the truth. "And I don't mind."

"I'm not intending to kill any more of them," Arthur said, wanting to be truthful.

"I'm glad," Iris said. "But I'm not so glad that you thought you had to kill yourself because of what I said to you."

"I'm still not sure it won't come to that," Arthur admitted, not meeting her gaze.

She put one hand on his arm. "But you're not alone anymore. You have *me* now."

Arthur sucked in a breath. "I'm sorry I cut off your braid," he whispered.

Iris smiled, but her smile was worried. "All is forgiven," she said, and they never discussed it again.

Maya proved true to her word. She provided the trophies and Arthur's father never discovered their secret. She also provided instruction--to both Iris and Arthur--with Blossom's help, and sometimes the help of other fairies and small folk. Sometimes Arthur didn't understand what they were trying to teach him; sometimes he stormed out of the cave (which had become a school, of sorts) and sulked in the forest until Blossom or Iris came to fetch him. Sometimes it was too hard to pretend that his life was anything other than terrible, especially when his father required everyone to watch the executions, and expected Arthur to stand right beside him while he wielded the blade or watched from the doorway as the hapless vampire burned to death in the cold light of dawn.

He learned to compartmentalize his life inside the household and his life with Iris. He learned to close all emotion away and pretend to be the son his father wanted, only to discard all of that when he was alone, or out in the forest, or with his only friend.

Iris proved to be a stalwart companion, and her smaller fingers made delicate work seem simple. Despite the horror she'd expressed at first, she did not hesitate to help him prepare the trophies Maya provided, and Arthur grew to rely on her talent and budding expertise.

He *wasn't* alone anymore. That much was true, but he knew that his carefully built world would crumble instantly if his father caught wind of the Secret.

And yet, a year passed. Then two.

When Arthur turned fourteen, his father deemed him old enough to help with the executions. This was, of course, the path Arthur had seen in his future two years before, and Iris stopped him this time before he could harm himself, and she hid all the poisons away until the panic subsided enough for him to think.

Although, in truth, he *couldn't* think, because it had been two years since he'd killed a fairy or one of the small folk, and he didn't know what he could do to refuse to obey his father's decree, other than to die himself, and Iris wouldn't let him do that.

"How do they usually die?" Iris asked.

Arthur stared at her. "You've never gone?" He'd supposed that everyone was required to go; there were crowds, most of the time, when his father deemed someone ready for execution.

"No," Iris said. "My mother won't let me."

"He doesn't use poison," Arthur told her. "He uses sunlight, or silver, most of the time."

"You're not him, though," Iris said. "Will he let you use poison?"

"What? I'm not--I can't--"

"And make it so they're dead so that we can sneak them out of the house at night and give them to Maya to save," Iris said quickly, just in case he thought she meant otherwise.

Arthur thought about what she had said. Wondered if it would work. Would Maya even agree to spirit the prisoners away? Would they have a place to go? She had not mentioned Arthur fleeing since that first day, and sometimes he wondered if the Secret was worth keeping if he would never get to utilize what Maya and Blossom and the others had taught him.

"We can ask her," he finally agreed, and they did, that night. Arthur's father had said nothing about the trophies, but Arthur half-expected him to refuse to allow him to hunt, now that he would be murdering those his father deemed enemies.

He *couldn't* do it. He knew he couldn't do it.

"Arthur," Iris said, and he realized she'd been repeating his name as he stood there, frozen with horror. Blossom hovered in front of his face, worried; he blinked at her and whispered, "We need to speak with Maya."

And Maya, when she arrived, listened to his concerns and Iris' idea and said, "Of course I know where they could go. Can you pinpoint the dosage so they'll seem to be dead?"

"I think so," Arthur said. The panic was subsiding a little now; faced with an actual plan, he only had to worry about pulling it off.

As if that were only a small worry.

But it worked; he stood up to his father and protested an audience; stated that he would only use poison, and his father did not object. And perhaps that was why he only had to dose a handful of unfortunates with the poison he'd developed over the course of the next year; his father still took care of the bulk of the executions.

After a while, though, Arthur began to pay attention to the condemned prisoner's crimes, and decided for himself which ones to request--to rescue--and which ones would be more likely to use the knowledge that someone in the household had freed them to return themselves to favor. That meant making choices he didn't want to have to make, and yet, he managed to save some lives. Not all of them, but some of them. And it was all he could do.

He never asked Maya where the prisoners ended up. Iris might have, but she did not share the information with Arthur. And perhaps they would have continued like that, for years, except--except one night, they were seen.

His name was Liam, and everyone believed him to be Arthur's younger brother--half-brother, really--although no one knew the truth. The story was that Liam and his mother had returned to the household after Liam's father was killed--much like Iris and her mother had returned years before. Liam's father was Arthur's uncle, so they were definitely cousins, but they looked enough alike to be brothers, even though they were four years apart.

Soon after Liam's arrival, his mother became ill, and so he was forever hanging around, unsupervised by anyone. Sometimes, Arthur suspected he had some sort of talent for invisibility, because he would be absolutely certain he was alone, but then have Liam appear in the next moment, standing against the wall or a tapestry as if he'd been there all along.

Arthur did not wish to encourage him, but he couldn't refrain from speaking to him since they were cousins, and since his mother had some sort of strange status, despite her illness. Arthur had spotted his father emerging from their small set of rooms on more than one occasion, something that never happened with anyone else.

They'd perfected their rescues by now; after the poison took hold, they would cast a spell to render themselves unseen, and slip out of the household without a murmur of suspicion.

Arthur had also--privately--inquired if Maya would be able to find someone to provide replacement weapons to the household's store of silver ones; he knew they wouldn't be able to do this forever, and he wanted to make their chances of survival higher by replacing as many of the silver weapons with harmless ones. Maya had not asked questions, but she had placed one hand on his arm and said, solemnly, "When you decide it's time for *you* to leave--and Iris, of course--know that we will help you."

And although he was not yet of age, Arthur realized that he would have a much better chance at not being sent back to the Morgan household now, if he did flee.

But then, if they fled, no one else would be rescued, ever again. The prisoners would have no hope at all, and his father would have complete control of the household. And although Arthur knew that his position was precarious--it would only take one mistake to doom them both--he could not allow himself to consider freedom just yet.

But then, Liam followed them into the forest one night. They'd just left the household wards behind; just carried their latest rescue into the forest, when Arthur heard something behind them; a twig snapped, or an indrawn breath; it wasn't much, but he lowered his half of their burden without a sound and vanished into the trees.

Iris followed him. The prisoner would keep; they never awoke until the next day.

Liam either didn't realize he'd been heard or Arthur was faster than he thought, because he was still crouched behind a tree when Arthur found him.

He gasped aloud at Arthur's appearance and tried to say something, but Arthur couldn't let him speak--or scream--this close to the household, so he covered Liam's mouth with his hand and pressed him up against the tree. "Not one word. No screams, either. Do you understand?"

Liam nodded convulsively, and Arthur realized he'd pressed the blade of the knife he always carried--just in case--against his throat. It wasn't silver, but Liam didn't need to know that.

"Don't hurt him," Iris said from behind them.

Arthur, slightly sickened at his reaction, slid the knife back into its sheath. "Not one word," he warned, and Liam nodded again.

He removed his hand. Stepped back.

Liam touched his throat, then looked down at his hand, as if expecting to see blood.

"How did you follow us?" Arthur asked quietly.

Liam opened his mouth to reply, then closed it, remembering Arthur's previous words.

Exasperated, Arthur said, "You can answer questions."

"I've been watching you for weeks," Liam said after a moment, and tensed, as if he expected Arthur to lash out at him. "That spell you use--I can see through it."

Arthur stared at him in dismay.

"How?" Iris asked when he didn't speak. "Another spell?"

Liam looked down at his shoes. "A talent," he mumbled, then, "Please don't tell anyone."

A talent for seeing through spells. Arthur's father could do a lot with such a talent; Liam would never have a normal sort of life (if one could have a normal sort of life in the Morgan household) if Arthur's father discovered his secret. He'd be locked up; used as Arthur's father's secret weapon against his enemies.

"We won't tell," Arthur said. "As long as you don't tell anyone about us, either."

Liam considered this for a moment, then nodded. "Okay." And then he asked the damning question. "What are you doing with them?"

"Rescuing them," Iris said after a moment. "And we'd be killed if you told *anyone* at all--you know that, right?"

"My mother has the same talent," Liam blurted out, then, as if he couldn't bear to keep it a secret any longer. "She--your father, he--he comes to her--" Miserably, he whispered, "That's why she's sick. He *made* her sick." He folded his arms. "I don't want the same thing to happen to me."

He looked so pitiful and young, standing there; helpless, even, but Arthur couldn't help but doubt his word. Not that his mother was sick; that was--well, that was likely not what was wrong with her; he suspected something a bit more nefarious, with his father involved, but he didn't want to say it aloud.

"Please," Liam begged. "I won't tell anyone. I swear. You can kill me if you ever think I'd betray you--"

"I hope that would not be necessary," Maya said from behind them, her voice quiet.

Arthur stepped away from him, suddenly cold. "I--"

"It's my fault," Liam said quickly. "I followed them; I shouldn't have--" His eyes were wide and frightened; he looked as if he wanted to run away as fast as he could possibly run.

Arthur didn't remember being frightened of Maya when they'd first met. She had been kind to him; covering him with a blanket against the sunlight; bringing him something to drink. And she'd been his friend ever since. "Maya is our friend," he said.

"Friend?" Liam asked. "What's--what's a 'friend'?"

"You have a lot to learn, young man," Maya said as Blossom flew up to hover beside her.

Liam gasped.

Iris gently took his arm. He started to pull away, then stopped himself, as if he realized that she wouldn't hurt him, despite what he had offered. "Come on," she said gently, but her gaze was on Arthur, as if asking permission to allow Liam to accompany them. "We can't stay here for long; we're too close to the house."

Arthur swallowed a sigh. "Come, then," he said, and the edge of wariness Liam wore like a badge crumbled to dust around his sudden smile. Had *he* ever been that young? That innocent?

That trusting?

"I will have your word," he said formally, resisting the urge to trust him completely.

"You have my word," Liam promised. His smile faded; he looked worried now, as if he feared Arthur would not accept his word for anything important at all. "I won't--"

"I know you won't," Arthur told him, and tried to pretend he meant it. "Come on." And together, they walked where they'd left the sleeping prisoner.

Despite Arthur's initial misgivings, Liam proved to be an invaluable partner in their little endeavor. Young as he was, no one really paid attention to him, and he soon became adept at hiding in plain sight; something he'd practiced while trailing after them all those weeks. He soaked up whatever Maya and Blossom chose to teach him, and didn't seem to have such a hard time with subjects Arthur had nearly abandoned, like empathy and caring. But for all he learned, he became even more adept at hiding what he had learned while home.

But despite Liam's assistance; despite his trust, Arthur felt as if a noose was slowly tightening around their necks. He couldn't pinpoint the source of their doom, because his father showed no sign of knowing or realizing what they had done. He assumed that Arthur dragged his victims out for the sun to take, and Arthur did not dissuade him.

And then, Isobel, Arthur's aunt; sister to Arthur's father and a highly placed member of the Morgan household, even though she didn't live inside the Morgan household, went crazy. Arthur did not hear the entirety of the story, but he heard enough of it.

She'd gone crazy, murdered her son Tobias twice times, and brought him back to life twice as well, with a spell.

The Council and the Hunt had gotten involved; two of the younger Richmond sons had died, and Arthur's father likely would have killed her himself, but Tobias did the deed, and then fled, resurfacing along with an errant cousin and the younger daughter of the Richmond household.

Considering his mother had killed him twice, Arthur didn't blame him for killing her. But Arthur's father did, and he put a high price on Tobias' head after Isobel's death.

He also forbade anyone from mentioning Tobias' name, which meant that the cells in the basement filled up quickly, and punishments were rife. Whether because of the fact that he couldn't reach Tobias himself or he hadn't seen this coming, Arthur's father became more cruel and even more violent than usual, if such a thing were *ever* usual.

He never actually did anything to Arthur; for some reason he seemed to trust his son, although Arthur wasn't certain why. He'd never actually defied his father to his face, after all, and the Secret had yet to be discovered. But when Arthur's father insisted he participate in punishments for such small infractions, Arthur knew that he couldn't keep the Secret a secret for much longer.

Nearly a year had passed since Liam had joined them. Arthur had no reason not to trust him now; he'd proved himself trustworthy time and time again. He had absolutely no indication what would happen, or what Liam had done until it was too late and he could do nothing about it; too late to help him; too late to save him; too late to dissuade him from his path.

Arthur's father became convinced there was a traitor in the household, feeding Tobias information.

Arthur had no idea that the traitor was Liam until he'd been imprisoned. Had no clue what Liam had done until he'd been shouted at and beaten and tortured, and sentenced to die at dawn.

Arthur himself wasn't suspect, but that could change, of course, with one slip of Liam's tongue; one hesitation; one--

"We can't allow this to happen," Iris said, shocking him out of the horrible spiral of his thoughts.

Arthur wasn't surprised that she'd appeared in his bedroom; despite the guard his father had put on the door--for Arthur's safety, he'd claimed--Iris knew all of the secret ways in and out and around the household by now. There were many secret passageways even Arthur didn't know about. He had no doubt one led directly to the basement, and had no doubt Iris had already looked in on Liam.

His father hadn't insisted he attend Liam's punishment. But he had no doubt he'd be required to attend Liam's death.

"Did you know?" His voice was hoarse. "Did you know?"

Iris' silence was answer enough. Arthur closed his eyes. Slumped back in the chair.

"It wasn't that he didn't trust you," Iris finally said. "He didn't want you to feel as if you had to become involved."

"How could I not?" Arthur asked hollowly. He'd thought--and dismissed--contacting Tobias himself, more out of fear than anything else, because if Tobias knew he was not with his father, Arthur feared he would be asked to do something he wouldn't be able to do, like kill him, or kill Grandmother Morgan, or worse.

"We have to leave," he said. "We can't stay here; not now; if Liam breathes one word--"

"He won't," Iris said quietly. "He knows it won't save him."

Arthur's father had come an hour before. Raging; furious; he'd spoken without thinking, and said something he shouldn't have said. Something he'd never admitted before.

He hadn't even noticed the slip, but Arthur had noticed it, and now, he wondered if he should tell Iris what his father had accidentally confirmed.

"He's my brother," he whispered, still stunned by the admission. "My father said 'sons' when he came here, Iris. He said 'sons'."

"Then that's all the more reason to save him," Iris said, unsurprised, which made him wonder if she'd already known the truth, or if she'd just assumed that the rumors were true, regardless of any proof at all.

"How?" Arthur asked, which was the most important question, really, because there were guards on Liam's door, of course, and while they had the spell to move unseen, Liam would be able to see him, and so would his mother. And Liam's mother, although still not well, had been taken down to the basement to keep watch over her son. And she was loyal to Arthur's father; fanatically loyal.

She would see them come, and she would tell Arthur's father, and then they would all die.

"Do you know the arrangements?" Iris asked. She didn't seem at all concerned about their inability to rescue Liam, or if there would be anything left to rescue, after Arthur's father finished with him.

"He is to die at dawn," Arthur said.

"Four hours from now," Iris said, and frowned.

Arthur couldn't cry; he wanted to, but the tears would not come. "I don't want him to die," he finally said, and heard his voice shake.

"Then let's make sure he doesn't," Iris said firmly.

"How?" Arthur asked again. He couldn't sit anymore; he stood and started pacing, back and forth, back and forth. "In four hours, I'll be standing beside my father while Liam is sentenced to death--" His voice trailed away. He stood, quite still, staring at the door, because he'd just realized what would happen when his father used the weapon he'd chosen to end Liam's life.

He'd taken care of nearly all of them at this point, and he knew that his father would choose something that would ensure Liam died in agony for his betrayal, only, since the weapons were no longer silver, unless he chopped off Liam's head, he would not die at all.

Which meant that he would then test the other weapons, realize that they weren't silver, either, and then the Secret would be uncovered, because he would *have* to suspect Arthur's duplicity. No one else had that much access to the hidden places; no one else could have done such a thing.

Arthur had switched out the weapons in the hope that they wouldn't be used on himself, or Iris, or Liam. But he hadn't thought past that; he hadn't realized what that actually meant. But now--

In a whisper, he told Iris what he had done. "My father will use one of them on Liam, and he won't die from silver poisoning. He won't die writhing in agony. He won't die at all, unless my father cuts off his head."

Iris' mouth had dropped open. She stared at him in shock, as if she couldn't quite believe he would even attempt such a scheme; or, more likely, that he'd been stupid enough to try.

"You do realize we'll have to leave?" Arthur asked. "We won't be able to stay here?"

"I don't want to leave my mother," Iris said. "But I understand why I have to. If I could get her to come with us--"

"It's too dangerous," Arthur said automatically.

"It will be dangerous for her if I leave," Iris said, but she did not back down; she folded her arms and stood firm against Arthur's fear.

He took a deep breath. "I know what I will need to do," he said. "To save him, I mean. But afterwards--if what I think will happen happens, you'll--you'll have to rescue both of us from the basement." Another breath. He had to take deep breaths or he would hyperventilate, and then be good to no one at all.

Iris stilled. "What do you intend to do?" she asked.

"It's probably best if you don't know," Arthur managed to say, and she glared at him until he told her, haltingly, of the dangerous plan that had suddenly appeared in his mind; a plan that could go wrong so many ways, but, perhaps, with a little luck, would go right.

"It's very dangerous," Iris said softly.

"I know," Arthur told her. "But I can't see any other way to save him."

"Maya would say you're purposely putting yourself in danger to save him," Iris said. "And that you're leaving me to pick up all the pieces, afterwards."

"I won't die, either," Arthur told her. "Unless--"

"Unless they cut off both your heads," Iris said, her voice quiet. "Yes." And then, quite unexpectedly, she threw her arms around him and held him tightly. Since Iris was usually the calm and collected one, Arthur wasn't sure what to do, at first. But then she sniffed, and wiped her eyes, and stepped back, and said, "I'll be there, afterwards. I--"

"Don't promise," Arthur said, interrupting her. "Too much could go wrong."

"I won't promise," Iris told him. "But I'll swear. I *will* be there, afterwards. You have my word."

And somehow, even though he knew too many things could go wrong, Arthur believed her, and loved her for it.

And then, too soon, it was almost dawn.

The entire household was required to attend, with no excuses. And they packed the meeting room--once, long ago, it had been a ballroom, but it hadn't been used for that purpose for many years. And as the members of the household trickled into the room--Arthur, his father, his grandmother, and Arthur's father's five lieutenants, two of which had once been vampire hunters, stood up front in a line, awaiting Liam's arrival; he'd be paraded in so that everyone could see him, forced to walk if he still could; otherwise, he'd be dragged--they were silent. There were no whispers. No murmurs. Just footsteps, as everyone filed into the room and awaited the horror therein.

Liam was almost upright when they brought him into the room. They were moving too quickly for him to actually keep his footing, so they half-dragged him down the suddenly empty middle of the room, where everyone had left an open space in front of Arthur and his father and the others. Arthur didn't see Iris at first; he had to steel his face not to show his sudden panic, but then he spotted her near the back of the room with her mother--with absolutely no expression on her face.

Considering everyone else looked properly horrified by Liam's appearance, Arthur felt as if his father would pull her out of the crowd and accuse her of being Liam's accomplice without a second thought.

But he did not. He seemed to be satisfied that Liam had worked alone, and apparently, Liam had not said one word about Arthur or Iris or the Secret. In fact, Liam's gaze slid right past Arthur as his guards left him standing in the middle of the circle, alone, barely able to stand upright.

All at once, Arthur realized that Liam's mother wasn't present, and wondered when his father would notice. But then, he realized that his father was waiting for something--some*one,* and when she stepped into the room and walked through the throng to stand beside him, Arthur knew that what he'd suspected was true.

Liam's mother did not even seem to see her son standing there, swaying, barely able to hold himself upright. She stared--glared, really--out at the crowd until Grandmother Morgan, who had--up until now--remained silent--pushed her aside and snatched up the bow Arthur's father had intended to use.

"This traitor--" Arthur's father spat. "Colluded with our enemies--"

"Cousin," Liam said clearly. "Our cousin."

"Whose name has been struck from the family!" Grandmother Morgan snapped. "Who is guilty of murdering his own mother!"

"She murdered him!" Arthur blurted, unable to stop himself. "And brought him back to life! Twice!"

"Silence!" Arthur's father roared as murmurs drifted across the crowd. To Arthur, he added, "We'll discuss this later."

"No," Arthur said, and stepped forward to stand in front of Liam. "We will discuss it now. I don't think my brother did anything wrong."

Liam drew in a shocked breath. Those who heard Arthur's declaration stepped back, fearful now, because Arthur's father would just as well kill them all to keep the secret safe. The *stupid* secret, really, because who really cared if Liam was or was not Arthur's brother? Why keep it a secret at all?

"It's true," Liam's mother said unexpectedly. "It's true."

"Regardless of his parentage, he has betrayed the family," Arthur's father said tightly. "Stand aside."

"No," Arthur said, dimly surprised that his voice did not shake. That he didn't immediately obey his father's order, out of fear.

Grandmother Morgan, never one for long conversations, snatched an arrow from the quiver and notched the arrow onto the bow. Arthur tried to watch both her and his father at the same time; he never expected one of the lieutenants to act without a direct order. The man stepped out of line and lunged for Arthur, who stepped back, away from him, and collided with Liam, who fell backwards.

Perhaps Grandmother Morgan had intended to shoot Liam, not Arthur. Perhaps she merely wanted to end the bickering, especially in front of the entire household. Either way, she let the arrow fly, and Arthur found himself falling backwards onto Liam, staring up at the shocked faces around him; one hand reaching up to touched the feathered shaft that now stuck grotesquely out of his chest; the other scrambling, as if he intended to get up and throw himself at his father, a suicide attempt if there ever was one.

There was no pain, at first. Just a bone-deep numbness that could not--*would* not--last.

And chaos. Above and around them. His father shouting for order. His grandmother's cackle. The *snap* as his father broke the bow in two.

Someone grabbed Arthur's arm, presumably to pull him upright. The abrupt movement awoke a deep and tearing pain that robbed both breath and sense and left Arthur reeling in its wake.

He had not--quite--expected it to hurt so badly.

"...away," his father growled. "Take them both. I will deal with them later." He threw the broken pieces of the bow in Arthur's face. "Or let them rot." Raised his voice. *"I will have silence!"*

Arthur screamed when they pulled him to his feet. He saw his father's fist right before it connected with the side of his head; heard Liam moan as the guards jerked him upright and dragged him away.

And then, blessedly, nothing more, not even pain. Arthur let himself fall into darkness.

He awoke sometime later to voices overhead and the taste of blood in the back of his throat. Not nourishment, but his own blood. For a moment, he felt no pain, but it was only a moment. One very *short* moment.

His eyes snapped open, or tried to. He couldn't seem to open his left eye all the way. He drew in a sharp breath. Choked on it. Moaned aloud.

"Don't try to move," Liam said, somewhere to his right.

He sounded--beaten. Exhausted and hopeless and *beaten.* Arthur doubted they'd fed him, so his wounds would not heal as quickly as they would, otherwise. Not that they were supposed to have healed at all; Liam certainly wasn't supposed to be alive right now.

Neither was Arthur, really, considering the arrow should have been silver.

"Are we alone?" Arthur asked.

"Blossom was here," Liam told him. "She came in through the window, where the glass is broken."

"Why did you do it?" Arthur asked. "Why didn't you tell me?"

"There's a guard outside the door," Liam said. "I tried to cast a spell, but I don't know if it took."

Arthur didn't have enough strength to check. "Answer my question," he said, but when he tried to raise his voice, the pain choked away anger and left him dizzy and sick in its wake. He realized, then, that the arrow no longer stuck out of his chest, or shoulder, or wherever it had entered (since everything hurt, it was difficult to tell) and someone had placed a bit of cloth against the wound, to soak up the blood.

There was a lot of blood.

"Please," he managed, and Liam said, "Because he deserved to know. He's no more a traitor than you or I. He had no choice but to do what he did. Do you blame him for fleeing?"

"I don't blame him for anything at all," Arthur whispered. "Where's Iris?"

"I didn't tell you because I didn't want you to try to keep that from your father as well," Liam said after a moment. "You're already hiding so much." He paused. "I'm sorry. I didn't tell them anything about--about the Secret."

"I know," Arthur said, and closed his eyes. He couldn't keep them open. "Where's Iris?"

"I don't know," Liam whispered. He sounded like he was crying. "Will you die?"

"Did you remove the arrow?" Arthur asked.

"It's on the floor beside you," Liam told him. "Blossom helped--she told me what to do."

As far as Arthur knew, Blossom had never actually ventured into the household before. How had she known to come? "Are we alone?" he asked again.

"I told you--there's a guard outside the door," Liam said. "I tried to cast a spell so he wouldn't hear us talking, but I'm--I can't--" He took a deep breath. "There's a body. A human. I think he's dead, though."

"Which cell?" Arthur asked.

"The second one from the end, on the left," Liam replied, because they'd marked them all long ago, in their quest to become more efficient in their rescues.

"There's a passageway into the one beside this one," Arthur murmured. "Is he dead or unconscious?"

"I don't know," Liam said. "I can't hear his heart beating." He paused. "He's just--just a child, though, Arthur--younger than me. A little kid."

A child. Younger than Liam. "How much younger?"

Arthur heard a rustling sound, then Liam's gasp. "Someone's drunk his blood." And then, "He's still alive. Barely."

"Don't--" Arthur opened his eyes. Tried--and failed--to sit up. "Don't hurt him."

"He's just a little *kid!"* Liam sounded shocked. "I wouldn't--"

"That never stopped my father," Arthur interjected, and Liam fell silent. *"Our* father, I suppose. Can you help me sit up?"

"I don't think that's a good idea," Liam said after a moment. "You should lie down. Maybe then--" He was crying again, and Arthur suddenly realized why.

"The arrow wasn't silver," he said quickly. "I'm not dying."

Liam sniffed. "What? Your father said it was--"

"He doesn't know," Arthur said. "No one was to know. *Iris* didn't know, until I told her. I switched them out. Nearly every weapon I could find. Maya helped."

Liam was silent. Arthur again tried to sit up. This time, he managed to prop himself up against the wall, even though the movement made the room dip and sway around his head. At least he could *see* Liam now, though. And while he'd expected Liam to look relieved, he had *not* expected anger.

"I'm the one who should be angry at *you,"* he said quietly. He could see the human boy now, too, although he wanted to *unsee* the boy as soon as he saw the bite marks on his filthy neck; his wrists; no doubt even his ankles. And--elsewhere.

Vampires were very thorough. And no one liked to open old wounds to feed, although it looked as if that had happened more than once. Arthur felt sick just looking at him.

"That's true," Liam allowed. "But you could have told me. Us." He glanced at the boy, following Arthur's horrified gaze.

"I didn't want you to have to lie to anyone because of it," Arthur said. He wanted to help the boy, but he didn't know how; he'd had very little interaction with the humans the vampires kept for food. Although if the boy's condition was any indication of how they were treated--Arthur shuddered. Then the faint rumors were true, and he'd drunk their blood without question. For all he knew, he'd drunk the *boy's* blood as well, and that seemed too horrible to contemplate.

"What happened, after I--after my father hit me?" Arthur asked, and reached up with his hand to touch the side of his face. He didn't try to move his left arm; he didn't want to dislodge the sodden dressing, and he knew it would hurt worse if he tried to move it.

"He kept hitting you," Liam said quietly. "And so did the others. And your grandmother wanted to chop off our heads, but *he* wouldn't let her."

"I see," Arthur said, and tried not to feel...well, anything at all, because none of this was a surprise; he *knew* how his father treated traitors, and to his father, he would be the worst sort of traitor of them all. "How long have we been here?"

"I'm not sure," Liam said. "I think it's still the same day. I wasn't awake when they brought us here, though, I--" he took a shuddering breath. "Arthur, are we going to die? I thought *I* would die; they almost caught Tobias when they caught me, and I tried to get away--"

"We're *hopefully* not going to die," Arthur said. "Depending on if Iris finds us or not." He paused. "But we're going to leave. Forever. Okay?"

"Okay," Liam said without any hope in his voice at all.

"Come sit by me," Arthur said. "If the boy's not lying in water or anything, leave him there. We can't help him right now." The floor seemed to be fairly dry, but he knew that the basement leaked when it rained. He'd found more than one prisoner lying in a puddle of brackish water and bloody vomit over the years.

"He's lying on a blanket," Liam said. "It's not a very nice blanket, but it's dry. Except for blood, but that's dry too. Mostly." He hesitated, then asked, softly, "Did *we* do that to him?"

"Yes," Arthur said. "If you mean did we, as vampires, do that to him. Yes. But did we *personally* do that to him? I don't know if there's any way to find out." He waited until Liam had joined him against the wall, then said, "When we leave, I want to take him with us."

"But he's barely alive!" Liam protested. "And wouldn't they--wherever we're going, wouldn't they think *we* did that to him?"

Arthur closed his eyes again. Leaned his head against the wall. "If we can get him to a Healer, then perhaps he'll live," he said. "And if--if others find out about what happens here, then perhaps they can do something about our father and Grandmother Morgan." He wasn't certain that anyone would care what happened to humans in the Morgan household, but he *hoped* someone would care. And, maybe, if someone *did* care, the Morgan household might not be so terrible anymore.

But he was too tired to think about that right now.

"I always hoped I was really your brother," Liam said after a moment of silence.

Arthur smiled. And, with Liam's steady presence beside him, allowed himself to slip away.

He awoke with the taste of blood on his lips, but it wasn't his blood, this time; it was from a cup, and fresh enough to be from the boy. He opened his eyes, reaching up to push the cup away, and Iris said, "Don't waste it. Liam told me--" she glanced over her shoulder. "What happened. I got this from the kitchen, so there's no way to know."

"He's coming with us," Arthur told her, then realized they weren't alone in the room. Iris' *mother* knelt beside the boy, her back to Arthur, doing something he couldn't see.

"She's not hurting him," Iris said quickly before he could move to the boy's defense. And then, softer, "I--I had to tell her, Arthur. She's trustworthy; I swear."

"You had to tell her *what*?" Arthur asked.

Iris' mother glanced back at him. "Nearly everything, I think," she said. "Is this the time I tell you that I won't betray my daughter's trust?"

She spoke softly, her voice unthreatening. And, perhaps, it was too late now to worry about her presence. After all, Arthur doubted Iris would be able to help them both to freedom while carrying the boy as well.

"This is the time, yes," Arthur said, and she smiled, briefly.

"I don't believe we've ever officially met," she said. "I'm Fern."

"Arthur," Arthur said. "And Liam. And we don't know *his* name."

"But you want to take him with us," Fern said, firmly establishing herself as part of their team.

"He'll die if we leave him," Arthur said.

"I gave him some water to drink," Fern said. "And he drank it, but he needs more than we can give him here. Can either of you walk? Iris tells me she knows a secret way out of here, and I don't think we have much time."

"We can't leave until the sun sets," Arthur reminded her.

"But we can *hide* until the sun sets, and not in here," Iris told him. "This isn't a safe place to stay. *Can* you walk?"

"I don't know," Arthur admitted.

"My mother can see through any spells you might use," Liam whispered, his eyes half-closed, his head leaning against Arthur's shoulder.

"So can you," Iris said crisply. "We're *not* leaving you here; your father will kill you long before dusk."

This was true. Arthur was rather surprised he hadn't shown up already. Perhaps he still believed the arrow had been silver; perhaps he would expect Arthur to be dead when he *did* arrive. "Liam? Can *you* walk?"

"Here," Iris said, and held out another cup. "You didn't drink nearly enough before; drink this now."

Liam took the cup. Made a face, no doubt because of the boy, but did not refuse to drink. "Arthur needs it more," he said.

"I don't think so," Iris told him. "And anyway, he drank half of it."

Arthur sat and drowsed for a bit, knowing that he should make the attempt to rise but realizing that he would likely be unable to do so. Despite the blood, everything still hurt, and the wound in his chest did not seem to be healing very quickly. The smaller wounds healed first, and there were many of them; at least he could open his eye all the way now, and his vision wasn't blurry anymore.

Something clattered at the window. He watched, mutely, as Blossom slipped inside and flew over to where he sat.

In a perfectly neutral voice, Iris' mother said, "That's a fairy."

"I *told* you," Iris said. "It's not my fault if you didn't believe me."

To Iris, Blossom said, "Maya wants to know if you know about the tunnel."

"The tunnel?" Iris asked. "There's a tunnel?"

"To where?" Arthur asked, struggling to stay awake.

"A cave, in the forest," Blossom said. "Your ancestors created it, to aid in their escape if the household was ever destroyed by Hunters."

That made sense; Arthur's ancestors were nothing but paranoid when it came to Hunters. And there had been a few close calls. But for Iris to not know about a tunnel in and out of the house; could they have used it in their rescues?

Iris asked the same question.

"Maya said it wasn't passable, and it isn't yet," Blossom said. "But we're working on clearing the rubble, and you can hide down there until dark."

Until dark. "And then what?" Liam asked.

"This boy won't be alive by dusk," Iris' mother said. "He needs a Healer's help, and there are no Healers here."

Blossom flew over to where he lay. Settled on his chest, and inspected his wounds, which were cleaner now; Iris' mother had been busy. She frowned. Opened her mouth to speak.

"We didn't--" Arthur began.

"Of course not," Blossom said hotly. "But *someone* did. More than one person, I'd say. Does this happen often?" She looked at Arthur, as if he would know.

In fact, *everyone* looked at Arthur, as if he would know.

Defensively, he said, "I have no contact with the humans who live here." And then he wondered why he felt so defensive, since he hadn't known. Was it just because he was a vampire? Would he feel that way for the rest of his life? Haltingly, he said, "I thought that if we saved him, we might be able to--help the rest of them, somehow. I thought that maybe someone would help us help them."

It was practically a speech, and in his current state, utterly exhausting. He closed his eyes.

"You can't sleep now," Blossom said, and touched the side of his face.

Arthur jerked awake. "I wasn't asleep."

"No, you weren't," Blossom said. "Maya would be proud of you."

"May I ask about Maya?" Iris' mother inquired. "Is she another fairy?"

"No," Arthur said. "Not a fairy. Not like Blossom." He tried to focus on her face, but it was blurry now; he'd apparently reached the end of his strength. "Can you help him?"

"I can--" Blossom touched the side of his face again when his eyes slid shut. "I can bring a Healer here, and *she* can help him."

"Then why can't the Healer also help Liam and Arthur?" Iris asked sensibly. "Do they just help humans, then?"

Arthur supposed that could be true. He'd never heard of a Healer wanting to help a vampire; he'd never actually seen a Healer before, in truth. They tended to keep away from the vampire households, and he did not blame them.

"They don't just help humans," he heard Blossom say. "I'm not sure that she could take the boy *and* Liam *and* Arthur."

"And Liam and Arthur aren't going to die before the sun sets, unless we're caught, and then you will die, too," Arthur pointed out.

Liam was silent. Arthur suspected he was asleep. Or unconscious; he seemed to still be in pain, which was worrying. How would they walk all the way through the forest to wherever Maya intended to take them? How could they possibly get away without someone noticing? How could they--

"Arthur," Blossom said, as if she could read his mind. "Stop thinking so hard."

"I can't help it," Arthur murmured, but didn't open his eyes.

"Liam?" Iris asked, and when he didn't answer, repeated his name until he stirred. "Can you walk?"

"I don't know," he whispered miserably. "I don't think so. Not very well."

"See?" Iris asked. "They both need a Healer's help."

"The boy needs one now," Arthur said. "Where is the entrance to the tunnel?" He opened his eyes. Pushed away the weariness. The pain wouldn't leave; he couldn't do anything about that, but he could--and did--slowly stand, using the wall for support. Holding his arm against his chest so not to jar his wound.

"I think I can find it," Blossom said, hovering in front of him worriedly.

"You'll get the Healer to come for him?" Arthur asked.

"I will," Blossom said. "I promise."

"Thank you," Arthur said. "Go with Iris. Find the entrance. And then come back for us. Please."

When Arthur stood up, Liam slumped sideways but managed to catch himself before he fell. He stared up at Arthur with wide, wounded eyes as if he had done something impossible, like walk out into the sunlight or survive a silver wound. Iris' mother helped him stand. Arthur had expected her to protest that he'd sent Iris away, but she did not.

"I'll help Liam if you can walk on your own," she said, and what seemed to be only seconds later, Iris and Blossom returned.

"Come on," Iris said. "I know where to look, now." She paused. "It's a trapdoor, though. You have to climb down a ladder."

"I'll manage," Arthur said, although he wasn't certain how.

Blossom stayed with the boy. Arthur could only hope that she would fetch the Healer to save him; he would have no way to know until the tunnel had been reopened so they could escape.

Somehow, he made it down the metal ladder. Somehow, Liam did too, although he insisted on going last, just in case he fell so they could catch him. Somehow, he found himself stumbling through a brick-lined tunnel in darkness so thick he couldn't see his hand in front of his face; Iris had called up a light, but it had only reached a foot or so into the darkness, hardly enough for all of them, and Arthur had no strength to cast spells.

They stopped when they reached the blockage. It seemed to be unyielding; Arthur heard nothing from the other side.

"Sit down," Iris told him, and he sat on sandy soil, damp and cool against his skin. Liam sat beside him; Iris on his other side. Arthur couldn't see either of them, but he heard them breathing, and he felt--for some strange reason, he felt safe.

"I should have brought supplies," Iris said after a moment. "Blankets. Food."

"Flashlights," Liam rasped, then cleared his throat noisily.

"There was no time to gather supplies," Iris' mother said quietly. "You did what you could. Why don't you all try to get some rest? I'll keep watch."

Perhaps before he was wounded, Arthur would have found her suggestion suspicious, and he would have refused. But now, he obediently closed his eyes and let himself drift away with his two best friends beside him and his father none the wiser to his location.

For now, at least.

Malachi

"This is how you see?"

"No," the Protector said. "This is how you perceive how I see."

Malachi hadn't noticed much of a difference, at first, especially after his trip into the Mists where the Protector's peculiar sight and his own talent's adaptation of the spell Josiah had used had likely saved more than one life. He'd returned to the room he shared with Josiah; returned to his quiet existence with Eri and the others, and the only remarkable thing at all was that he no longer had to rely on his family to make his way into the world. He'd learned to adapt, yes, but even then, he'd still felt, sometimes, like a burden.

But then, after only two days of this newness, he realized that something *had* changed, and not necessarily for the better. It began when he answered unasked questions, unthinking; at first, it was as if the bond itself had expanded to include thoughts as well as actual speech, which was concerning enough. But even thoughts would have been preferable to what he saw when he looked directly at someone; when he met their gaze, and found their every secret exposed as if they'd spoken them aloud.

The Protector had seemed to know a lot it should never have known. Now Malachi knew why, and how.

His first mistake was to look directly at Nathaniel, who had pulled himself away from Amalea's home to return to the Hunt for a short time. Malachi did not understand why he wanted to stay there; the elves were notorious for their disdain for Hounds, and Jordan's status as a guest in their castle could not have been the only reason why. But he'd been loathe to ask the truth, because he was afraid of what Nathaniel would say. And he felt, even now, that this separation was between Nathaniel and their Master and no one else; that they could all (if they wished, nowadays) live elsewhere and Gabriel would not deny them their request.

But when he looked at Nathaniel; when he met his gaze for the first time in months; when the words of welcome died on his lips because he *saw* what Nathaniel didn't want anyone else to know just yet, only Josiah's quick response to his distress saved him from having to explain himself.

And later, as Malachi lay in his bed, wide awake in the darkness, he felt Josiah's gaze on his back, and he whispered, "I saw--something Nathaniel would rather have kept to himself. Inadvertently."

"This has something to do with the Protector, and its gift to you," Josiah guessed, but did not ask him to betray Nathaniel's secret.

"I imagine it is the reason the Protector seemed to know so much about so many people," Malachi said. "I--I don't think I want that kind of a gift."

"Perhaps you're still getting used to it," Josiah said optimistically. "Perhaps it won't happen again."

But it *did* happen again. And again. And again. Three times over the span of the first week, and Malachi kept his silence because he wasn't certain what else to do.

Ben and Riala had been taken--together--to Sennet's house, where they lay in the same room, but in different beds, a concession to Riala's parents, who had wanted to take their daughter back to the dragon's territory as soon as they discovered she was alive. Sennet had refused, outright, to allow them to take her. Malachi, who felt responsible for their survival, since *he'd* made the bargain with the Protector for their lives, thought she'd made the right decision, because the dragons would have closed ranks, and Ben, Riala's companion for nearly sixty years, would have awakened alone in a world that had forgotten him, and he likely would never have seen her again.

Malachi, who still hoped Josiah was right in his optimism, had taken to spending most of the day and some of the night at Sennet's house in a solitary and guilty vigil, because he could meet Sennet's gaze without any issues at all, and he'd already seen too much.

Sennet, apparently, had no terrible secrets. Neither did Josiah, or Eri. Malachi hadn't quite summoned up enough courage to meet their Master's gaze quite yet. He wasn't certain he wanted to see any sort of secret that Gabriel had been hiding, especially now that he had no choice but to see them.

It was an uncomfortable situation, but not an impossible one, because Malachi wasn't the most outgoing of Hounds to begin with, and avoiding nearly everyone by sitting vigil at Ben and Riala's bedside seemed more of a solution than he could have ever hoped. Still, he felt guilty for pretending he was only there to keep them company when, in fact, he hoped that by the time they awoke, his sight would be if not normal, then at least manageable.

And then, a little over a week after the rescue, Tobias knocked on Sennet's door. Not for her help, but to join Malachi in his vigil, something Malachi had not expected at all.

Sennet did not protest his presence, but then again, Malachi hadn't told her what he could now see, either. She knew *something* was wrong; Healers were very astute at noticing distress, after all, but Malachi wasn't certain how he could tell her without branding himself a pariah until (if) he could learn some sort of control.

He did not protest Tobias' arrival, although Tobias seemed both uneasy and hesitant to join him.

Malachi was careful not to look at him directly. "There's a spare chair on the other side of the door," he said.

"Has there--they haven't woken up at all?"

"No," Malachi told him. "Not yet. But Sennet says they're sleeping, and I didn't want them to wake up alone."

"Because you're the one who bargained for their lives," Tobias said. "You think they'll blame you for being here." He spoke softly; simply, stating facts, not blaming Malachi for anything at all.

"Yes," Malachi said, because Tobias' words were true.

"After almost sixty years--" Tobias sat down in the chair, but didn't move it closer to either bed.

"Riala's parents wanted to take her away," Malachi said. "Sennet refused to let them take her."

"But she's a dragon," Tobias said.

"She was, yes," Malachi agreed. "But is she still?"

"And Ben was seen in sunlight," Tobias murmured. He hesitated, then added, "I--I'm not sure why I came here, really. I was on my way back from--" he paused. "There's a cousin. I can talk to. Who gives me information." Another pause. "I probably shouldn't be telling you this."

"You don't have to explain yourself," Malachi said. "Either where you were or why you're here."

Tobias was silent for a moment, then said, "I feel as if I should. Explain myself, that is. This isn't--something I would normally do."

"Neither was volunteering to go into the mists with Michael," Malachi pointed out.

Tobias smiled briefly. "But that was not bravery, or self-sacrifice," he said. "I gave my word that I would bring Michael back, and I did."

"Because you feel you are expendable," Malachi said, which was what Josiah had told him after their return.

"I've been told I am not," Tobias told him. "Vehemently. Although I'm not certain I believe them." He looked down at his hands. "I thought--I felt--" he sighed. "I'm not good at this."

"You'll find no judgment from me," Malachi said. "We had to learn to be more--compassionate--just as you are learning."

Tobias thought about this for a moment. "But what if it's not something I can learn?" he finally asked.

"You're here, aren't you?" Malachi replied. "For some reason you can't quite fathom, but you're *here*."

"I'm worried about my cousin," Tobias admitted. "And the others don't approve of my meetings with him, and they wouldn't--well, they *would* understand why I'm worried, but they feel as if I'm putting myself in danger just talking to him."

"Are you?" Malachi asked.

"He approached *me*," Tobias said. "I didn't approach him. But he's younger than Cecilia, and likely would be killed if my uncle found out about his betrayal." He paused. "And he didn't come to our last meeting."

Malachi knew a bit about the Morgan household, but not many details. From the little he'd heard, he wasn't sure he *wanted* to know the details. And he certainly did not want to know any secrets about the Morgan household that Tobias might be hiding. "Could your cousin flee?" he asked instead. "And come to live with you?"

Tobias shifted on his chair. After a moment, he stood, and walked to the window, staring out at the forest outside Sennet's little house. "I asked him," he said. "He said that if he fled, then I would have no information at all from the household. And no one to warn me, if they planned an attack."

This was likely true. The price on Tobias' head had doubled, then doubled again. Malachi had heard questions, however, and doubts that Ichabod Morgan would agree to pay the price, even if someone managed to deliver Tobias to him, dead or alive.

"I'm not used to worrying about anyone but myself," Tobias continued. "And I'm not sure what to do about it. Or my cousin. If he dies because of me--" He hesitated. "Is that compassion?"

It was an honest question, and one Tobias had not wanted to ask, Malachi thought, and wondered if he'd expected him to laugh, or worse, deride him for attempting to pick his way through emotions he was not accustomed to feeling.

"Yes," Malachi said. "And probably empathy, too." Now it was *his* turn to hesitate. But he felt as if he should share--*something*--with Tobias, since he'd risked Malachi's scorn by sharing his own confusion. "I'm not here just to keep them company or because I feel responsible for their presence here."

Tobias turned. "Oh?"

Malachi avoided his gaze. "You may not want to stay here if I tell you. It has to do with the Protector, and the gift it gave me to help me see." He paused. There was no good way to tell him, and Malachi fully expected Tobias to leave as soon as he realized the import of Malachi's abilities. "It helps me to see too well."

"Too well?" Tobias asked curiously. And then, "Why are you telling me this?"

"Because I know you have secrets you don't want anyone else to know," Malachi said. "I'm giving you the option for me not to know them." He turned to look at Ben, lying so silently in the bed. Waiting for Tobias to leave. "It won't work unless I meet your gaze, so you needn't--"

Tobias sat back down. "I see," he said, interrupting whatever Malachi had intended to say. "The Protector gifted you with sight, but now you see too much. When before, you saw nothing at all."

"Before, I used a spell to see, and those of my family helped me see," Malachi said. "Now, I can see using everything around me, but I--when I agreed to this, I didn't expect for this to happen." He kept his gaze on Ben. "I'll understand if you don't want to stay."

"You're hiding here, aren't you?" Tobias asked. There was no fear in his voice; wariness, yes, but not fear.

"I already know things--accidentally--that others would rather keep to themselves," Malachi said. "I had hoped that this ability would go away, eventually."

"I see," Tobias said. And then, "What if my secret is one I want to share, but don't know *how* to share?" He paused. Took a deep breath. "To the others, I mean. I don't--" His voice cracked. "Perhaps I would rather you know." Another pause, then, whispered, "I don't know how to tell them." He lowered his head to his hands.

Malachi stared at him in surprise. He hadn't thought that his new sight might *help* someone find the courage to speak or to tell a story; he'd merely thought about the secrets no one wanted to share. Like Nathaniel's feelings for Amalea, which Malachi would honestly rather not have known.

"You could tell me," he finally said. "Of your own accord."

Tobias sighed. "You know that before I came to them, your Master and Lucas and Aaron's father left me in my mother's house. With a bottle of garlic-laced olive oil and a pair of gloves."

"I heard, yes," Malachi said.

"That was after she killed me and brought me back to life," Tobias whispered. "Twice. And drained my blood to make Greta into a vampire." He paused. "They left me there. To kill my mother. I could barely *move*, and they left me there."

He wouldn't look at Malachi, but not, Malachi suspected, because he feared what he would see.

"In hindsight," Malachi said, "I think they regret that decision, especially after what happened later." He knew no such thing, but suspected it, especially after Tobias had volunteered to go with Michael into the mists and asked nothing for himself in return.

"Oh," Tobias said, surprised. "I--ah--I hadn't thought that they would--is that why everyone has been so *nice*?"

"I've been told that Aaron's mother is naturally that way," Malachi said, having been on the receiving end of her concern, albeit indirectly. "And you made no bargains, when you volunteered to go into the mists with Michael. You demanded nothing of the Council, and Lucas notices these things."

"I didn't feel as if I was in a position to demand anything," Tobias said. "I am there by their sufferance, after all; the Council's, I mean, and your Master's, and--"

"No," Malachi said. "Not by their sufferance. You don't want to go back, do you?"

Tobias' smile was small and fleeting. "The correct answer would be 'of course not', but that's also the true answer. I would like to stay. I find it--refreshing that they care so little about status, and that I don't have to--" He sighed. "I can trust them. But I--"

Malachi thought about what their Master had said about what they had found inside Tobias' mother's house. How Tobias had been chained, lying in a pool of blood. How the girl, Greta, who was--even now--quite mad, had answered the door covered in his blood. How Tobias' mother had not seemed concerned for her son; how she'd told them that she'd used Michael's spell three times--

And he was still sane, after that, which had surprised Gabriel greatly.

And then, Tobias had appeared at Erialas' front door, restored--

"Oh," Malachi said.

Tobias raised his head. Malachi automatically glanced away, but Tobias said, "No. I'd rather you see. If you don't mind to look."

After a moment, Malachi met his gaze.

Tobias had fled from the house once his mother was dead. Although fled was probably not the right word. Staggered, perhaps. He'd barely made it to the cabin before dawn. Didn't even have the keys, but the door was open, and someone slept inside.

An old man. A vagrant. He'd found the broken window where he'd gained entry later, when he'd awakened. There were no wards, so he'd spent the day in the only closet, because he had no time for any sort of preparations.

The old man hadn't even opened his eyes. Tobias had later removed seventeen bottles of cheap wine from where he'd made his bed. And he'd buried the body in the garden and covered the space with rocks from a flowerbed.

His mother had liked her flowerbeds.

They'd left him alone. Half-starved. He'd returned to them a few nights later, restored. And both Erialas and Cecilia were vampires.

He hadn't intended to stay. Had only intended to ask for help with the wards. If they would help him. Otherwise--he knew both the Morgans and the Richmonds wanted him dead. And he'd already made contingency plans. If they refused to help him, then he would have returned to the cabin and opened all the windows and doors and he would have--

But he'd tarried too long. Fearful of rejection. That they'd drive him away. And by the time he actually spoke to Erialas, his only option had been to return to his mother's house that night, and he couldn't bring himself to do that, and then they'd let him stay.

And six months had passed, and no one had asked how he had come to be so restored, afterwards. No one had asked.

"I think, perhaps, they already know," Malachi said gently. "Or they suspect. Cecilia and Erialas are vampires, after all, and they would realize what you had to do to heal yourself when the Council and my Master and Aaron's father left you with no other option."

Tobias let out a long breath. "But I didn't *tell* them," he said. "I *haven't* told them." And then, softer, "I haven't told them much of anything at all. And now that Erialas and Michael are members of the Council--"

"You feel as if you should," Malachi said, and Tobias nodded. "Our Master kept his entire family a secret from Lucas for years. And yet, they are good friends, now." When Tobias did not reply, he added, "You won't be cast out for this, and you won't be cast out for caring about your cousin. Or anyone else, for that matter."

Sennet knocked on the door. "I've brought tea," she said when Malachi opened it.

Tobias had stood up at her knock. "I should be going," he said quickly. "I--I didn't intend to bother anyone--"

"It's no bother," Sennet said, and set the tray on the table beside Tobias' chair. "Truly," she added when he would have protested. "You can stay as long as you wish."

Malachi had tried to protest after the first day. Sennet had refused to listen. "If you're here, I'll feed you," she'd said. "It's a failing of mine. But if you feel you have to repay me, you can help me feed *them,* okay?"

She said the same thing to Tobias.

"You wouldn't mind if I came back?" he asked.

"Not at all," Sennet said.

"I wouldn't mind either," Malachi commented, and poured Tobias a cup of tea before pouring one for himself.

Tobias cradled the cup in his hands, staring down at it. "Thank you," he finally said. "I would like to come back. I'm not certain why--I can't explain it, but--"

Sennet touched his arm. It was only a little touch, but he stiffened nonetheless. "You don't have to explain yourself to me," she said.

"I feel as if I should," Tobias admitted. "As if you would expect me to."

She looked at him closely. "Are you well?"

"I'm--worried," Tobias said, and then, in a rush, he told her everything, as if telling Malachi--and Malachi's sight--had loosened some dam inside of himself that had blocked him from speaking, before.

When he was finished, Sennet asked, "What is your contact's name?"

"Liam," Tobias said, and drank a sip of tea. He sighed. Sat back down, since it was obvious Sennet had no intention of kicking him out of her house for his past transgressions. "He's--nearly thirteen, I think. There are rumors that he's one of my uncle's bastard sons, but I don't know if the rumors are true."

"And your uncle's legitimate son is Arthur, right?" Sennet asked. "And he's about sixteen?"

"Yes," Tobias said. "But I don't think Arthur is involved in this." And then, hesitantly, "Is he?"

"Mmm," Sennet said, and at first, Malachi thought she would stay silent, but then she said, "Are you willing to talk to me about the Morgan household?"

"Has something happened to Liam?" Tobias asked; almost demanded. "He missed our last meeting--"

"Earlier this afternoon, I brought a young human boy out of the Morgan household," Sennet said. "Healers go where they are needed, and a fairy named Blossom promised your cousin Arthur that he would be saved. And so I saved him."

She had said nothing of this when Malachi had arrived to sit by Ben and Riala's beds.

"He's very young," Sennet continued. "And very weak." Before Tobias could ask about Liam again, she said, "I believe Liam is alive. Maya is involved, and she has everything in hand, although my services might be needed once they are rescued."

"Rescued?" Tobias whispered, and set down his cup so he wouldn't drop it.

"There's a tunnel, under the Morgan household," Sennet said. "It was an escape tunnel, originally, according to Maya. For use in Hunter attacks. The tunnel collapsed somewhere in the middle over the years, but there are trolls involved now, working to open the way again."

Reluctantly, Tobias said, "Humans are used for food in the Morgan household. But--how young?"

"It's hard to say," Sennet said. "He's very small and undernourished. He may be less than seven years old." She paused. "I don't need to tell you what happened to him, do I?"

Malachi felt sick, just thinking about it. Tobias closed his eyes and shook his head. "No." And then, as if he felt he had to say it, "I--I never *knowingly* drank from a child--"

"And I am not accusing you of doing so," Sennet said quietly. "What I'm asking, however, is if this happens regularly. I know you didn't live inside the household, but--"

"To be honest, I don't know," Tobias said slowly. "I would imagine that yes, it happens frequently, if the boy's condition is any indication. My uncle would rather pretend bottled blood doesn't exist, but he *does* use it. For those--" he paused. "Status is everything in the Morgan household. Humans are lower than low. And those vampires who displease him, or are seen as useless burdens won't ever taste fresh blood. He cannot feed everyone on the humans who live there."

"In your mother's house--" Malachi began.

Tobias' lips twisted. "We fed on the servants. I suppose they were treated better than the humans in my uncle's house; there were no children, at least." And then, "I realize that doesn't really make it any better to stomach."

Sennet's frown deepened. Tobias said, softly, "I cannot change the past."

"None of us can," Malachi said.

"How willing are you to try for a better future?" Sennet asked.

"My uncle has a price on my head," Tobias said after a moment. "It's--quite large, or so I've been told. If I set foot anywhere *near* the Morgan household and they catch wind of my presence--"

"The cave is half a mile away," Sennet said. "I could take you there." She glanced at Malachi. "Both of you, if you wish. Maya might need help, once the tunnel is clear."

Malachi didn't want to go, and it wasn't because he didn't want to help. Despite Tobias' words; despite what he had done, he still felt as if this new sight would not gain him anything but trouble. He opened his mouth to tell Sennet that, and then, through the bond, he heard Gabriel say, *Maya has asked for our help to rescue someone she cares about from the Morgan household. I believe Sennet may be involved.*

Not long ago, Gabriel would already have known this, because he would have been listening in through the bond. But that rarely happened now.

We are speaking about it now, my lord, Malachi said. *Tobias is here as well; he stopped to sit with me.* Among other things.

She gave no details, Gabriel continued. *But I told her we would help. If you are not willing, I will go.*

"Will you go?" Tobias asked.

It's not that I am not willing, Malachi said through the bond. *It's what I'm afraid that I may see, my lord; I'm sorry I haven't told you this before.* Aloud, he said, "Someone should stay with Ben and Riala. Maya has asked for the Hunt's help with this--"

This has to do with the Protector's gift? Gabriel asked.

Yes, my lord, Malachi said. *It makes me see too clearly. It makes me see things that others might not want to be seen.*

I see, Gabriel said. *This is why you won't look at anyone?*

Malachi hadn't realized it was so obvious. *Yes, my lord. I believe that is how the Protector and its other knew so much. It's not quite reading thoughts, not like Jordan. But close enough that I can sympathize.*

Tobias and Sennet had obviously realized that Malachi wasn't ignoring them, but conversing through the bond. Still, Tobias looked uneasy and unsure of himself, no doubt because of his secret, and what Gabriel would think of what he had done.

"I have told no one what I've seen," Malachi said aloud, for Tobias' benefit.

And what do you see when you look at me? Gabriel asked.

I haven't, yet, Malachi admitted. *I've been too afraid.* And there, he'd used that damning word.

Do not be afraid, Gabriel said calmly. *Is what you've seen so terrible?*

Malachi thought about his question for a moment. Terrible? No. Not terrible. Surprising? Yes. Shocking? Yes. Distressing? But terrible? *No, not terrible. But these secrets were not shared. It's as if I've stolen them.*

And this is why you've hidden yourself in Sennet's house these past few days, Gabriel said. *Not only because you feel responsible for Ben and Riala.*

Yes, Malachi said, because that was the truth.

And how does Tobias feel that you know his secret? Gabriel asked, then added, *I did not look, if he needs reassurance.*

Relieved, Malachi said.

And how do you think Nathaniel will react? Gabriel asked, as if he *had* looked into Malachi's mind; as if he had--

You knew? Malachi asked, because that was the only answer.

Yes, Gabriel said. *Nathaniel has spoken to me.*

"Oh," Malachi said aloud. Through the bond, he added, *I didn't want to pry, my lord. I wouldn't have asked for this sort of sight.*

I know, Gabriel said. *I have no secrets from you, regardless. Will you go? They may need your help, in more ways than one.*

"I'll go," Malachi said aloud.

Tobias looked relieved. "Thank you," he said in a way that made Malachi wonder how many times he'd actually spoken those words.

And if I need to come as well, you would only have to call, Gabriel added, and Malachi felt the bond fade again to the back of his mind.

"And you needn't show us the way," Malachi said to Sennet. "I can find them."

"Very well," Sennet said. "I will wait here, with my patients."

"May I--before we leave, may I see the boy?" Tobias asked, almost tripping over the words.

"Yes, of course," Sennet said. "Follow me." She led them both down the hall to another room--Malachi didn't quite understand it, but her house, which seemed so small on the outside, was much larger on the inside. Inside this room, on a narrow bed, lay a small, wasted child, his eyes closed and sunken in his face, his skin tinged with gray. There were bandages on his neck and on the one wrist Malachi could see. The clothes he wore swamped his thin frame; he seemed to be on the brink of death, even in a Healer's care.

"He'll live," Sennet said softly. "He drank a little broth, earlier. I don't want to give him too much, because it wouldn't stay down."

Malachi thought that Tobias would speak; to protest the boy's treatment, but he did not. His lips thinned; he seemed almost furious by the time he tore his gaze away from the boy and looked at Sennet.

"I will help in any way I can so that this never happens again," he vowed, and Malachi could hear the truth in his words.

"Thank you," Sennet said. "When Liam and the others are rescued, they'll need a place to stay. Maya said something about the Walker household, but there might not be enough time to get there tonight. Do you think--"

"Erialas won't mind," Tobias said. "But I'll call him on my way to make sure. We have beds enough for half my cousins, if it came to that."

"It may come to that," Sennet said, and Tobias reluctantly nodded, still looking at the boy. And then he shook himself, and glanced at Malachi.

"I'm ready if you are," Malachi said, and Tobias followed him out the door.

They walked into the forest without speaking, and then Tobias said, "I meant what I said."

"I know you did," Malachi told him. "That may be a large undertaking, and best not done alone."

"I don't plan to attempt it alone," Tobias said. "And I need to talk to the others about it, but--not right now."

He seemed more certain of himself now that neither Malachi nor Sennet had condemned him. But he was wary, walking through the forest, as if he expected his cousins to be out in force. Not necessarily looking for *him,* but perhaps for his contact, Liam, and Ichabod Morgan's son.

But they met no one as they made their way closer and closer to the Morgan household. They kept to the forest and to the shadows, moving quickly; Malachi found he had no trouble keeping up with a vampire's pace.

And then, out of the darkness, Maya appeared. "Come," she said, and led them into a well-hidden cave.

The ceiling was low enough for Tobias to have to duck his head at times, but Malachi and Maya could walk easily.

"You are responsible for this?" she asked after a moment of silence.

"Liam is the cousin I've been speaking to, yes," Tobias said evenly. "He contacted me and offered to pass me information I might need. I did not refuse him."

"He's very young," Maya said. "And he almost died." She sighed. "There is more to this; did Sennet tell you about Arthur?"

"Sennet said someone you care about is in need of help," Malachi told her.

"I care about all three of them," Maya said. "But it began with Arthur, and then Iris, and then Liam. Although Iris' mother is with them as well, and she'll be coming, too."

"*What* began with Arthur?" Tobias asked, and Maya explained. It seemed extraordinary that no one had suspected anything until now; even more extraordinary that they were still alive after what Arthur had done. Tobias' mouth fell open; Malachi saw both guilt and wonder in his gaze, as if he couldn't quite decide if Arthur and the others were very brave or very foolhardy.

Malachi suspected the guilt stemmed from the fact that Tobias himself would never have thought of such betrayal while he lived with the Morgan household's grasp. He never would have considered it. That Arthur had not only *considered* it, but had been rescuing prisoners for years was almost unbelievable. But Maya had involved Ethan Walker, and while Malachi had yet to meet the head of the Walker household, he'd heard plenty of stories, most of which were true.

"Are they to flee to the Walker household, then?" Tobias asked.

"Not tonight," Maya said. "They'll need a place to stay tonight." She glanced into the darkness where Malachi heard movement; sliding sounds, and grunts, and--chewing. "Provided we can open the tunnel by dawn."

"Provided they're still in the tunnel when it's open," Tobias pointed out. "Is someone of yours with them? Are they hurt?"

"Iris and her mother are unharmed," Maya said. "Liam and Arthur, however; Arthur was shot with an arrow that was supposed to be silver. Both were beaten."

Tobias had sent a message to Erialas, who had responded with a text, then called. The person on the other end sounded like Michael, though, although Malachi heard voices in the background, which probably meant they all were listening in.

He explained almost everything. Not about his secret, but about the boy, and Liam, and what Maya had told them about Arthur and Iris as well. His tone was not questioning, or hesitant, but firm. And no one asked any questions at all.

This was the person Malachi thought Tobias would become. Despite his upbringing, he was used to getting his way, and that showed in his voice and his bearing. He was not used to rejection, or failure, although he'd bounced back rather quickly once he found his balance again.

But then, he said, "I know it's not my place--" and Malachi knew that he wasn't quite as certain of himself as he pretended. Not yet, at least.

"It *is* your place," Erialas said, his voice slightly tinny through the phone's small speakers. "And we have no objections."

"Thank you," Tobias said, and glanced up at Malachi. "I have something else to tell all of you, once Liam and the others are safe."

"You'll call if you need us?" Cecilia asked from the background.

"I'll call if I need you," Tobias said. "Malachi's here with me, and Maya--unless my uncle is waiting for us past the blockage, we should be fine."

"And if he is?" Michael asked.

"We have trolls," Maya said. "And small folk, as well."

"Keep us informed," Erialas said simply, and Tobias promised he would and hung up the phone.

The trolls were massive, hulking things who should not have been able to stand upright in the tunnel, but somehow managed to do so nonetheless. Tobias wanted to be as close to the blockage as possible; no one protested, but Malachi felt they were in the way. But then, one of the trolls managed to pierce all the way through, and in a small shower of pebbles, the way--albeit small, and too narrow for anyone except, perhaps, the boy who lay in Sennet's house--was clear.

There was silence from the other side; torturous silence, and then Tobias asked, "Liam?"

"Liam's asleep," a voice said out of the darkness. "They're all asleep. I'm Fern, Iris' mother." She spoke in a whisper. "I think the searchers have found the tunnel. Is there any way you can get them out of here quickly?"

"The hole's not large enough yet," Tobias said, and looked at the trolls, who looked at Maya, who said, "Quickly? No. But we could collapse the other side of the tunnel."

"And guarantee the whole thing won't collapse on top of them?" Malachi asked.

"Do it," came a cracked, exhausted voice from the other side. "I'd rather take my chances with you."

"Arthur," Tobias said, naming the speaker. He spoke softly, almost reverently.

"Liam will be happy you came for him," Arthur said.

"I came for all of you," Tobias said. "Even though I had no idea you would dare to do something like this."

"We may not have to," Maya said as the ground shook beneath their feet. "They may do it for us. That tunnel has never been very stable."

A cloud of dust burst from the hole the trolls had made. Malachi stepped aside, but Tobias didn't move; he reached through the hole as if to snatch Liam and the others out of harm's way, and then, softly, asked, "Are you okay?"

There was no answer, at first, and then, a whisper, "It's--hard to breathe." That had to be Liam, which meant Iris was the only one who hadn't spoken.

Coughing, Arthur whispered Iris' name. When she answered, Tobias removed his arm from the hole, then asked, "The tunnel collapsed?"

One of the trolls stepped forward. The other had vanished; Malachi hadn't seen it move from where it had stopped against the wall. It grumbled at Maya, who looked at the remaining bits of blockage critically. "It's thin enough; it might work." To the four on the other side, she said, "You'll need to move back away from the blockage, okay? As far as you can." To Tobias and Malachi, she said, "And you'll need to--"

"I want to stay," Tobias said, as Malachi knew he would.

Maya looked as if she wanted to argue, but she stared at him for a moment, then nodded. "You'll need to watch out for yourself, then," she said. "I can't be responsible for your safety."

Tobias nodded. "Understood."

The troll--melted into the stone. One moment it was there, standing in front of them; the next, it had stepped forward, and disappeared. Malachi tensed, but then he saw the troll reappear, super-imposed over the stones that blocked them from Liam and the others. For a moment, Malachi had no idea what it intended to do, but then it--somehow--took hold of the rocks and *stood up*. Taller and taller, until the hole leading to the other side widened; until the rest of the blockage crumbled and fell away.

"Quickly, now!" Maya said, and Malachi helped Tobias as he reached into the darkness and pulled out first Liam, then Arthur, then Iris, then her mother. Covered in dust and dirt and blood, they looked less like vampires and more like the trolls who had saved them. But they were alive, and despite what seemed to be major injuries, they managed to follow Tobias and Malachi to the mouth of the cave.

And then, from behind them, a thunderous roar. The ground shook again, harder this time, and they fled from the cave to the forest.

Maya stepped up beside them to steady Arthur when he swayed. Malachi did not see the trolls anywhere.

"They can't be killed by collapsing tunnels," she said, as if he'd asked the question aloud. "Is everyone okay?"

Liam looked at Arthur, who looked at Iris, who didn't protest when her mother wrapped her arms around her.

"Everyone's okay," Arthur said, but he looked both exhausted and ill, and Liam wasn't much better.

Iris and her mother seemed to be unwounded, at least.

"There's not much time until dawn," Malachi reminded them. "And we walked here." In fact, dawn was quickly approaching, which meant two things: they had a very short amount of time to get everyone to safety, and the possibility of searchers in the forest would be small, since the Morgan household only relied on their humans for food and nothing more.

"I'm sorry," Iris' mother said. "I don't think they can walk very far."

"No, *I'm* sorry," Tobias said. "We should have brought supplies."

Arthur's gaze kept straying to Tobias, as if he couldn't quite reconcile the cousin he'd known with the one who stood in front of him right now.

"I don't think supplies would have helped very much," Malachi said. "They need to rest." Liam was swaying where he stood, his eyes half-closed. None of them had asked Malachi's name, or identity, and he had to wonder what would happen if they discovered he was a Hound.

"It's about five miles to Erialas' house," Tobias said. "Part of the way can be through Faerie--" But that wouldn't help them once they reached the edge of the lawn, which was past the Veil.

"It's less than two miles to our house," Malachi said, "And they would be welcome." And the Hunt had entrances both in Faerie and past the Veil, if needed.

"*Your* house?" Arthur asked curiously.

Of course they could come here, Gabriel said before Malachi could ask.

Malachi hesitated. "My name is Malachi," he said. "You would be guests of the Hunt."

Iris' mother gasped. Although she didn't protest, it was clear that she'd heard some of the stories. Iris, on the other hand, looked interested, brightening up for the first time since the rescue.

Liam didn't say a word. His eyes were closed now; he'd leaned back against the wall, but as Malachi watched, his head fell forward and Tobias had to catch him before he toppled to the ground. He did not wake up.

"We should go," Maya said to Arthur, who hadn't spoken. "If you need my assurance that the Hunt will keep you safe, consider it done."

"I know you're not what the stories say," Arthur whispered, although he didn't look completely convinced. "I'm just not certain I can walk that far right now."

"Then we'll help you," Malachi said. "That's why we're here."

Arthur nodded. "Thank you," he said, and did not pull away when Iris took his arm.

It was a silent walk through the forest. Malachi kept his eyes and ears peeled for any sign of pursuit, but there was none. After a little while, a fairy flew up and reported that the tunnel's collapse had brought down part of the house, so that was likely why there had been no pursuit.

"This is not your fault," Maya said to Arthur, as if she expected him to feel responsible.

"My father won't feel that way," Arthur replied, and Iris mother glanced back the way they'd come.

"No, he won't," she said, subdued now, as if she'd just realized they could never go back. "Um. We didn't bring anything with us--"

"Nor did I," Tobias said.

"How much do you know about what we did?" Arthur asked abruptly, and for a moment, Malachi thought he'd asked Iris' mother, who apparently had not been involved until now.

"Maya told us some of it," Tobias replied. He was silent for a moment, then added, "If I had discovered your secret before my mother's death, I would have reported you to your father. That information would have eliminated a lot of bother before my mother went mad."

"Is it true, then?" Iris' mother asked hesitantly. "What she did to you?"

"It's true," Tobias said. "All of it." He paused. "And it's not something I like to talk about."

Malachi watched as their conditioning eliminated any additional questions they might have had; even Arthur looked uneasy, as if he thought Fern's question had gone too far. And he watched as Tobias realized this; and a flash of annoyance crossed his face. Annoyance and frustration, as if he thought he should have known how they would react, and he had forgotten.

"Of course that doesn't mean you can't ask questions," he said, but Malachi wasn't certain that would be enough. Not yet, at least.

"Blossom said that the human boy was safe," Arthur said instead of pursuing that line of questioning. "In a Healer's care."

"Yes," Malachi said before Tobias could respond. "Safe and comfortable. Do you know his name?"

"No," Arthur said. "No, I'm sorry--but I don't. I'd never seen him before, but I couldn't leave him there."

They were almost to the cave that led to the Hunt's house in Faerie. The sky was still dark; they'd made good time.

"And I feel I have to ask," Arthur said as Josiah stepped out of the cave to meet them. "Is it a good idea for you to let us stay with you? The price on *our* heads is likely to be much higher than the price on Tobias' head--"

"We would welcome you nonetheless," Gabriel said from behind Josiah. "Please--come in. You needn't worry about politeness or status here; you are here to rest."

If Malachi hadn't been watching Arthur's face, he wouldn't have seen the fleeting shift; the small tightness around his eyes releasing; the tension in his shoulders suddenly gone. He swayed; staggered back. Malachi caught his arm.

"I'm sorry, I--"

"Go and rest," Maya said, and wrapped her arms around him, hugging him tightly. "I'll not come with you, but I'll see you soon. Okay?"

Tobias had already walked inside, following Josiah, no doubt eager to settle Liam down onto a bed. Iris and her mother were right behind them; Arthur stopped in front of Gabriel.

"Thank you," he said.

He managed to walk inside under his own accord, but only just; when Malachi showed him to a room, he was asleep almost before his head hit the pillow.

There weren't enough beds for everyone without someone giving up their own, but Malachi didn't mind, and no one else protested, either. Iris' mother was the only one who didn't fall asleep; Emle took her in hand and she emerged from the bathroom, clean, with borrowed clothes less than thirty minutes after their arrival.

"What now?" she asked when Emle handed her a cup. "I'm sorry--I only found out about this tonight; Iris was intending to leave with Arthur and Liam, and I couldn't--" Her voice cracked. "She's all I have left. I couldn't let her go without me."

"I would feel the same way," Emle said firmly. "You've done nothing wrong, and no one will fault you for this."

Iris' mother burst into tears. Emle put her arm around her shoulder and led her into the kitchen, away from everyone, but not before Malachi accidentally met her gaze--and saw what she'd never told her daughter; why they had returned to the Morgan household after her husband's death.

"I should go," Tobias said, and Josiah offered to walk him home, and Gabriel took one look at Malachi's face and said, "And we should talk," which released Malachi from accompanying them.

Even Eri was asleep; despite the fact that they had guests, the house was quiet, save for the low murmur of Emle's voice in the kitchen.

"My lord," Malachi said as soon as they were alone in the library.

"You saw something, just now." Gabriel's voice was quiet and calm. "What was it?"

"Should I tell you?" Malachi asked. "Or keep it to myself, where it's likely to do less harm?"

"Hmm," Gabriel said. "Good question. Is it likely to do harm? To anyone here?" And then, as if he'd just now noticed, "Look at me, please."

"It was easy, in the dark," Malachi murmured. "I didn't actually have to look at anyone; not closely."

"Malachi," Gabriel said, ever-patient.

Slowly, Malachi raised his head to look directly at Gabriel. What he saw in his gaze; what he *knew* was not, at all, surprising. Or distressing. After all, he'd been a Hound for many, many years. And there was little to be hidden in such a relationship as theirs.

"You've spoken with Lucas," Malachi said.

"I have," Gabriel told him. "And I've explained the situation."

"And he said--" *Lucas had not realized what he had asked when he'd offered Gabriel a place on the Council. Despite that, in the end, he had not reneged the offer.*

"And he said he would welcome all of you, as well," Gabriel told him. "Although I understand his point of view, I also realize that gives you little choice, if I were to accept. And I would rather you have that choice, so I have not accepted."

"I see," Malachi said, and tried to comprehend what it would feel like to be a member of the Council. The *Council,* who had kept the Hunt bound for so many years. And Lucas, who had very nearly cost Malachi his life, there at the beginning.

"As for any secrets you thought I'd hide from you--" Gabriel waited a moment to see if Malachi would protest, or deny this, but he was silent. "I have nothing to hide, as you can see."

"I'm sorry I didn't tell you, my lord," Malachi said.

"Now," Gabriel said. "Iris' mother?"

"Her husband was not killed by Hunters, at least, as far as she knows," Malachi said slowly. "That's what she told everyone; that's what Ichabod told her, I mean, but she doesn't know if it's true. He'd gone to visit the Morgan household and never came back. She thought that he might be a prisoner, because Ichabod had never approved of their leaving, but she hasn't been able to find out what happened to him. And now, even though she refused to be left behind, she thinks she'll never know." Malachi paused. "Iris doesn't know anything about this."

"What was his name?" Gabriel asked.

"Carroll," Malachi said. "Ichabod's younger brother."

"And Grandmother Morgan's youngest son," Gabriel said. "We met once, a very long time ago." He paused. "I don't think it unlikely that she is correct, and that he came to harm inside the household, not from the Hunters. How long has she been looking?"

"Since they arrived, six years ago," Malachi said. "Although from what I could tell, her movements were curtailed, and she had no idea Iris was involved in this until it was too late."

"Since they were freeing prisoners, it's likely Carroll is either dead or was held elsewhere," Gabriel said. "My bet would be dead, after this long. Even if they kept him captive while holding his family as bait for his cooperation, someone would have known of his presence, unless Ichabod and Grandmother Morgan's hold on the household is that complete."

"Your hold on *us* was that complete, once," Malachi said.

"True," Gabriel replied. "But you were not an entire household of humans and vampires. And you could shift shape, and did so without my knowledge."

"This may not be over," Malachi said, and told him what Tobias had said after he'd seen the human boy. "I don't think he has a plan; not yet."

"And you wish to be involved?" Gabriel asked. "We've never involved ourselves in household business, and neither has the Council."

"Sennet said he's maybe six years old," Malachi told him. "Tobias said it's likely this happens often to the humans who live inside the household, young or old. The Council cannot look the other way if they know something is wrong, can they?"

"If we go after the Morgans, even with Council approval, what of the Richmonds, then?" Gabriel asked. "They're no better, although they've been quiet, of late. If they discover what we've done, provided we succeed, then they will likely assume they'll be next. And we may have a war on our hands, because none of them will go quietly."

There was no easy answer. Malachi knew that, but he also knew that without their help, Tobias and the others would likely fail, provided he managed to convince his housemates that they couldn't turn a blind eye to the Morgan household any longer. He thought, perhaps, that Michael would side with Tobias, but Cecilia, not being a Morgan, was a cipher, and he wasn't certain what Erialas and Aaron would say. And the fact that both Erialas and Michael were members of the Council only complicated everything even more. Malachi wasn't certain if one member of the Council could go against the others without the whole Council breaking apart. And he already knew what Lucas would say, because he'd said it before. The Council did not get involved in vampire matters.

But surely, once Lucas saw the boy lying in Sennet's house, surely he wouldn't turn away. Malachi knew Tobias was right; this couldn't continue.

"If you'd like me to speak to Lucas about this, I will," Gabriel said. "But I fear I already know what he will say."

"May *I* speak to Lucas about this?" Malachi asked.

"Of course," Gabriel said. "And I assume Tobias will want to go with you, as well."

"And Sennet, I think," Malachi said, then asked, "What if *I* feel as if we should be involved?"

"Since you obviously do, I will say only one thing," Gabriel told him. "I will not stop *you* from pursuing this, but *I* will not go against Lucas." He paused. "Although, I would not abandon you if you were in trouble, either."

"Thank you, my lord," Malachi said.

"For now, however, the human boy is safe, and you should get some rest," Gabriel suggested. "I have a feeling that the day ahead of us will be trying, in more ways than one."

Since they'd given up their beds to their guests, Malachi joined Thomas out in the cave where the sand was soft and, at least in the form of a Hound, quite comfortable. And, mindful of what lay ahead, he fell asleep.

Tobias

They were all waiting for him in the library when he arrived, with tea on the table, despite the late hour. He'd seen Josiah off and let himself inside the house--the *silent* house--but he had no illusions that they wouldn't have waited up for him.

But when he hesitated in the doorway, he only saw concern on their faces, nothing more. Perhaps a little fear, especially from Cecilia, which confused him.

"They're safe," he said. "Hopefully asleep by now, in the Hunt's house. It was too far for them to walk here."

"Tell us what happened," Erialas suggested, and Tobias did. And then, after that, he told them what he had kept secret for so long, and waited for their judgment.

After a moment of silence, Cecilia asked, "Do you think we're stupid?"

Shocked, Tobias looked up at her, and realized that they all were smiling; not judging him for what he had done, but *smiling.* In relief that he had trusted them enough to tell them.

"I--er," he managed to say, because he couldn't manage to say anything else.

"Dad wanted to ask," Aaron said. "After you came here. But Erialas asked him not to." He looked around the room, presumably for support. "I mean, they didn't leave you with *anything.*"

Tobias felt a lump form in his throat. "No, they did not." His voice cracked. "I'm sorry I didn't tell you. I thought--"

"You thought we wouldn't let you stay," Erialas finished his sentence when he couldn't.

"Yes," Tobias said, because that was the truth. "And I--I *want* to stay." He'd told them about the human boy, but not what he'd promised Sennet, so he told them now. And again, they surprised him.

"My question would be how the Richmond household would react if something were to happen to the Morgan household," Erialas said. "I'm not the only one who will have that question, either. It's the same one Lucas will ask."

"I kind of assumed Lucas would refuse to help," Tobias said. "The Council doesn't usually involve itself in vampire households."

"There's a vampire on the Council now," Erialas said. "That changes things."

Tobias hadn't considered that. "I see," he said.

"Er," Cecilia said. "About the Richmond household. While we're--er--confessing secrets and everything--" She looked a bit embarrassed now as she took a folded envelope out of her pocket. "I got a letter in the mail yesterday. From my brother, Tristan."

"I thought your brother's name was Jericho," Tobias said, trying to remember why the name Tristan sounded so familiar.

"It is," Cecilia told him. "My half-brother Tristan, I suppose." She paused. "Who is currently head of the Richmond household." Miserably, she added, "They told me not to tell anyone what happened. And no one asked, so I didn't."

"And the letter says you can tell us now?" Michael asked, and Cecilia nodded.

"Would you read us the letter?" Tobias asked. "And tell us what happened?"

"I don't know everything," Cecilia said. "My brother Jericho had a talent for music, and our mother sent him away. Tristan was sent after him and never returned. There had always been rumors that he was my half-brother, but no one knew the truth. Ten years later--almost a year ago now--one of the searchers brought Jericho back. He was--" Her breath caught in her throat. "Almost killed. And left out in the forest to die, but he was rescued. I haven't seen him, but Tristan said he would make a full recovery." She whispered the next part. "Tristan came to avenge him, and killed my father."

"You told us you were a prisoner, too," Erialas said gently. "Did he free you as well?"

Cecilia shook her head. "No, he--there was another vampire there. His name is Alexander Ross; he took Jericho in, and Tristan, later. He's very old. I mean, he looks like he's a little older than Aaron's father, but he's been a vampire for a very long time."

"He repairs musical instruments," Erialas said. "I met him once, a long time ago. He came here to look at my grandmother's piano; the one in the second parlor. But I don't think my father knew my mother had called him, because he never came back. I think I was about five years old when he came."

"Huh," Tobias said. "I wonder what he's doing in the Richmond household, then."

"Apparently, making sure that the transfer of power goes smoothly," Cecilia said. "And giving violin lessons. Tristan says there's only one student who's any good. Minerva was there, too, and an elf; Minerva's a cousin, I think. She was always nice to me. I'm not sure where the elf fits in. He didn't introduce himself." She looked down at her hands, which lay in her lap. Formed them into fists. "My father was not happy that I'd refused to marry--"

Tobias closed his eyes. "I'm--"

Quickly; fiercely, Cecilia said, "Don't you *dare* apologize to me again!"

Tobias opened his eyes and ventured, "But--"

"You were just as much a pawn in that arrangement as I was," Cecilia said hotly. "You might not have known it at the time, but it's the truth."

"You're right," Tobias said, surprising both himself and Cecilia. "The difference was that I was not unwilling. But I had just as much of a choice as you did, which was none."

And he thought he would continue to apologize, nonetheless, because she hadn't deserved what her father had done to her to force her to marry him.

"Anyway," Cecilia said pointedly, to change the subject, "They told me you were here, Erialas, and that it might be best if I asked you for shelter. I'm not sure how they knew."

"'They'?" Erialas asked.

"Alexander Ross, really," Cecilia said. "Minerva and the elf were busy with Tristan, who had collapsed; I think my father did something to him, but I didn't ask any questions."

"And he's apparently okay, since he wrote to you," Michael pointed out just as Tobias remembered where he'd heard Tristan's name before.

"Oh," he said. "There are *stories* about Tristan. Something about a nest of Hunters, most recently. I think Liam might have told me, although I have no idea who he heard it from."

"Since that story wasn't passed around, Tristan would probably like to know where Liam heard it as well," Erialas said. "Regardless, I assume we have nothing to worry about with the Richmond household?"

"Tristan specifically said he had removed all bounties," Cecilia told them. "Especially for you, Tobias."

"Well, that's one good piece of news," Tobias said.

"I can read the letter, but I've told you just about everything that's in it," Cecilia said. "Except for the part about sending students to Darkbrook. He wants the Council's permission."

"My mother didn't ask the Council's permission to send *me* to Darkbrook," Erialas said. "Does he know he doesn't need it?"

"He says he'd rather have it, since they're Richmonds, and he also said he intends to ask Lucas to visit the household. I assume to show his goodwill." Cecilia sounded a bit doubtful of this, but Tobias could see where it would be to Tristan's advantage to show the Council that he intended to be an ally and not an enemy of their desires.

And then, the part Tobias knew would be coming: "He also said I could come back if I wanted to, but I would rather stay here."

He hadn't really expected her to say that last part. "You would?" And *that* slipped past his internal censors before he could stop it; he wondered if she would be annoyed now, or worse. But if she had a place in the Richmond household, why wouldn't she return to it? Why remain in exile?

Tobias wondered if *he* would go back to the Morgan household if his uncle and grandmother were dead. If there was no price left on his head; if he had no qualms about returning. He hadn't grown up within its walls; his mother had moved out when he was small, after his father's death. But despite that, there had been a twisted sense of family there. Familiarity. And yet, he couldn't really imagine ever going back to stay.

Perhaps Cecilia felt the same way.

"Michael and I have something to discuss as well," Erialas said into the silence, since Cecilia had chosen not to answer--or to ignore--Tobias' question.

Somehow, this statement seemed more ominous than anything Tobias or Cecilia had shared.

"Unless, of course, you're not finished," Michael added.

"I'm done," Cecilia said quickly. "But Tristan did ask for me to call him. Or write back. He--um--said he didn't think I would want to come back, and he called this 'our household'." Her eyes were bright now, whether with fear of what Erialas and Michael would say or from shock that Tristan would say such a thing in the first place, because everyone knew that they were not--

"Lucas thinks we should form our own household," Erialas said calmly. "And to be honest, I agree with him."

Tobias had just decided to risk drinking a sip of tea. And he barely had enough control not to spit it across the room; in fact, his hand hardly shook when he lowered the cup to its saucer.

"That's--" *stupid. Impossible.* He couldn't decide which word to use, so he asked, instead, "And how do you propose we manage to do that?"

He *had* said to Sennet that the house had enough room for dozens of cousins, but he hadn't really thought that through.

"Aren't we kind of a household right now?" Aaron asked curiously. "I mean, we're all living under one roof, and we all take care of this place--"

"Not a recognized one," Tobias said. "To every single household that exists, we're a bunch of exiles, nothing more. Lucas has no idea what he suggested, and I mean no disrespect, but neither do you, Erialas."

"Tell me what I don't understand, then," Erialas said. He'd apparently expected an argument; Tobias could see it in his gaze. And he started to respond, almost harshly, at first, but then he stopped himself before he could get angry about a mere concept; an impossibility that would never actually work.

"Because it isn't *done*," he finally said. "Vampires don't just go out and create their own households."

"Why not?" Michael asked reasonably.

And of course it would be Michael who'd ask 'why not?' Michael, who had created wards that allowed them to walk out in the sunlight, and a spell to bring the dead back to life; Michael who was still tweaking the recipe for bottled blood to make it more palatable. Michael would not understand why households could not be created at whim.

But on the other hand, Tobias couldn't answer his question, because he did not know how to answer it.

"It's just not done," he finally said. "No other vampire household would recognize us as a household, for one--"

"I imagine Tristan would," Cecilia commented.

"And the Walkers," Michael said.

"Of course, neither Michael nor I could be head of household," Erialas said. "Since we're members of the Council. Even Lucas agreed with that."

Which left--

"*I'm* not interested," Cecilia said firmly.

"Can humans be head of households?" Aaron wondered aloud.

"Ethan Walker's parents were both human," Tobias told him. "And they were joint heads of the household before they died in a Hunter attack."

Aaron smiled, and Tobias had the feeling he'd known this already. In fact, it seemed they'd discussed this without him, which meant-- "Oh, no. Not a chance."

"You're eldest," Erialas pointed out.

Tobias opened his mouth to protest, then closed it again. "You've already discussed this, haven't you?" he asked.

Cecilia looked guilty. Aaron frowned; only Erialas and Michael seemed calm.

"We mentioned it, yes," Michael said.

"And saw no issues?" Tobias asked. He could not stay seated; he stood and paced, back and forth, back and forth, wanting to laugh at their naivety but also not wanting to admit that he craved the familiarity of a household.

"How would it differ from how we live already?" Cecilia asked. "Especially if the Richmonds and the Walkers recognize us as a household?"

It would make things easier, truly. It would. But Tobias couldn't see how it would work.

"And anyway, why can't it be a more democratic household?" Aaron asked.

"Because the person you've chosen to be head of your household knows nothing of democracy," Tobias said, and sat back down. It was either that or flee, and while he *wanted* to flee, he knew he could not.

"Anyone can learn," Erialas said. "Even you."

This was true. He'd learned so much already; what would it hurt to learn a little more? And were his excuses just excuses or honest and clear-eyed opinions? He'd dismissed the suggestion out of hand without any thought at all, but what if the Walkers and the Richmonds *were* willing to recognize their nascent household?

"You--ah--there's no good way to ask this--you trust me enough to ask me to do this?" Tobias asked. "Because I'm not sure *I'd* trust me enough--"

"Democratic means you wouldn't have absolute power," Aaron said. "And we'd have to vote on things, and the majority should rule unless you have a very good reason to go against us."

"I trust you," Cecilia said simply, and she meant it; he heard the truth in her voice and saw it reflected in her gaze. And that, just that small thing; the fact that he had her *trust* after all he had done (even after what she'd said before, he couldn't stop the guilt from rising every time he thought about what had happened to her) shocked him into complete and utter silence.

"You know that *I* trust you," Michael said, which was true. After their visit to the Mists and what had happened there, Michael was quite possibly the only person Tobias could consider to be a friend. Erialas didn't count, because he was a cousin, but--

"Do I really need to answer that question?" Erialas asked after a moment of silence.

"Then I thank you for your trust," Tobias said humbly. "And I hope I never betray it."

"So you're agreeable to this?" Michael asked.

Tobias thought about it. Thought about all of the reasons that this wasn't a good idea, and found them wanting. "On one condition," he said. "Heads of households are normally only replaced when they die. Either from natural causes or because of a coup. I want the option to step down if I decide I can't do it anymore."

"Agreed," Erialas said, and the others echoed him, one by one.

"Will Arthur and the others come here to stay?" Cecilia asked.

"I don't know," Tobias said. "They've been taking the prisoners to the Walker household, so they might want to go there. But they'd be welcome here, wouldn't they? Even Iris' mother? She seems nice."

"We'd have to clean out a few more bedrooms," Aaron said.

"Of course they'd be welcome here," Erialas told him. "Even Iris' mother. I'm sure Aunt Amy would be happy about that, too."

Erialas' Aunt Amy had opined that there were not enough female members of the household. Tobias hadn't wanted to respond to that, since he wasn't certain how to rectify that without kidnapping other cousins, but if Arthur and the others moved in, perhaps she'd be satisfied.

"I probably should go back to the Hunt's house before dark," Tobias said. "Although they might sleep for most of the day. I'd really like to know more of how they managed to pull this off right under Uncle Ichabod's nose; it would be unbelievable if I didn't know it had really happened."

"You said they'd been doing this for years," Michael said. "And you had no idea?"

Tobias shrugged. "I wouldn't necessarily have known, since I didn't live there. But I heard nothing; no rumors; no nothing. The last I remember hearing about Arthur was that he was to help with the executions; I suppose that's when they decided to put their plan into place."

"How many executions are we talking about?" Aaron asked curiously.

"I have no idea," Tobias told him. "Anyone who angers Uncle Ichabod. There are rooms in the basement; cells, really. That's where they keep the prisoners." He hesitated. "Liam told me that Uncle Ichabod forbid anyone from saying my name after--after my mother's death."

"Saying your name would have gotten someone killed?" Michael asked in surprise.

"I hope not," Tobias said honestly. "But considering the price on my head, I wouldn't be surprised."

Silence reigned for a moment; a comfortable silence, not one begging to be filled. Tobias sipped a fresh cup of tea and tried not to think about how much needed to be done; what would *have* to be done if Sennet had been serious about the health of the humans in the Morgan household.

He'd never known her to joke, but he hadn't been around her very much at all; she'd spoken to him, of course, after his arrival, but he'd been fine by then.

Fine. He'd been *healed* by then, but he still had nightmares, sometimes; it had been easier to hide the fact that he wasn't sleeping well when Michael awoke screaming every night, but now, since that had faded, he was finding it harder and harder to hide.

Perhaps he didn't have to hide it now.

"You look tired," Cecilia said. "Why don't you try to get some rest and we'll call the Hunt's house to check on Arthur and the others in a little while? They're safe enough; they can sleep for as long as they need to sleep."

"I probably wouldn't be able to sleep," Tobias admitted.

"I imagine you'll sleep just fine," Erialas said, leaving Tobias to wonder if he'd suspected something after all. "After all, you've told us everything you've been hiding, and that *has* to lighten the burden on your dreams."

"Oh," Tobias said. "I hadn't thought about it that way." He hesitated. "And I probably haven't told you everything. But I--"

"You've told us what's important," Michael said, and everyone else seemed to agree.

Cecilia stood and started to gather the tea things. Aaron went to help her; Michael made a show of yawning, as if he wasn't used to staying up half the night as it were. But then, he said, "Oh, I almost forgot. Can I talk to you for a moment, Tobias? Privately?"

"Of course," Tobias said, and followed him down the hall.

Michael had claimed--if that was the right word--a few rooms in the basement, now that he had no trouble going up and down the stairs. He was always very polite about visitors, even going so far as to tell them to stay away if he was working on something that would harm a vampire. (Aaron helped him in those cases; Cecilia had been helping him otherwise.) But lately, he'd been working on the formula for the bottled blood they drank; tweaking it and adding things to it, sometimes with disastrous results.

But the last formula was close enough; Tobias had told him so, but he'd persisted in trying twice more, each time even closer. But considering the human boy who lay in Sennet's care and what had happened to him, Tobias almost didn't want to try another attempt at this point. He would almost rather drink bottled blood that tasted *almost* right, instead of something indistinguishable from fresh.

Almost.

Michael poured a small glass and presented it to Tobias solemnly. Tobias didn't have to drink it to know he'd perfected whatever formula he'd used, because it smelled so much like fresh blood that he--at first--suspected Michael had drained it out of his own veins.

"I hope you wrote that one down," he said hoarsely after he'd emptied the cup. "Although it's--almost *too* convincing."

"I thought you might say that," Michael said. "So I wrote the last one down, too. Just in case you thought it was too much."

"I'd be curious to know if it works the same on us as fresh blood," Tobias admitted. "Healing faster, and all; it would be nice to not have to rely on fresh blood at all."

"I'm not sure you'll get around that with this," Michael said. "I tweaked the formula more for the taste, not for its--nutritional values."

"Thank you," Tobias said.

"You're welcome," Michael said. "I have bottles, if you want one."

Tobias almost refused, more because of the boy than anything, but then he realized he could not help him and the rest of the humans in the Morgan household without feeding himself first. And although bottled blood was a perfectly nourishing substitute for fresh, especially with Michael's tweaks, those vampires who had made the attempt *not* to drink human blood had never succeeded. Humans could become vegetarians and not eat meat, or vegan and not eat any animal products at all, but vampires did not have that sort of luxury.

They could pretend all they wanted that they were civilized, and drink blood in glasses and from bottles, but the fact remained: they could only drink one thing for true nourishment, and that one thing ran through human veins.

"Thank you," he said aloud, and accepted the open bottle from Michael. He left him there, in his workroom, and retreated up the stairs to the first floor, carrying the bottle with him. And then, only a moment later, he closed the door to his bedroom behind him, set the bottle on the table beside his bed, and felt his shoulders slump. He was--truly--tired enough to sleep in his clothes, but he undressed, nonetheless, and lay down, expecting to have trouble falling asleep; expecting the dreams to return as they did nearly every night, but they did not.

Proving Erialas right yet again, but who was counting?

Tristan

Over the past six--nearly seven--months, Tristan had worked out a sort of system with Minerva. Someone would come to him, usually with a mundane or annoying question, and instead of snapping at them, Tristan would call Minerva. She would appear in the doorway, listen to the question or concern, and usually solve it within five minutes, leaving Tristan's reputation (not that he *cared* about his reputation, but truly, he had a sneaking suspicion that Miriam had decided to send *all* petitions his way, thus proving her point that being Head of Household was not just about the complete control of those who lived within the household) intact and unsullied.

He had, after the first few, started sending them back to Miriam with handwritten notes of his suggestions, but Alexander had put a stop to that fairly quickly. Tristan still didn't understand why.

He had not *ever* intended to become the head of the Richmond household. He still wasn't certain he truly wanted the position; Miriam knew this, and that was why, he suspected, she would not leave him in peace.

Jericho had ventured his opinion that Miriam was merely trying to teach him patience and understanding in her own way, but Tristan had had it up to--well, he'd *told* them he wasn't any good at diplomacy or anything like that, but that he would *try*. And the first thing he'd done was to promise that he wouldn't kill anyone, and he'd kept that promise (although it was difficult, sometimes; he would be the first to admit that) and some of them actually summoned up enough courage to approach him first, instead of Miriam.

And that was how he came to write two letters--one to Cecilia, and one to Lucas--after two of the children ventured into his lair (okay, office; he'd claimed the most interesting library for himself) to request--on their own--to attend Darkbrook.

Up until then, Miriam had kept the children away from Tristan. He wasn't quite certain why; he certainly had no reason to harm any of them, but he did not protest. She'd allowed Alexander to take a handful of students, only one of which showed any promise, at least to Tristan's admittedly not very musical ear, but the rest of them had stayed out of his way.

Until two days ago, when he'd been sitting at the desk he'd claimed as his own, looking over ancient receipts and files and diaries from before his father's ascent to head of the Richmond household, trying to determine exactly what had happened when Connor Richmond had come into power.

He still had trouble calling him his father. He'd been without one for so long, and truly, Alexander was more of a father than his own would ever have been.

And then he'd glanced up, and he wasn't alone in the room any longer.

A boy stood in front of his desk with a girl beside him. They seemed to be about the same age, although the girl was taller. The boy wore an oversized hooded sweatshirt and sunglasses, as if it were bright in the room, but the girl's head was uncovered, her gaze direct.

"Hello," Tristan said. "I apologize for keeping you waiting; I wasn't aware of your presence."

The girl looked surprised. The boy's expression was harder to read; Tristan thought he saw faint traceries of scars on his cheeks, hidden by the sunglasses, but that could have been shadows, due to the hood.

"Will you sit down, please?" Tristan asked. "I'm assuming Miriam knows you're here?"

"She doesn't," the boy said. "She'll be angry with us."

"Not so angry," the girl murmured, as if she thought Tristan would send them away for fear of Miriam's anger. "Annoyed, perhaps."

"Then we'll both be in the same boat," Tristan said. "I seem to annoy Miriam without even trying."

The girl looked cautiously optimistic about this; the boy just as inscrutable as before. Tristan motioned to the two chairs that sat in front of his desk. Only Minerva had ever sat in them; everyone else tended to hover in the doorway. "Please, sit down, and tell me why you want to speak with me." One--or both--of them was a wizard; they'd managed to sneak up on him, and not many people could do that. Since they hadn't moved to sit, he said, "If you won't sit, then may I have your names?"

"Christopher," the boy said uneasily, sounding as if Tristan should know his name.

"Ada," the girl said, and Tristan *did* know her name; she was Miriam's daughter; Minerva had told him about her niece late one night, murmuring the story in his ear in response to something he'd complained about; how his father had--at one point--ordered the deaths of all children under the age of two and how Miriam had saved almost all of them and hidden them away in the depths of the house, feeding and caring for them until they grew old enough to care for themselves. Tristan had no idea why his father had ordered the deaths other than the fact that the Richmond household was practically hemorrhaging money and they were the weakest mouths to feed. Years ago, some of the household members had jobs with incomes outside the household, and they contributed to the whole, but Connor Richmond had put an end to that after he'd assumed his parents' position. And whatever money they'd had left had been spent since then, with wild abandon.

And yet, Minerva and Miriam had managed the impossible: to feed their charges without any trouble at all.

Minerva had told him that the small things had been sold first. There was enough silver, even in a vampire household, to bankroll a few years, and Tristan and Alexander had even ventured into the attic to uncover furniture to sell; apparently, Tristan's grandparents had purchased quite a few pieces from a now well-known furniture maker, and with Alexander's contacts, a desk, two chairs, and a table had brought in nearly twenty thousand dollars, which had quelled Miriam's concerns about family heirlooms and the like.

After all, the Richmond household couldn't eat furniture.

The children sat down, gingerly; Tristan waited a moment, then said, "If you've come to me for a reason, don't hesitate to ask, whatever it may be. The worst thing that could happen is that I refuse your request."

Ada glanced at Christopher, whose face was in shadow now. His hands were hidden by the long sleeves of the hooded sweatshirt, and he made no move to free them; Tristan couldn't even see the color of his hair.

"How do you feel about Darkbrook?" Christopher finally asked, casually, as if Tristan's reply did not really matter.

"It--has its place," Tristan said. "And serves a valid purpose."

That must have been promising, because Ada said, "Christopher wants to go to Darkbrook, but my mother doesn't think you'll agree to send him."

Christopher scowled; the only expression Tristan had seen him display, as of yet.

"Why not?" Tristan asked.

Solemnly, Ada said, "You know about the children who were slated to die and how my mother saved them?"

"Yes," Tristan said. "Minerva told me that story."

"Did she also tell you about the ones my mother couldn't save?" Ada asked. "Or the ones she saved, but not before they were badly hurt?"

"No," Tristan said. "She did not. *How* badly hurt?"

"How do you feel about damaged vampires?" Christopher asked abruptly, and with enough emotion that Tristan would have been *blind* not to know this was the crux of the matter. And, if he didn't believe Miriam wouldn't stoop so low, he would have suspected that she'd sent the children herself, just to see how he would react.

"When the Hunters captured me, they tortured me with drops of molten silver that burned into my flesh and left me in agony," Tristan said quietly. "The scars will very likely be with me for the rest of my life." He paused. "If you are talented--and it's obvious that you are, since not everyone could sneak up on me--and wish to attend Darkbrook, then I see no reason why you should not, although I would like to contact someone about it, since I'm not certain of the protocol. And I would wish, of course, that you could attend without issue from anyone who might see the Richmond household as the enemy."

"But you don't know--you haven't seen--" Christopher spluttered the words.

"Show me, then," Tristan said evenly, just as someone knocked on the door.

Christopher stiffened.

"Ignore them," Tristan suggested. "Show me why I wouldn't allow you to go."

The knock came again. Ada half-turned to the door. "It's my mother," she said quietly.

"Then I suppose I should try to appease her before she gets worried enough to break down the door," Tristan said, and stood. "Wait here, please; I'll ask her for a few more minutes."

Angry, more likely than worried, Tristan thought. But if she intended to lash out at anyone, she could lash out at him, not Christopher, who had shrunk down in the chair as if to make himself a smaller target. Was it merely the fact that he'd disobeyed? Tristan had found no evidence at all that Miriam abused her charges, and so he'd left her--and them--alone, other than to give them some of the money.

Abruptly, he asked, "Are you *afraid* of Miriam? Will you be punished for disobeying her order?"

"She'll be disappointed in me," Christopher said after a moment. "Because she asked me to wait, and I didn't want to wait. But no, I won't be punished. Not--like you're thinking."

"I can tell her you're not here and that I haven't seen you," Tristan offered.

"That--won't be necessary," Christopher said, and sat up a little straighter in his chair.

Tristan opened the door, surprising Miriam in mid-knock. She stepped back, suddenly wary, as if she hadn't expected him to answer at all; had she *intended* to break down the door and accuse him of something terrible? He saw nothing of the sort in her gaze, just concern, no doubt for her daughter and Christopher.

"They're both here, unharmed, and we're in the middle of negotiations," Tristan told her before she could speak.

The wariness fled from Miriam's gaze. "I see," she said. "Might I sit in on those negotiations?"

"Let me ask," Tristan said, and closed the door. To Christopher, he said, "You need not have her here if you think she'll try to twist you from the path you've chosen."

Almost inaudibly, Christopher said, "She can come in."

Tristan opened the door again and stepped aside. "You may come in."

Miriam stepped inside. Her lips tightened when she saw Ada, but Tristan saw something else in her gaze when she looked at Christopher; something he could not interpret as easily as annoyance, or frustration.

"Christopher has asked to attend Darkbrook," Tristan said without giving her a chance to take control of the conversation.

"Yes," Miriam said, her voice completely neutral. "He has."

"And I told him yes, of course," Tristan continued. "But he seems to think that I will not allow him to go if he shows me whatever my father did to him."

That last part was a guess, of sorts; Tristan didn't know for certain that his father had wielded the blade to kill the children or if he had ordered someone else to do it. Or, even, if it had been a blade at all. It would have been much more efficient to carry them out to the lawn and let them burn. But Christopher's visible skin did not seem to be burned.

"He's also your half-brother," Miriam said. "I imagine he didn't tell you *that,* either."

"And his mother?" Tristan asked, unsurprised. So far, he'd been told of one other living half-sister--Calliope, who, at their awkward first meeting, had asked Tristan if he intended to allow the tradition of arranged marriages; when Tristan had said no, and that any arrangements were null and void from that point on, she'd burst into tears and had to be escorted from the room.

Later, Tristan had asked Minerva about it, and she'd explained that Callie had been promised to an older vampire in the Morgan household, not unlike Cecilia. The Morgans were, apparently, paying for their brides, which was one of the ways Connor had managed to keep the household afloat. Tristan had no use for that practice now, but he'd decided to refrain from telling the Morgan household right away, because it seemed to have been a lucrative arrangement, and he did not wish to have a war on his hands.

"Dead," Miriam said, then hesitated. "She died trying to save him. He was an infant at the time. That was eight and a half years ago."

Tristan sat back down behind his desk. Miriam didn't have a chair; the only two were occupied, but she didn't seem to mind. Christopher had slumped in his seat again, his head down and hidden by the hood. Ada looked worried.

"Show me," he said gently. "Please."

Slowly, ever-so-slowly, Christopher pulled back one sleeve, then the other. His left hand was unmarked and whole; his right missing the last two fingers; from the scar tissue, this had happened with a very sharp blade and a long time ago. And then he glanced up, and carefully removed the sunglasses.

The scars weren't as bad as Tristan had feared. Perhaps it was the age of them; if this had happened when Christopher was an infant, then they'd had years to smooth out and become less--obvious. But the fact that his eyes--No. His *lack* of eyes. Both of them, gone, the skin smooth across the holes where they had been, slightly puckered at the edges as if someone had attempted to make it look less ghastly and more--acceptable. His hair--blonde, not red like Tristan's, fell across his forehead, where there was another scar, this one trailing down one side of his face and near his ear. And a thinner one, across his throat.

"I was supposed to have died," Christopher said, his voice emotionless. "But Miriam found me, and saved me."

"His mother *did* die," Miriam said. "I found him in her arms, covered in blood--" She glanced away, as if remembering the moment when she realized he wasn't dead. "His mother was sixteen years old."

"Why did you think I would refuse to allow him to attend Darkbrook?" Tristan asked, knowing what she had thought; how *couldn't* he know, but he wanted to hear her say it.

Miriam folded her arms and glared at him. Tristan stared her down, unrepentant. "Because he's not whole?" he snapped. "Because he's damaged?" He shrugged. "So am I. Or haven't you seen my scars?" He would have taken off his shirt to show her, but he did not, more because of Ada's presence than any show of modesty. "The only reason why I can *move* right now is due to the elves, and the king of the kingdom that borders Richmond land." She did not reply, so he continued, angrily, "This household *needs* the talent it holds. If Christopher wishes to attend Darkbrook, then he shall, but I would request that we contact Lucas Lane about it first, so that he doesn't think *I* did this to him."

She'd left--or *he'd* left--the door open; and Tristan saw someone lurking in the hallway. He suspected it was Alexander, waiting until he was finished shouting to make his presence known. Or waiting to see if his presence was *needed,* more likely; just in case Tristan lost his temper, or Miriam said something unforgivable.

Or vice versa.

Miriam noticed him too. For a moment, Tristan thought she would argue with him, but then she said, simply, "I have no objections, of course. However, he'll need a sighted guide."

A vampire's senses could only compensate for so much. "What about Ada?" Tristan asked, since she'd come with him in the first place.

Ada's eyes widened. She glanced at her mother, then at Christopher, who had replaced the sunglasses; they dwarfed his face, really; Tristan had to wonder where he'd found them.

"Ada could go," Miriam said reluctantly.

Ada beamed. Christopher allowed himself a small, satisfied smile.

"You would, of course, represent the Richmond household at Darkbrook, and I would expect you to conduct yourselves accordingly," Tristan warned, and motioned Alexander inside. "We were just making arrangements to send Ada and Christopher to Darkbrook, per their request, nothing more."

"Mmm," Alexander said. "You were shouting. And this hallway echoes quite nicely."

"I meant what I said," Tristan told him, and tried to remember exactly *what* he had said. Hopefully nothing too terrible.

"I'm glad," Alexander said, and that was that.

After Miriam had ushered Christopher and Ada away, Tristan had taken out a sheet of paper and a pen, and written letters--one to Cecilia, which was long overdue, and one to Lucas. The one to Lucas requested a meeting; something he wondered if Lucas would even consider.

"Now that you're telling them the truth, he has no reason not to consider a visit," Alexander said. He'd vetted both letters, declared them suitable, and had sent them away with a fairy for delivery, one very useful perk from their new relationship with the small folk, considering the fairies would do nearly anything for sugar cubes.

"We're not the Council's allies," Tristan pointed out.

"We're not their enemies, either," Alexander responded, and that had been the end of the conversation.

Tristan knew the letters had been delivered, but two days later no one had called; no one had contacted them by other means, and while Alexander advised patience, he said so with the knowledge that Tristan's *lack* of patience was very near legendary now.

"You can't just--*call* the Council," Minerva said, staring at him in surprise.

"Why not?" Tristan asked.

"Do you know Lucas Lane's phone number?" Minerva countered.

"No," Tristan admitted. "But I imagine I can find it if I look hard enough." He paused. "I could just go to his house--"

"You can't just show up at--" Minerva began, but he was smiling now, because he knew she would protest and she'd walked right into it. She sighed. "I can find his phone number. But I think you should give him a day or so longer to call."

"Christopher is impatient," Tristan said, although that wasn't really true; he'd only asked that morning, and had not seemed too disappointed that Tristan had no news to give him.

Minerva folded her arms. Tristan waited a moment, then said, "I asked for a reply. If I didn't know that the letters were delivered, I would have thought they'd gotten lost."

"You haven't heard from your sister, either," she pointed out.

"No, I haven't," Tristan agreed. "But I'm not certain I will; I think she's happy with her household of exiles."

"I think so too," Minerva said with a certainty that made Tristan wonder if she'd spoken with Cecilia. As if he'd asked, she added, "I saw her once, in passing. She didn't see me, but she seemed happy."

"I want her to be happy," Tristan said. He meant those words, but he wasn't quite sure what they were supposed to mean; no one could be happy every single day of their lives, after all, and, for example, *he* wasn't happy at the moment, because no one seemed to want to call him in response to his letters or send letters themselves. He scowled.

Minerva rummaged through a stack of oddments on the desk. Pulled out a telephone book; outdated, but even so. "Here. I bet his number's listed."

Without speaking, Tristan looked it up. As she predicted, Lucas Lane was listed, and as he wrote down the number, he said, "Do you really think I should wait? Alexander thinks I should wait."

"Are you *willing* to wait?" Minerva asked, then smiled. "I could, perhaps, help you forget that you're waiting."

There wasn't a telephone in Tristan's office-cum-library. And while mobile phones were useful--Alexander had one, of course, and Tristan used it often to call Jericho--Tristan had yet to get one of his own. He'd put the house phone number on the letters. *That* phone was in the kitchen, and technically Miriam's territory, but she had promised to come and find him if it rang.

And of course, things were just getting--interesting between Tristan and Minerva when someone knocked on the door.

"My sister," Minerva sighed, and straightened her clothing.

Tristan stole a kiss before opening the door. The look on Miriam's face was almost worth the interruption, but her news was not.

"We have a--visitor," she said, looking very uneasy.

Surely Lucas wouldn't have--

"Not Lucas Lane?" Minerva asked before Tristan could speak.

"No," Miriam said. "I'd say worse, but I'm not quite certain what's going on. A human. She's in the parlor. She's from the Morgan household. She's carrying a letter addressed to your father, which I have read, by the way--it wasn't sealed--"

"I don't mind," Tristan said. "What did it say?"

"It's an inquiry about a certain Fern Morgan, born a Richmond. Ichabod wrote the letter, and he thinks she might have come here last night."

"Did she?" Tristan asked.

"Not that I know of," Miriam said.

"Does she have relatives here?" Tristan asked. "Other than being a cousin, I mean?"

"No siblings that I can remember," Miriam told him. "No parents, either. I don't remember her very well, but she was one of the brides your father arranged, and she married Ichabod's younger brother."

"Carroll," Minerva said. "He was actually the sane one of the family."

"Was?" Tristan asked. This was all new; he'd never really paid attention to the Morgans before, other than the obvious players in their rather sick little drama. Grandmother Morgan was said to be the worst, but Ichabod wasn't far behind. That Tobias had managed to extricate himself from their clutches was not only surprising, but also miraculous.

"I heard he died," Minerva said. "But there seemed to be some question of how. I'm sorry I don't have better information to give to you."

"Ichabod will want a reply," Miriam said slowly.

"Then we'll send his human back to him with one," Tristan said, and she countered with, "No, we will not." Very quietly, as if she expected him to protest.

Tristan started to say something he would likely regret, but stopped himself just in time. "Why not?" he asked.

"Will you allow me to handle this?" Miriam asked. "Or ask Alexander?" She hesitated. "You've done much better than I expected, but--"

"But?" Tristan asked. "What did they send us?"

"A child," Miriam said reluctantly.

"I promised I wouldn't kill anyone, and I've yet to break that promise," Tristan said, puzzled as to why she wouldn't want him to interact with this person. "And I don't make it a habit to murder innocent children or anything of the sort."

"I know you don't," Miriam said. "But this girl--the letter--"

For the first time, Tristan realized she held the letter in her hand. He held his hand out for it, and she reluctantly relinquished it.

She hadn't lied. The letter asked after Fern Morgan, born a Richmond and mentioned nothing else. But at the bottom, after Ichabod's signature, was the part that Miriam had not wanted him to see.

"Is she in the parlor?" Tristan asked. Miriam nodded. "Good. Follow me."

He didn't lead them to the parlor, but to a passageway that led to a tiny room that held a single chair and the other side of what looked to be a mirror *inside* the parlor, where the watcher could sit and observe, entirely undetected, even by vampires. Tristan and Alexander had tested it after its discovery; up until now, however, Tristan hadn't told Minerva or Miriam about his find.

"I haven't been spying on anyone," Tristan said, since the parlor was mostly used for meetings. "Not often, at least."

"Mmmm," Miriam said. "This does explain why your father knew some of the things he knew."

"Yes," Tristan agreed. "I thought so too." He looked through the mirror at the human the Morgans had sent. "I see."

The girl's hair had been recently brushed; she wore a clean dress with a very high collar and long sleeves. She could have been anywhere between twelve and fifteen; Tristan wasn't a good judge of ages, so she could have been younger, despite the fact that she wore makeup to hide the bruises on her face. He had no doubt the high collar and long sleeves of her dress hid scars, and perhaps even marks from a vampire's attention.

"What is her name?" he asked.

"I don't know," Miriam said. "She wouldn't speak to me. Do you understand? She expects--"

"Wait here, please," Tristan said. And then, because he expected them to protest, "You can watch and ensure I do not mistreat our guest."

He knew why Miriam had wanted to take care of this herself; the girl had been abused; had *grown up* in abuse, and expected the worst from the vampires she served. He had no doubt at all that she would submit to him without a single protest if he asked her to do so; Ichabod had not wanted her back. A 'token of my appreciation of your cooperation', indeed.

Nowadays, Tristan's fury was slower to build, but it was well on its way to a conflagration now.

Miriam caught his arm before he could leave. Before she could speak, Tristan said, "I will not harm her. If I must swear--"

She released him. "No," she said, her voice soft. "I believe you."

"And you're right," he added. "She won't be returning." And with that, he left them and exited out the other door that led into the hall; if you knew where the latch was to open the secret door, it was obvious, but no one else knew.

The girl started to stand when Tristan appeared in the doorway, but he waved her back down. "Did you read the letter you brought here?" he asked.

"N-No," she whispered, her eyes downcast now, as if she expected him to punish her for some invisible crime.

Tristan handed it to her. She stared at it blankly, her hand shaking now, as if he'd given her a bottle of poison. And then, she said, almost tripping over the words, "I--I can't read it."

Her hands, though clean, were rough and chapped. A servant's hands, Tristan thought. A pretty one, yes, but still a servant. "Will you unbutton your sleeve and pull it up for me please?" he asked, struggling to keep the anger from his voice.

She heard it anyway, but obeyed without question, pulling her sleeve up to show unbroken skin, and then, without asking, doing the same for her collar. Moving her hair aside to uncover her throat.

Tristan saw her pulse jumping under the pale skin, and wondered why she hadn't been touched. "Have they tasted you?" he asked roughly.

"No," she whispered. "I am a favor. An offering. And must be pure."

"I see," Tristan said. He walked away from her. Towards the mirror, first, then swung away lest they see something horrible in his gaze.

"Do I not please you?" the girl asked innocently.

This was why humans hated vampires. *This* was what the Hunters fought against, and at this moment, Tristan didn't blame them.

"I do not wish to drink your blood," Tristan said. "Do you understand?"

The girl's chin wobbled a bit. "I am not worthy?" she asked, her voice almost plaintive. "You do not find me a suitable offering?"

"I would rather you live," Tristan grated. "Do you understand? No one will touch you here. No one will drink your blood, or--or do other things to you." He was almost shouting now. *"Do you understand?"*

She cowered against the back of the couch, clearly expecting violence, and at that moment, Tristan would have lashed out at her just because of what she stood for; just because of how she'd been--brainwashed into thinking that her life was not worth anything at all.

He didn't understand why he cared. Why it mattered. Why *she* mattered, since she was only a human girl and nothing more. She'd be dead in less than a century; less than seventy-five years at best, forgotten like so many others.

The door opened behind him. Alexander. "Tristan."

"I'm not going to hurt her," Tristan said as Miriam slipped in behind him to go to the girl.

"I know," Alexander said.

She was sobbing now, holding out her wrists in supplication to him; twisting away from Miriam to throw herself at Tristan, tearing at her flesh with her teeth, flinging the blood in his face.

It was all he could do not to--

"Sleep," Alexander suggested, and the girl collapsed into Tristan's arms. He very nearly dropped her, but Miriam took over, gently removing her from Tristan's grasp and lowering her onto the couch. Minerva appeared with bandages and they took over; Tristan stood there covered in blood and tried not to hyperventilate.

"Come with me," Alexander said, and ushered Tristan out of the room.

He was covered in her blood. It was sticky on his face; his hands; covering his shirt. "What happened in the Morgan household last night?" His voice was too high; too fast; too panicked.

"Let's find out," Alexander suggested, and opened the door to Tristan's room, almost forcing him inside. "Sugar cubes?"

"On the desk," Tristan said.

Alexander opened the window and placed six sugar cubes on the edge of the windowsill. Considering Tristan had never told him *how* he contacted the fairies or the small folk, it would have been intriguing to ask how he knew, but since he was still covered in blood, he decided not to ask.

Only a moment later, a fairy appeared, one of the usuals; a tiny little being with purple hair and iridescent wings. She hesitated at the sight of Alexander, then saw Tristan and fluttered into the room.

"You are covered in blood." the fairy commented.

"It's not mine," Tristan said. "Do you know what happened in the Morgan household last night?"

The fairy glanced between Alexander and Tristan. "I can ask," she finally said.

"Ask who?" Tristan inquired, then scowled when Alexander said--as if he couldn't help himself-- "Whom."

"Someone who might know," the fairy said after a moment.

For some reason Tristan could not explain, he suspected that the fairy already *knew* what had happened, but had been told--by someone--not to tell anyone without permission. This made him feel a bit--annoyed wasn't the right word, but it would do. But it wouldn't be right to take his annoyance out on the Faerie. "Thank you," he said instead, and she zipped out of the window, taking another sugar cube with her. And then, to Alexander, he said, "I wanted her to know she was safe. And that no one would hurt her here. But she--"

"It was a spell," Alexander said. "And suggestion. She had no choice but to offer herself to you, and she saw no issue--there was no question in her mind that she deserved anything but to sacrifice herself to obey."

"Can she be fixed?" Tristan asked.

"With patience, yes," Alexander said. "And preferably no contact with vampires in the meantime."

Tristan ran one hand across his face. Stared down at the blood on his hand. "I need to wash this off. And change my clothes."

Alexander nodded. "Send for me when the fairy returns," he said, and let himself out.

Tristan took a shower in the attached bathroom and emerged with a towel wrapped around his waist and nothing else. He didn't even notice he wasn't alone until a voice emerged from the shadows.

"Oh, I'm sorry. I should have knocked."

It wasn't a fairy's voice.

Tristan clutched at the towel around his waist and turned around. The woman--fairy--whatever she was with her green-tinged skin and long ropy hair was nearly as underdressed as Tristan, considering she wore a skirt and nothing more.

His first inclination was to cover his scars, but that would mean dropping the towel, and she'd already seen them, after all, so what did it matter now? And he'd left the window open, which was an invitation, so it was his own fault. "The window was open," he said. "But I'll admit I expected the fairy to return."

"The fairy came to me," the woman said. "As I requested them to do if anyone asked about what happened at the Morgan household last night."

"I should call Alexander," Tristan said. "So he can hear this too." He started towards the door.

"I would--perhaps--get dressed first," the woman said. "I'll turn my back."

"No need," Tristan said. "You've already seen the worst of what you're going to see." But he did not dawdle while dressing; pulling on clean pants and a shirt; socks and shoes could wait.

"May I ask you about the scars?" the woman asked, carefully neutral.

Tristan paused. "Do you know who I am?"

"Your name is Tristan Richmond," she replied. "The small folk are quite enamored of you. *My* name is Maya. I--keep care of the small folk."

"And you know what happened at the Morgan household last night," Tristan said.

"I do," Maya replied. "I was there."

"I see," Tristan said, then, since she seemed to be waiting, added, "The scars are part of a very long story, but I was captured by Hunters and tortured with silver and left to die, but I didn't die."

"How long ago was this?" Maya asked.

"Not yet a year," Tristan said. "And before you ask, the spells that enable me to be mobile are held by the Veil, with the permission of Nefir, who is king of the kingdom that is closest to here."

"That explains why you seem of Faerie, even though you are clearly not," Maya said. "Call Alexander; I'd like to meet him as well. I've heard a lot about him."

All Tristan really had to do was open the door, interrupting Minerva before she could knock. Alexander had set something into place, just in case Tristan needed him, and it had something to do with the door. Tristan wasn't quite certain how it worked, but it had never let him down.

"Come in," Tristan said to Minerva. "We have a guest. How is the girl?"

"Still asleep," Minerva said. "I came to see how *you* were--" Her gaze widened when she saw Maya, but then, apparently recognizing her, she relaxed.

"Of *course* you would know each other," Tristan said grumpily.

"We've met," Maya said. "What girl?"

"The Morgans sent a girl here, looking for a certain Fern Morgan, born a Richmond; apparently they thought she might have come here," Tristan said, seeing no reason not to tell her. "Where have you met?"

"A *human* girl?" Maya asked.

"In the forest, of course," Minerva said. "And once in Faerie."

"Yes," Tristan told her. "A human girl. Who gnawed through her own flesh when I refused to drink her blood." He nodded to the pile of bloody clothes on the floor. "Hence the reason why I was in the shower when you arrived."

"You were in the *shower* when she arrived?" Minerva asked, her eyebrows raised.

Maya grinned. Her teeth were pointed; all of them, and made her look quite ferocious. "I saw the scars," she said. "And heard the abbreviated story of how they came to be."

"And she offered to keep my virtue intact, but I explained that I don't have any virtue," Tristan said, and grinned at the look in Minerva's face. "We're waiting for Alexander so that Maya can tell us what happened last night."

"They sent a human girl to ask after Fern?" Maya frowned. "And didn't mention Iris or Arthur or Liam?"

"Arthur's name is known to me," Alexander said from the doorway. "He's Ichabod Morgan's son." He paused. "*You* are known to me, too. It's likely the letter did not mention Iris or Arthur or Liam because they are children, or nearly so."

"That may be true, but Fern wasn't even aware of their movements until--" Maya began, then stopped. "I should tell you the entire story, I'm afraid. Starting at the beginning, not at the end."

"Is there time for that?" Tristan asked.

"What do you mean?" Maya asked.

"Are they in danger?"

"No." Maya shook her head. "They're all safe, for now." She hesitated. "Do I need to ask if you are their allies? The price on their heads is likely to be--"

"Astronomical," Tristan interrupted. "Considering the price on Tobias' head is half a million dollars the last time I checked."

Maya's eyes narrowed. "The last time you *checked*?"

Tristan waved his hand, as if to brush away all thoughts of cashing in the bounty. "The last time I asked one of the small folk. Just out of curiosity, although I don't doubt we could use the money, I *do* doubt that Ichabod would pay."

"Tristan!" This from Minerva, who sounded as if she wanted to smack him. Since she sounded like that a lot, Tristan wasn't overly concerned.

"I'm speaking plainly," he said in protest. "Maya has been forthright with us--"

"Maya hasn't told us the whole story yet," Alexander pointed out. To Maya, he added, "You needn't worry, however. We have enough to do here, without involving the Morgan household. And we have no designs on the bounty."

Maya folded her arms. "Four years ago, Arthur Morgan, Ichabod's eldest son, tried to kill himself in the forest because he did not wish to become his father's executioner. He was twelve years old." She paused. "He'd been trapping and killing the small folk for years at that point, and the fairy he freed before he tried to kill himself came to get me when she realized what he intended to do."

"How--" Tristan began, but Minerva elbowed him to shut him up.

"He took the poison he used on the fairies," Maya said. "It didn't kill him, but made him wish he were dead for a little while, at least. Once we convinced him to listen to reason, he realized that his friend Iris would die if he did not return, and he went back to save her life."

"How old was he at that time?" Tristan asked, which seemed to be a better choice of questions; or he sidestepped Minerva's elbow this time, at least.

"Twelve," Maya said. "Since then, he and Iris, and later Liam, have smuggled prisoners out of the Morgan household and I've transported them to the Walker household to recover safely. But after Tobias' defection, Liam became his contact in the Morgan household, and when he was discovered and sentenced to die last night, Arthur and Iris had to flee. Fern is Iris' mother, and she hadn't been involved until last night. But she seems to be wholly supportive of her daughter's activities, even though she knew nothing about them."

"You can close your mouth now," Minerva said to Tristan, who did so, then sank down on his bed.

"You-- How old is Liam?" Tristan asked, trying to wrap his mind around three children outsmarting Ichabod Morgan and Grandmother Morgan without really getting caught, since Liam had been caught contacting Tobias. "Does Tobias know Liam is alive?"

"Tobias was there with me," Maya said. "He insisted. And Liam is twelve."

Tristan felt his eyes narrow. He didn't know Liam or Arthur or Iris; he didn't know Tobias, really, just from the stories, but he couldn't believe Tobias would have allowed a twelve-year-old child to become his contact, knowing that child would likely die if he were discovered.

"Apparently, Liam approached Tobias, and Tobias had every intention of offering him a place in exile," Maya said quietly, correctly guessing the source of Tristan's sudden anger. "But Liam didn't want to leave Arthur or Iris behind. Tobias was very concerned for Liam's safety, and the safety of the others once he knew what had happened."

Tristan had never met Tobias. But considering that Cecilia seemed to be getting along with him and the others who lived in Erialas' house, he'd assumed that Tobias had abandoned his former life without a single glance behind him. "I rather assumed they'd have created their own household by now," he said. "I don't think Cecilia will want to come back, although I told her she would be welcome." He paused. "I also told her that all bounties were null and void as far as the Richmond household was concerned. I wrote her a letter. She hasn't contacted me yet."

"You also wrote Lucas Lane a letter," Maya said. "I'll admit I was a bit curious as to why."

Tristan was honestly surprised she hadn't read it. "I have two children here who would like to attend Darkbrook," he said. "I wanted to ask Lucas Lane about the proper procedure to send them."

"You wanted his permission," Maya said sagely.

"Well, the Richmonds aren't known for their love of the Council," Tristan said. "Or of Darkbrook. And we're in a precarious position right now."

"Changing sides will do that," Maya said. "Are you intending to ally yourself with the Council?"

Tristan glanced at Alexander. "I would hope we could come to some sort of an alliance," he said. "I invited Lucas to come here, but I doubt he'll accept the invitation."

"Not by himself, at least," Maya said. "If he comes, he'll likely bring a Hound with him, or maybe even Gabriel."

"We would welcome anyone, I'm sure," Tristan said to cover his shock at the thought of the legendary Wild Hunt inside the Richmond household. Even knowing that Lucas would be merely prudent about any potential visit and would likely not intend any harm, it was difficult to believe that the Hunt--and the Council--were not threats.

"Would you really?" Maya asked as if she knew exactly what he was thinking.

But if he withdrew now; if he embraced the paranoia that always fluttered on the edge of his vision, Christopher would never openly attend Darkbrook and Miriam would probably lock him up somewhere in a room no one else had access to, just to get him out of her way.

"Yes," he said, then, more firmly, "Yes."

"Okay, then," Maya said. "I'm *certain* the Council would rather have the Richmond household as an ally and not an enemy."

"I would hope so," Tristan said.

"Are there any--objections about this?" Maya asked. "From anyone not on your side? Here, I mean?"

Tristan raised an eyebrow at Minerva, who shook her head. "Not really," she said. "My sister Miriam took a little while to warm up to Tristan's tactics, but she won't disagree with this path." She paused. "Especially if this household is to survive."

In retrospect, perhaps he should have invited Miriam to this little meeting, but--

"She was with the girl, still, when I came to find you," Minerva said, as if reading his mind.

"I want this household to survive," Tristan said, and, to his surprise, realized his words were not just words to placate Maya or Minerva or Miriam. He *wanted* the household to survive, just not as it had before.

Minerva was smiling now. Tristan suspected Alexander would be smiling, too, but Tristan didn't dare look. Instead, Alexander said, "I imagine there will be others, after dark? Searching for the runaways?"

"And some searchers will likely come here," Maya said.

"That might pose a problem," Tristan said slowly. "No one else knows that my father is dead; the Morgans still think he's head of this household."

"I assume you had a reason for doing this?" Maya asked curiously.

"Preventing a war was rather high on my list of things to avoid," Tristan said. "Along with honoring any bargains my father might have made with the Morgans. Fern was one of those bargains."

"She was married to Ichabod's brother Carroll," Alexander said. "I haven't made any inquiries, but I assume he is dead?"

"That's an interesting question," Maya said. "I think Fern might have had some doubts about his death, but he hasn't been seen in almost five years. He disappeared after visiting the household; Ichabod claimed he left and was on his way back when he vanished. Considering he wanted to raise his child outside of the household and he seemed to love his wife, Grandmother Morgan might have had a hand in his disappearance."

"Well, if they used Hunters, perhaps they stole the idea from my father," Tristan said.

"I doubt they 'used' Hunters," Maya said. "If he didn't die in an actual Hunter attack, then I wouldn't be surprised if Grandmother Morgan killed him. Or kept him captive until he died."

"There's no reason to think he might still be alive?" Alexander asked.

"For his sake, I hope he isn't," Maya said. "Considering how they treated Liam--"

"Who *was* considered a traitor," Tristan pointed out.

"He's twelve years old," Minerva countered.

"I had killed plenty of people by the time *I* was twelve years old," Tristan said.

"And how many people have you killed since you became head of household?" Maya asked.

"Just one," Tristan said. "Well, that was *before* I became head of household, to be honest--and I did promise I wouldn't kill anyone else." He glanced at Minerva. "Although if needed, I could break that promise."

"As Alexander said, you have your hands full here," Maya said.

"Yes," Tristan said slowly. "But what are Arthur and the others intending to do? Remain in exile?"

"We haven't discussed it yet," Maya said. "They may go to the Walker household. They may stay here."

"With Tobias," Tristan said.

"Perhaps," Maya replied, then, curious, "Why?"

"No reason," Tristan said. "Just curiosity, nothing more."

No one was fooled, of course. But he had no real reason to ask; he had no plan in mind for the answers to his questions. Other than the nebulous thought that the Morgan household could potentially become a problem for everyone--with dire consequences.

"I should go," Maya said. "I trust you will be able to handle any--influx of searchers?"

"We can handle them," Alexander said.

"And if they don't believe us and launch an attack?" Tristan asked.

"A part of the house fell when the tunnel collapsed," Maya said. "I imagine they'll be busy for a little while. As far as they know, Arthur and the others are buried under the rubble."

"I think since they sent someone here, they know they're not buried under the rubble," Tristan pointed out.

"Perhaps," Maya allowed. "Even so, they're likely to be busy for a little while."

"Where are Arthur and the others?" Tristan asked.

"Guests of the Hunt until dark," Maya said. "After that--well, I'm sure they'd be welcome in the Hunt's house until they decide where they're going to go."

"And may I ask for notification of where they end up?" Tristan asked.

"You may," Maya said. "And I will tell you, once they decide."

Tristan nodded. "Thank you," he said.

She was gone between blinks, vanishing as quickly as she had come. Tristan waited for a moment, but no one else appeared in the window, so he closed it and stepped back. "Well."

"Well," Minerva echoed.

Alexander was predictably silent, but not because he didn't have anything to say. Sometimes, Tristan tried to *guess* what he would say and say it first, just so that he could feel as if his lessons in civility were paying off. But he wasn't quite certain what Alexander would say in this instance.

Cautiously, Tristan ventured, "I *do* want this household to thrive. And I would like for us to be allies of the Council, if that's what it takes to ensure our survival. I have no real quarrel with anything the Council holds dear. But surely the Morgan household deserves just as much of a chance as us?"

Alexander's smile was swift and barely registered on his face. "Do you realize what you're proposing?" he asked.

"That we go to war against the Morgans instead of waiting for them to go to war with us?" Tristan asked.

"What?" Miriam asked from the doorway. Crossly, as usual. "Are you mad?"

"Obviously it would have to be some sort of a joint effort," Tristan said, ignoring her.

"Obviously," Alexander agreed, and just by that one word, Tristan knew he'd said the right thing.

"What are you talking about?" Miriam asked, alarmed.

Quickly, Minerva told her sister what had happened. She left nothing out, and neither Tristan nor Alexander interrupted her explanation.

Surprisingly, Miriam did not protest or interrupt at all. She stood there, arms folded, listening politely, and then, she said to Tristan, "Do you have a plan?"

"What?" Tristan asked, completely sidelined by her question. He'd expected her to protest; to say something cutting; to call him an idiot, perhaps; or something like that.

"I don't like to repeat myself," Miriam said. "But I will, this once. Do you have a plan?"

"Not yet," Tristan told her. "Not really."

"Well, I suggest you come up with one, and quickly," Miriam said. "If that means creating alliances with the Council and the others so that you don't destroy this household while you're attempting to save the Morgans from themselves, then I suggest you do that, too."

Tristan stared at her, openmouthed.

Miriam's lips twisted slightly. It might have been a smile, but Tristan didn't want to push his luck. "I want this household to thrive as much as you do," she said into the silence. "Maybe even more."

This was true.

"But I also understand that if you declare us allies of the Council; if you truly change how we've been seen--and lived--for many years, then the Morgans will feel threatened, and they will retaliate," Miriam said. "And I don't want that to happen without having a plan in place."

"I would rather that not happen at all," Tristan said honestly. "But you're right; it will."

"For what it might be worth, you'll have my support in this," Miriam said.

"Your support is worth a lot to me," Tristan told her, again being honest, although she narrowed her eyes a bit as if she suspected he was being facetious.

"The girl--what was done to her--" Miriam fairly spit out the words. "Humans are malleable. Their minds can be twisted and broken and bent beyond fixing. I'm not sure I can fix this child."

"There will likely be more of them," Tristan said.

"I might be able to help her," Alexander said quietly.

"I'd hoped you might say that," Miriam admitted.

They walked off together, leaving Minerva and Tristan alone.

"Should we--" Tristan began.

"No," Minerva said, and firmly closed the door. "We shouldn't."

"But--"

"No," Minerva repeated, and took his hand. "They'll be fine without us." She kissed him for good measure, which was distracting enough to cast the girl's fate out of his mind, at least temporarily.

He *did,* however, remember to make sure the window was closed before drawing the curtain and joining her on the bed.

"We should make some sort of plan," he said to try to protest, but she pulled him down and said, quite kindly, "Shut up."

So he did.

Arthur

Arthur opened his eyes.

It was dark in the room, but he could see clearly, and he knew he was alone. He lay in someone's bed with a blanket over his body and a soft pillow under his head.

Both, he feared, would have to be cleaned quite extensively once he managed to get up, because he hadn't changed his clothes or washed or anything, and he was covered in filth and blood and dust from the tunnel.

And he probably smelled horrible, too, but at the moment, his nose was all stopped up, making it difficult to breathe, much less smell anything at all.

He vaguely remembered the Master of the Hunt, Gabriel, welcoming them into the Hunt's home. He remembered Malachi more clearly, and Tobias, who had surprised him by carrying Liam all the way through the forest.

Tobias had been surprising in *every* way. Arthur remembered him from before his mother's death, and he seemed to be a completely different person now. Before, he would have turned Arthur and the others in without a single hesitation. Now, though, he'd almost seemed--respectful of what they had done.

Arthur levered himself upright, using his good arm, although the wound from the arrow should have been healed by now. He touched his face; felt dried blood but little else; the bruises were gone; the puffiness faded.

There was an open bottle on the table beside his bed, and a cup. Clearly, someone had been feeding him while he lay there, asleep or unconscious, although there was no sign of that person now.

He swung his legs over the side of the bed. Poured the rest of the bottle into the cup and finished it off. And then sat there, because he wasn't quite certain what he was supposed to do now.

Maya had left; he remembered that. They were to stay at the Hunt's house for the day, and then what? Arthur would never admit this to Iris or Liam, but he hadn't really expected to survive, and so he hadn't made any plans for afterwards.

But could he *really* have made plans? He slipped out of bed and walked to the door. Hesitated, not wanting to disturb anyone; they'd disrupted the Hunt's lives so much already. But then, as he stood there, paralyzed by indecision, the doorknob turned.

The door opened. Arthur backed away, towards the bed.

It was Gabriel's lady, Emle, carrying a small stack of clothing in her arms. "Oh! I'm sorry; have you been awake for long?"

"No," Arthur said. "I just woke up--a few minutes ago."

"You can have a bath if you're feeling up to it," Emle offered. "I think I have some clothes of Josiah's that will fit you."

"Thank you," Arthur said, and found himself perilously close to tears. "I can't repay you for your kindness--"

"I know," Emle said, and smiled at him. "It's awkward, isn't it? But perhaps that tradition is growing outdated; we would find it acceptable if you build a better life outside your father's household and think of us as allies."

"I--I would like that," Arthur said. "And I would also *love* to have a bath."

"Follow me, then," Emle said. "I'll wash your clothes, as well, so just set them outside the door."

The bathroom was antiquated; the faucet a pump, but the water was hot when it came out; the perfect temperature for a bath. And there was an assortment of herbal soaps in a basket on the edge of the tub; Arthur chose one, undressed, set his clothes outside in a pile, and then washed the physical evidence of the last day away.

When he was clean, he put on Josiah's clothes; the pants were a little long, but the shirt fit perfectly, and brushed off his shoes as well as he could. Emle had provided socks and underthings as well, so he actually felt *clean,* not just halfway.

When he opened the bathroom door, his clothes were gone, and since Emle hadn't told him what to do once he was finished, he ventured the opposite way from the bedroom and emerged into the living room, which he remembered from that morning. Sunlight poured into the room through a large window that overlooked the garden outside; the door was closed and the window's glass blocked the effects of the sunlight, but--

"This house sits on the border of the Veil," Gabriel said from behind him. "So the sunlight you see will not harm you, as the garden--and the bulk of this house--lies in Faerie."

"Thank you," Arthur said, and then, "It's still very bright." He stared out at the garden; it seemed a peaceful, if wild, place, with the forest all around it. "I'm not sure my eyes will ever adjust."

"I've been told that a hat helps, and sunglasses," Gabriel said. "You're free to go outside if you wish."

Arthur nodded, but made no move to leave the shelter of the house. After a moment, Gabriel said, "Your cousins are asleep in other bedrooms; Iris's mother is sitting with Liam, as he has no idea you came here, and might be distressed when he wakes up. Tobias has returned home; I'm sure he intends to come back later."

"And what--" Arthur heard his voice crack. "What will become of us?"

"From what Maya tells me, Ethan Walker would take you in without question," Gabriel said. "However, your future is entirely up to you, and if you would feel more comfortable staying with Tobias and the others, I'm certain you would be welcome there as well."

A small white puppy bounded into the house just then with a ball in her mouth and deposited it at Arthur's feet. When he did not react in the way she wanted, she shifted shape, pointed at the ball, and said something unintelligible.

An older girl--they were both obviously Gabriel's daughters--followed her inside and smiled at Arthur. "Sorry," she said. "She just gets excited. It's her favorite toy." She paused. "I'm Eri--short for Erianthe, and that's Chloe."

"I'm Arthur," Arthur said. "What--what does she want me to do?"

"Throw it," Eri said. "And she'll chase it and bring it back." Then, quickly, "But you don't have to."

Arthur smiled. "I don't mind." He bent to pick up the ball. "But--"

"I'll get you a hat," Gabriel said, and disappeared down the hall. "Unfortunately, we don't have any sunglasses." A moment later, he returned with a rather battered leather hat with a brim wide enough to shelter Arthur's eyes, at least, which helped as he stepped outside, carrying the ball.

"Don't throw it past the wall," Eri instructed, and Arthur saw a low stone wall, apparently a work-in-progress, outlining the perimeter of the garden.

"I won't," he promised, and sat on one of the benches that circled what looked to be a fruit tree of some sort as Chloe bounded back and forth. Her joy was infectious. For a moment, okay, nearly an hour, Arthur forgot about his father and grandmother, his worry about the future, and everything else, and found himself smiling and laughing along with Eri as Chloe tried her best not to miss.

She wasn't always successful, but she never gave up. And after that hour, she collapsed at Arthur's feet, panting, grinning up at him, first as a hound, and then as a little girl.

And then she climbed up beside him on the bench and fell asleep with her head against his hip.

Arthur sat very still, not wanting to disturb her; he'd never been so *trusted* before by someone so small, and that made him feel very--strange.

"I can carry her inside if you'd like," Eri said quietly. "She usually takes a nap around this time anyway, so she'll be asleep for a while."

"Could I--could *I* carry her inside?" Arthur asked hesitantly. He wasn't really certain *why* he wanted to; she wasn't *his* little sister, after all, but she trusted him. And that meant more than he could possibly explain.

"Sure," Eri said. "Have you ever carried a toddler, though? She can be kind of floppy, and sometimes she shifts shape in her sleep."

"I've never even held a *baby*," Arthur said, wary now. "Maybe I shouldn't-
-"

Eri smiled. "Maybe you should. Go ahead; pick her up. Like this." She mimed holding something in her arms.

Arthur carefully lifted her up. Chloe nestled herself against his chest and murmured something, but did not awaken. And then, just as carefully, he carried her inside.

"Follow me; I'll show you where you can lay her down," Emle said softly from where she sat repairing Arthur's shirt. She stood up and led the way down the hall.

Arthur carefully lowered the sleeping girl into her bed and stepped back. "Thank you for trusting me with her," he said, his throat suddenly tight.

Emle looked at him levelly. "Why wouldn't I trust you with her?" she asked, and Arthur found that his eyes had filled with tears. He couldn't speak; couldn't explain, but when the expression on her face softened, he realized that she already knew.

After all, the Hunt had once been distrusted. In some places, they still were.

Emle hesitated, then held out her arms. "You needn't tell anyone, but if you'd like some comfort, I will oblige."

Iris had been the only person who had ever hugged Arthur before. But he stepped into Emle's embrace and let her hold him as he cried.

"I didn't--I didn't think we'd make it this far," he sobbed against her shoulder.

She stroked his hair like she would if he were a little child, and he found he did not mind this simple kindness. Eventually, his tears slowed, then stopped, and he loosened his grasp on her and stepped away.

"Thank you," he whispered, his voice hoarse.

Emle smiled. "You're welcome. Will you take a small piece of advice from me?"

Arthur wiped his eyes with the cloth she handed him. "Yes," he said without any hesitation at all.

"You must not focus your life on others' expectations," Emle said. "Focus your life on how *you* want it to be." She paused. "Prove those who would doubt you wrong."

It was good advice. Arthur could only hope that he would be able to follow it. "I'll do my best," he said, unable to promise her anything, especially now when their futures seemed so uncertain.

"That's all you can do," Emle said, and held out her hand. "Come. Let's look in on your friends. I believe Iris is with her mother in Liam's room; she took a bath while you were outside with Chloe and Erianthe."

Arthur took her hand and let her lead him from the room. Iris was, indeed, seated beside her mother, watching over Liam, who still lay asleep--and filthy--in his borrowed bed.

Arthur heard voices in the living room now; wherever the Hounds had been, they had apparently returned.

"Arthur!" Iris jumped up and threw her arms around him when he appeared in the doorway, then stepped back and looked at him critically. "You look much better."

"I feel much better," Arthur said. "How is Liam?"

"Still asleep," Iris' mother said. "Although just asleep, nothing more. Once he wakes up, Emle says he'll have some clean clothes to wear, too."

Cautiously, Arthur said, "I expected you to be angry with me. About Iris. And what we've done."

Iris' mother seemed to think about her reply for a handful of seconds, then said, "I suppose I *should* be, but I'm not. Not really. I was frightened when Iris told me what you had done. Frightened for your lives, and mine. I should probably thank you for allowing me to come with you."

"Sit down," Iris said, and brought him a chair. Arthur sat, not because he was tired, or needed to rest, but because he would pace, otherwise, and he didn't want to pace.

"I'm not sure what happens next," he admitted, and Iris' mother smiled.

"No one ever knows what happens next," she said. "You can hope for a certain outcome, but there's never any guarantee." She paused. "I understand that you probably don't want to be separated--"

Arthur didn't dare look at Iris. "That's true," he said. "We--I always thought we would be together."

"Do you know where you want to go?" Iris' mother asked, almost casually, as if she wanted to ask him a different question all together.

"I thought we could discuss it," Arthur said. "All of us. And make a decision." And then, softer, he added, "I wasn't sure we'd get to *have* a say in where we ended up. I wasn't sure what would happen if we managed to get away." He paused. "I didn't think we would. Escape, I mean."

"I wouldn't have abandoned either of you," Iris said loyally, and folded her arms.

"What do *you* think we should do?" Arthur asked curiously.

"If I ask you a question, will you answer it truthfully?" Iris' mother asked abruptly. She looked uneasy as soon as she asked, as if she expected him to refuse. Or, perhaps, as if she thought he would refuse to answer her question.

"I have no reason to lie to you," Arthur said, which was true.

"Do you remember your Uncle Carroll?" Iris' mother asked solemnly. "Iris' father?"

Arthur had known the identity of Iris' father, but they'd never discussed what had happened to him. The story was that he'd left the Morgan household and had been killed by Hunters. Arthur had never heard anything otherwise.

"I remember him, yes," Arthur said. "But he disappeared before you came back. He came to visit, and never made it back. That's all I know."

Iris' mother took a deep breath. "I came back--*we* came back--because I thought he might not be dead," she said quietly. "I thought that maybe

Ichabod--your father--had done something to him; I know he wasn't happy when we decided to leave the household. And neither was your grandmother."

Arthur closed his eyes and tried to remember everything he could about his uncle's last visit. He would have been seven years old, and this would have been before Iris; before Maya; before his suicide attempt in the forest. He remembered his father and grandmother talking about his uncle, but nothing more; nothing to indicate that the story they told everyone wasn't true.

"I'm sorry," he said, and opened his eyes. "I heard the same story you heard. If they did something to him, they never told me about it. I haven't even heard any rumors." He paused. "My grandmother isn't one to share secrets, though, so if she *did* have a hand in his disappearance, she wouldn't have told *me*."

"There aren't any--places? In the household? That they might have kept him captive?" Iris' mother asked.

"You never told me you thought my father was still alive," Iris said quietly.

Iris' mother sighed. "It was only a hope, nothing more," she said. "I found no sign he was in the house; I looked as well as I could without any luck at all."

"I'm sorry," Arthur said. "I wish I did know something; even a rumor. But I've heard nothing at all, and he wasn't in the basement; we would have found him."

"There are secret rooms all over that house," Iris said matter-of-factly. "If Daddy is alive--"

"We can't do anything about it now," Iris' mother said, and turned her face away to wipe her eyes.

"You must have loved him very much," Arthur said quietly.

Iris' mother tried to smile. "I did," she said. "He was--nothing like your father." She reached out to touch Iris' hand. "He loved you very much."

"I know," Iris said, her voice soft. "I didn't want him to go. I remember not wanting him to go." She hugged her mother, then, and Arthur looked away, wondering what it would have been like to grow up with parents who loved him, but he couldn't really imagine how it might have been if things were different. Because they weren't.

Liam opened his eyes then, anyway, and Arthur spent the next few minutes telling him what had happened, and where they were, and everything else. And then, after Liam had taken a bath and changed his clothes; after he hesitantly accepted a hug from Emle as they trooped out into the Hunt's living room; after he stared around him with wide eyes--

After he said, "I didn't expect the Hunt's lair to look like *this*." And after the embarrassment had passed and Gabriel said, gravely, "Things are seldom what they seem," Arthur knew that he'd be okay. That *they'd* be okay, whatever happened next.

No matter *what* happened next.

Tobias

It was after noon when Tobias awoke; the sun peeked through the opening in the curtains, but there was no shaft of light on the floor, so it wasn't too late yet. And he'd slept; apparently soundlessly, and as he lay in his bed, he realized that he felt a bit--lighter than he had before.

He looked around his room. It was nearly empty; he'd come with nothing other than the clothes on his back, after all, and even after clearing out and selling his mother's house, he'd kept very little of the contents. His room contained a bed, a dresser (half empty) and a lamp; the table beside the bed and an upholstered chair were the only other furniture. All of his clothes fit in one drawer of the dresser; he had one pair of boots, and very little else except for the money he'd stored in the bottom drawer of the dresser, inside a fireproof box, just in case.

Vampires weren't known for their love of banks, after all.

He'd purposely not purchased an excess of clothing. Purposely limited the furniture he'd carried into the room he had chosen after the first few nights where he'd slept on the couch in the library. Purposely kept his possessions at a minimum, because he'd fully expected to have to flee again.

But that hadn't happened. And now, it seemed that he would have a purpose here; a reason to stay; something to work towards, and he found he didn't mind that at all. Which was odd, because he'd spent his whole life, up until now, confident about his place in the hierarchy of the Morgan household, until his mother had killed him and brought him back to life. Until he had abandoned everything. Until he had fled.

And yet, here he was, and they wanted him to be the head of their newborn household. They *trusted* him enough to ask him to be head of their household, and he--still--could not believe that their trust wasn't misplaced.

He had no *intentions* to betray them, but--

A soft knock on his door interrupted his train of thought. That was likely a good thing, because Tobias didn't really want to think about what might occur to force him to betray his new--well, his new friends. For want of a better word, his new *family*.

He sat up, threw back the covers, and slipped out of bed. Hesitated before pulling on the previous night's pair of jeans; they were filthy, but he hadn't showered, either, so he knew he wasn't exactly clean to begin with. And he couldn't answer the door in his underwear, especially since the person standing outside of it was Erialas' aunt Amy.

He opened the door, not quite certain what to say. "I wasn't asleep," he finally said, since she probably intended to ask.

"But you slept," she countered. "And slept well?" She raised an eyebrow at him, which meant she'd either known or guessed that he hadn't been sleeping well. Or, more likely, someone had told her.

"I think so," he said, then noticed she held a bag from a local secondhand store. When she noticed he'd noticed, she held it out to him without comment.

The bag was heavier than he expected. And he knew better than to protest, or try to argue with her; he knew she wouldn't hear of any compensation, but he also knew he had to try. "You don't have to do this," he said. "I have money--" And then he looked inside the bag and his breath caught in his throat. Along with a new pair of jeans and a couple of t-shirts was a pair of boots almost identical to the ones he'd arrived in; the same boots he'd worn when he'd fled his mother's house; the same ones he'd carefully cleaned and which now lay at the foot of his bed, much the worse for wear.

"I know you have money," Aunt Amy said implacably. "And I know I don't have to buy you clothes. But your boots are falling apart, Tobias. And I'm pretty sure getting them resoled wouldn't help; the leather is cracked." She looked at them critically. "And I bet they leak."

"They do," Tobias confirmed. "I--I wanted to get a new pair, but--I've never actually--" Was it a horrible thing to admit that his mother had taken care of all of that? That he'd never purchased a piece of clothing in his life?

"I'd like for you to come with me, the next time I go," Aunt Amy said. "I think you'd be surprised at how much you could find."

"If Liam and Arthur and Iris and her mother come here, they'll need new clothes," Tobias said, not quite agreeing to join her. Not quite refusing, either.

"That's true," she agreed. "*Are* they coming here?"

"I don't know," Tobias said. "I haven't talked to them about it yet. There wasn't really any time to talk to them about it last night--well, this morning, really--they weren't in any shape for long conversations--" He was babbling now, so he shut up.

"I have a question to ask you, but I don't want you to get offended," Aunt Amy said slowly. "I know what they've asked of you, and I'm pretty sure I know what that would mean, in a normal vampire household."

Tobias wasn't quite certain *he* knew what she meant, but he had a hunch he knew what she wanted to ask him. "If it's about Cecilia, I wouldn't--I have no intention--" From the look on her face, he'd guessed correctly, and for some reason he couldn't quite determine, the mere thought of what she felt she had to ask was too distressing to contemplate. He very nearly shut the door in her face. Very nearly retreated into his room because of what they thought of him.

And then, he realized--remembered, really--that what she thought would have been true, not yet a year ago; he wouldn't have thought twice about taking Cecilia to his bed; she'd been promised to him, after all, and he would have been entitled to every inch of her. Now, the mere thought sickened him beyond belief; he could hardly draw a breath, his throat was so tight.

He *had* changed. For the better, he hoped, but time would tell about that. But even knowing that, *knowing* that he would never do such a thing or entertain even an *idea* of it--

And she'd said she didn't want him to get offended.

"Thank you for the clothes," he managed to say. "And the boots." He turned away from her stiffly, trying not to betray any emotion at all; trying to give her the benefit of his doubt that she'd felt obliged to ask him if he intended to act on his mother's arrangement now that he would be head of this household, and able to--technically--do whatever he wanted.

He neglected to close the door behind him. And perhaps she sensed some of his torment, or saw it in his gaze, or his bearing, because she followed him into his room.

"I'm sorry," she said quietly. "You--"

Tobias set the bag onto his bed. "No, you're not," he told her without turning around. Not letting her finish the sentence. "And you had every right to ask. To wonder." He felt--depleted now, and knew it wasn't just because of the previous night's events. "You're--concerned. I understand that." He was a little surprised that he wasn't angry, after that. But he wasn't angry. Numb, yes. Not angry. In a monotone, he told her what he'd told the others. About the old man, and what he had done to save himself. When she reached out to place her hand on his arm, he had to steel himself not to pull away. Not to lash out.

Not to hurt her, because it would be very easy to hurt her.

Perhaps he never should have gotten involved with Liam. Or insisted he accompany Maya and Malachi to the cave. Perhaps he should have stayed in the cabin, and taken his chances with the bounty on his head. Perhaps--

"I believe you," Aunt Amy said, her voice firm and low and utterly without doubt. "I believe you've changed, and I believe you wouldn't hurt a hair on her head."

All the words dried up in Tobias' throat. He stared at her mutely, his eyes suddenly swimming in tears.

"I believe you care about Liam, and your cousins," she continued. "And that you care about Ben and Riala, too. The question I intended to ask was *not* about Cecilia."

"Oh," Tobias said hoarsely. "It wasn't?"

She was the one who closed the door. He sank down on his bed. "No, it wasn't. Although I think I know why you thought what you thought. Thank you for telling me how you healed yourself. Thank you for trusting me."

"I told the others earlier," Tobias murmured, still drained; he wanted to lash out at something, but he didn't dare move for fear of hurting her.

She'd asked him to call her Aunt Amy just like everyone else. He'd never quite been able to bring himself to do so, but he decided to try it now. "What was your question, then, Aunt?" The honorific sounded strange on his tongue, but it helped; with a status, he was less likely to forget. Less likely to hurt her.

"I intended to ask about *you*," Aunt Amy said. "How you felt about all of this and if you were okay." She paused. "I don't think you're okay, however."

"No," Tobias said, deciding to be truthful. "I'm not." He took a deep breath. "I think I will be, though."

She looked at him critically. "You're not just saying that to get rid of me, are you?"

From somewhere, Tobias found a smile. "No," he said. And then, he felt he had to add, "I'm glad you didn't intend to ask me what I thought you intended to ask me--"

"So am I," Aunt Amy said soberly.

They sat in silence for a moment, considering this. Finally, Tobias said, "I should check in on my cousins."

"You should change your clothes first," Aunt Amy suggested.

"And take a shower," Tobias agreed.

"If you go to them today, may I come with you?" Aunt Amy asked.

Surprised, Tobias said, "Yes, of course. But I think waiting until dark would be prudent; there might be questions, otherwise." He paused. "Although I doubt they'll sleep all day."

"I think they'll be wondering what will become of them, and would like to know the answer to that question as quickly as possible," Aunt Amy said sagely.

That was a good point, and likely true. But Michael's rings were still a secret, and Tobias didn't want anyone to see him in the forest where no vampire should be seen.

"You *could* go in disguise," Aunt Amy suggested. "You're about the same size as Mark; you could wear his jacket, and a hat, and since I'd be with you, it wouldn't be so obvious that it's not Mark in the first place." She paused. "The likelihood that the Morgans would have humans in the forest isn't that high."

This was also true. "Okay," Tobias said, because he couldn't really think of any reason not to agree.

"I'll talk to Mark, then," Aunt Amy said. "Go take a shower and get dressed. Try on the boots. I'll probably be in the kitchen when you're ready to leave." She left him, then, sitting on the bed, still drained; he couldn't quite bring himself to do anything but stare after her for a few minutes, and then, slowly, he rose, and gathered his clothes, and carried them to the bathroom.

When he emerged, newly clean, he tried on his new boots (they fit perfectly, of course; Aunt Amy had said it was a gift, knowing what sizes to buy; Tobias hadn't questioned, and she'd never been wrong) and then walked down the hall into the kitchen.

Erialas was there, along with his aunt and uncle, waiting for him.

"We took the liberty of phoning the Hunt to see how their guests were holding up," Aunt Amy said. "Liam had just awakened. Gabriel said he'll be fine, and Erialas said that you carried him all the way through the forest."

"I did," Tobias confirmed, relieved that Liam was awake. "He was awake when we got to them, but didn't last long after that. I don't think he was badly hurt, but I--there was no time to check."

"And the human boy in Sennet's care has not awakened," Mark said. "Neither have Ben or Riala. Apparently, Malachi has already stopped by Sennet's house to check on them."

"He's been sitting with Ben and Riala," Tobias said, then hesitated, wondering if he should have shared that tidbit about the Hound. "He was there when I stopped by last night." Had it only been last night? It seemed like ages ago. "The human boy--Sennet said she couldn't let that continue, in the Morgan household. I had no idea--" He stopped, then, because it wasn't that he had no idea; it was more that he'd never bothered to find out. Ignorance was bliss, when it came to where the Morgan family sourced the blood they drank. No one *ever* asked. Or cared to find out.

"How does Sennet intend to stop this?" Mark asked.

"I don't know," Tobias said honestly. "I don't know that *anyone* can stop my uncle from doing whatever he wants--and my grandmother, too. She's no better; she--" He hesitated, then plunged on. "There was a rumor, once, that she liked children. The younger the better." To avoid their horrified looks, he turned away. "Even infants."

"Then you're well rid of them," Aunt Amy said firmly. "And so is Liam and your cousins."

"I told Sennet I agreed," Tobias told them. "That this couldn't continue."

"The Council will agree as well," Erialas said, without a single doubt, as if he'd already discussed it with Lucas.

"And then what?" Uncle Mark asked. "There's not enough of you to go to war with them--"

"No, there's not," Tobias agreed. "I don't know, 'and then what', but whatever is decided, I--I can't stand by and watch."

"*We* can't stand by and watch," Erialas said, and for a moment, Tobias thought he meant the Council, but then he realized he meant the household; their nameless household made up of exiles--strangers who were now family.

"We'll discuss this later," Uncle Mark said. "But now, you and Amy should probably head on your way; here's my jacket, and a hat I've been seen in before."

Tobias put on the jacket, feeling as if he were donning armor for a battle. It fit him perfectly, which, despite Aunt Amy's words, surprised him, because he'd always thought of Mark as taller; larger, somehow; he'd *loomed* larger in Tobias' mind, at least. And the hat fit as well, and the brim was wide enough to shelter his sensitive eyes from the sunlight without having to resort to sunglasses.

If anyone got close enough, they wouldn't be fooled at all, of course, but from far away, the disguise might work.

"Do you have your phone?" Erialas asked.

Tobias patted his pocket. "Yes, and it's charged."

"Let us know if we should start preparing rooms, then," he said. "And be careful."

"Always," Tobias said, and followed Aunt Amy down the hall.

That they didn't see the others wasn't surprising; Michael spent a lot of time in his workrooms, after all, and Cecilia had taken to helping him. Aaron might have been there, too, or he might have left on an errand or something; they weren't tied to the household, after all. Not now, with Michael's rings.

And then, outside, in the afternoon sunlight; he still felt a flutter of anxiety when he stepped outside during the day, despite the fact that he'd done the same thing many times before and the spell had never faltered.

They walked in silence to the edge of the lawn, then into the forest. It was easier to go through the forest at any rate; the Hunt's house was a bit of a hike, but not *all* that far away. The Morgan household was closer; but despite that, Tobias really didn't believe there would be searchers in the forest. Not during the day, at least.

So they walked in companionable silence; Tobias in his borrowed jacket, pretending to be someone he was not; Aunt Amy unconcerned, as if any thought of capture or pursuit would be too outlandish to even consider.

And she was right; they neither saw nor met anyone; the way to the Hunt's house was clear and quiet; the afternoon sunlight trickled through the trees, and no one challenged their presence.

On Tobias' insistence, however, they approached the house via the garden, in Faerie. More because Tobias didn't want to answer any questions, because he knew Arthur would have them if Liam did not. And Iris was more of a mystery; Tobias did not ever remember meeting her at all.

Anyone who had outwitted Uncle Ichabod and Grandmother Morgan, however, were bound to ask questions. And Tobias didn't want to have to explain the existence of Michael's rings just yet.

The garden wasn't empty; Eri and Josiah seated on the bench under the apple tree, but they stood when Tobias approached with Aunt Amy.

"Hi," Eri said. "They're inside; I'll take you to them."

"Thank you," Tobias said. There was a book open on the bench; Josiah noticed his glance and said, simply, "Eri and I are learning together." He nodded towards the pile of stones and the barely-begun wall. "We intend to build a gate as well, but this way, the garden will be more contained."

"Malachi's not back yet," Eri said as she led them inside.

Tobias wondered what Malachi would see--or had seen--when he looked at Eri. Was she the young girl she seemed? Or did she have secrets of her own? What about Gabriel? He realized, then, that his thoughts had to mirror Malachi's own, and knew why he'd been so reluctant to look into Tobias' gaze.

"We only came to speak with my cousins," Tobias said; someone had obviously told them they'd arrived, because Arthur appeared in the doorway just as Tobias finished his sentence, clean and apparently healed, his gaze wary. Iris was right behind him; Liam lagged behind with Iris' mother, whose face showed nothing but unease.

"You all look much better," Tobias said. He kept his voice calm and even, because he suspected Arthur would expect him to take advantage of his status, and he knew he wasn't wrong when Iris glanced at Arthur, concerned that he hadn't replied. "I came to talk to you, nothing more than that. This is my cousin Erialas' Aunt Amy." He smiled. "She's kind of *everyone's* Aunt Amy now, though--"

"That's true," Aunt Amy agreed, and Tobias saw Liam's surprised look before he hid it behind indifference again.

"You can, of course, use the living room to talk," Gabriel said from behind them, appearing out of a room Tobias suspected was his library.

"To talk," Arthur said. "About what?"

Tobias suspected he wasn't trying to be deliberately objectionable, but Iris apparently thought he was, because she scowled at him and said, "Our future, I assume?" At Tobias' nod, she continued. "I imagine we have two choices. Live with you and the others or flee to the Walker household where Maya sent all the prisoners we freed."

"Can we sit down and talk about this?" Tobias asked. "Please? I'm really not here to antagonize anyone--"

"Come," Aunt Amy said in the voice that brooked no argument. "Let's sit down. Talk. Over tea, perhaps?"

She'd spied Emle with a tea tray in her hands, carrying it out of the kitchen and into the living room as if someone had requested she make it. Tobias felt a bit bad about commandeering the Hunt's home for this; he would have felt more comfortable in the parlor at home--

At home. He realized, then, for the first time, that he truly thought of that as home. Not his mother's house; not the Morgan household, but their own little household, safe and secure.

They would definitely need a name, and soon, he thought, and watched as Arthur and the others filed past him, into the living room.

Tobias deliberately chose to sit on the hearth, which was a lower spot than the bench that stretched under the picture window. Aunt Amy poured the tea; Emle, Gabriel, and the rest of the Hunt made themselves scarce.

Arthur introduced the others to Aunt Amy. His voice was formal and stiff; Tobias suspected he couldn't really help but feel uneasy, considering they had little to offer anyone who might take them in.

But *he'd* come with only the clothes he wore, and nothing more, and so had Cecilia. And Michael, for that matter.

"Iris is correct," he said. "Although you likely have more than two choices, you would be welcome to join us in our household." He decided to get the shocking part out of the way immediately.

"Your--*household?*" Arthur asked slowly, as if he'd heard wrong. Disbelieving. But Liam's eyes lit up; he said, excitedly, "Really? Who will be willing to recognize a new household?"

And Arthur, Iris, and her mother stared at him as if he'd gone mad.

"We're assuming the Walker household will, although I haven't spoken with Ethan yet," Tobias said. "And the Richmond household, as well." He hesitated, not certain he should share the information about Tristan's coup, then deciding that he had to, really, to gain their trust. "You may not know this, but Connor Richmond is no longer head of the Richmond household."

Arthur's shock warred with his wariness; after a bit of a struggle, he asked, "When did this happen?"

"About eight months ago," Tobias said. "Right before my mother died." No one mentioned that he'd *killed* her; they all knew, of course, but Tobias doubted they knew the entire story.

"And who is head of the Richmond household?" Iris asked.

"His name is Tristan; he's Cecilia's half-brother," Tobias told them. "I only just found out about this, myself; he apparently swore Cecilia to secrecy when she fled."

"The Tristan who killed an entire nest of Hunters?" Liam asked.

"The very same," Tobias said. "I know you told me that rumor; it's apparently true, but no one was supposed to know about it. Do you remember where you heard it?"

Liam shook his head. "No; it could have been anywhere; no one really notices me, so I--" He hesitated. "I heard a lot of stuff I wasn't supposed to hear."

"That's all behind you now," Tobias said.

"Is it?" Arthur asked. "If we join you, then I don't think we'll be able to escape retaliation for long. And we might put you in danger."

"The last time I checked, there was a half a million dollar bounty on my head," Tobias said. "I'm--*we're*--used to danger. And looking over our shoulders."

Iris' mother said, slowly, "Can you protect them?"

Not 'can you protect *us*', Tobias thought.

"Two members of the Council--Erialas and Michael--live in the household," Tobias said. "We're well-protected." On a hunch, he said, "You could likely go to Darkbrook, if you wanted to, once--things die down a bit."

Arthur opened his mouth to speak, then closed it again as soon as he noticed the look on Liam's face--and Iris'. He frowned, very briefly, then said, cautiously, "Would Darkbrook want us?" And then, "I mean, we're *Morgans,* and likely to be hunted, no matter how much time has passed."

Tobias remembered what Sennet had said, and wondered what she'd meant. And how she planned to stop his uncle, or if she had a plan at all. "I think Darkbrook would welcome you," he said. "And you don't have to make a decision now, of course, but you'd be welcome to join us." He paused. "All of you would be welcome, of course."

Iris' mother smiled a little at this, almost sadly.

"There's plenty of room," Aunt Amy said.

"Who is head of household, then?" Iris wondered aloud, and Tobias felt the words dry up in his throat, because he couldn't quite voice them; couldn't quite believe they were true.

When he didn't speak, Aunt Amy looked at him oddly; he had to clear his throat to continue. "I am," he said. "They--ah--asked me to be head of household, and I accepted."

Arthur looked surprised by this. "They trust you that much?"

"They have no reason not to trust me," Tobias said evenly. "I'm not going back, even if your father offered me a complete pardon. I--I like it there. And I'd like to think we can build the household into a family--a *real* family, not one like you're used to."

"That would be--" Arthur began, then stopped. He folded his arms; took a deep breath. "Can we talk about it? Whether or not we want--"

"I do," Iris said, and Liam echoed her words, looking worriedly at Arthur, as if he expected him to refuse. And Tobias wondered how they would react if he *did* refuse; if he told them he'd rather flee to the Walker household. Would they join him?

Arthur wouldn't look at either of them. He wouldn't look at Tobias, either, or Iris' mother, who reached out, as if to put a hand on his arm--in comfort, Tobias thought--then hesitated, as if she thought he would react badly.

"Maybe I could speak to Arthur in private?" Tobias asked gently.

Arthur blinked rapidly; Tobias saw tears hovering on the edges of his eyelashes. "No--No, it's okay," he said, unconvincingly. "It's just--I didn't think--"

"I thought I'd be dead by now, honestly," Tobias said. "But I'm not, and it looks like my future might just be a little brighter. It seems that way right now, at least."

"I would like to join you," Arthur said slowly. "I want to stay here, if I have a choice; I don't want to go to the Walker household. Not right now, at least. I'd rather stay with family."

"Did you bring anything with you at all?" Aunt Amy asked.

"No," Iris replied. "Nothing. We borrowed these clothes--" She looked suddenly worried, as if Gabriel would appear to demand them back.

"I should probably warn you that Aunt Amy has a sort of gift when it comes to clothes," Tobias said. "She'll buy you new ones, and they'll fit perfectly, no matter what. I don't think she's ever been wrong."

"We don't have any money," Liam said practically.

"We're not exactly hurting for money," Tobias said. "I sold my mother's house, after--" He paused, not really wanting to go into detail. "Anyway, I have all that money, and you're cousins, so it will still remain in the family either way. And with forming our own household, I'm sure there are things you can do, if you feel the need for repayment."

Iris' mother had stayed silent, letting Arthur and the others do the talking. Tobias had to wonder what she thought of all of this.

"You'll come too?" he asked.

Iris looked at her mother when she did not reply.

"We really do have plenty of room," Tobias said. "And you would be welcome."

"*Mom*," Iris said insistently.

And then Tobias saw the knowledge in her gaze, and realized that while Liam and Arthur and Iris had taken his words at face value; had believed he'd changed, Iris' mother was older, and wiser, and had probably seen him at his worst.

"Your mother doesn't believe I've changed," Tobias said. "Understandably so; she's probably heard more stories about me than you have." He hesitated. "If I did something to you--"

"No, not to me," Iris' mother said. "But you're right; I've heard the stories, and I've seen you--do things." She took a deep breath. "And I'm willing to believe that what your mother did to you has changed you, with reservations."

"I'd expect nothing less," Tobias said quietly. "Your reservations are completely understandable."

"To be honest, I'm surprised you're not offended," Iris' mother said.

"I've had to learn a lot over the past few months," Tobias replied after a moment of silence. He'd half-expected Aunt Amy to say something, but she remained silent. "One of those things is that I have to accept that I wasn't a very nice person, before. And some people will still believe that I'm not a very nice person, and that's okay; I can't change their minds by finding offense in everything they say or do." He paused. "You would--will--be welcomed, as I was welcomed. And *I* did not deserve to be welcomed, then."

From the look on her face, Iris' mother doubted he should be welcomed *now,* but she didn't speak her thoughts aloud. Instead, she said, "Thank you. And if everything is as you say, then perhaps--perhaps one day we can be allies, if not friends."

"Then I'll look forward to that day," Tobias said. "If you're well enough to travel, I can return once the sun sets and we can walk back; it's not a difficult hike, really, even in the dark."

"How did you come here now?" Arthur asked curiously. "I didn't think the house was past the Veil."

"It's not," Tobias said. He didn't want to lie to them, but he'd hoped no one would ask. Trust Arthur, though, to notice, and ask, because he was used to knowing what was going on.

None of them were stupid. All of them realized what that meant, but no one really wanted to come right out and ask for fear of what door would be opened then; vampires were, of course, not supposed to walk in daylight. That had been truth for so long that it felt almost sacrilegious to consider anything else.

Even so, Tobias felt he had to say *something,* at the very least. "I'll explain, once you get settled in. You can hold me to that promise."

Arthur nodded. "I will," he said solemnly.

"Unless you have any additional questions, then, we'll come back for you after the sun sets," he continued, just as Malachi walked into the room via the cave; he stopped when he saw them, as if no one had told him they were to be left alone.

Not that Tobias minded his presence. He felt more--secure, for some reason, with Malachi there. Less likely to say something stupid; less likely to trip over his own tongue.

"You'll be happy to know that Sennet thinks the boy you rescued will recover," he said. "He hasn't awakened yet, but he's resting comfortably."

Relieved, Arthur said, "I'm glad to hear that." He twisted his hands together in his lap, then asked, "What will happen to him? Once he has recovered?"

"I doubt Sennet has thought that far yet," Aunt Amy said gently. "He'll be well cared for, regardless. And he'll have you to thank for not leaving him to die."

"I couldn't do that," Arthur said quietly.

"I know," Aunt Amy said, and smiled at him. He couldn't quite smile back, but he tried; Tobias suspected he hadn't quite rested enough, which wouldn't help on the journey back home.

"There will be searchers in the forest once the sun sets," Liam said. "Once they find out we didn't die in the tunnel collapse."

"You won't have to worry about searchers," Malachi said firmly. "And you *certainly* won't be alone."

Arthur's next question would be whether or not the Hunt was stronger than his father; Tobias knew that just as Malachi had known his secret.

"Your father's not all-powerful," he said. "And he would never come himself."

"That's true," Arthur said after a moment.

"We'll be back for you after the sun sets, then," Aunt Amy said.

Iris' mother looked surprised. "You'll be there too?"

"Yes," Aunt Amy said. "Unless Tobias has objections--"

"I have no objections," Tobias told her, which was true. He stood up, then, and said, "Get some rest. It's still a hike, and I'd rather not have to carry anyone this time." He smiled to take the sting from his words, but it didn't work.

Liam flushed. "I didn't say thank you," he said. "I'm sorry--"

"No need to apologize," Tobias told him. "I'm just glad I was there to help. We'll see you soon."

"Be careful," Arthur said.

"I'm always careful," Tobias replied, which was true, now, at least. And after thanking Gabriel for the use of his living room; after thanking Emle for the tea, he followed Aunt Amy out into the garden again. Josiah and Eri were fitting stones into their wall now, in no particular hurry, enjoying each other's company.

Malachi followed them out. "I'd come through Faerie tonight," he said. "Just in case there's trouble."

"We will," Tobias promised. "And we'll call before we leave."

"See you then," Malachi said, and stood there, watching, as they walked away into the forest. Tobias looked back once and he was still there; only then did he realize he hadn't asked after Ben or Riala.

But surely Malachi would have said something if they were awake.

"You did well," Aunt Amy said after a moment of silence.

Tobias adjusted his hat to shadow more of his face. "Did I?" he asked. "I'm not so certain. Iris' mother doesn't trust me, not that I blame her."

"You did," Aunt Amy insisted. "And she'll come around."

They'd met no one on the way to the Hunt's house; Tobias expected no less on their way back. But even so, he was alert, watchful; he couldn't let down his guard. And perhaps the forest *was* too quiet; he hadn't even spotted one of the small folk, and that was unusual enough to mention, but he kept his mouth shut for fear of someone recognizing his voice as they drew nearer to the Morgan household.

"Do you think it's safe enough to take a look?" he finally asked.

"Absolutely not," Aunt Amy said immediately.

"You're probably right," Tobias admitted, and despite the fact that he wanted to see the destruction, he did not press the issue and did not mention it again.

There would be time to see the destruction, if something were to happen to his uncle and his grandmother.

Until then, however, he could only wait.

Tristan

"I'm going to visit Jericho," he'd told them, which was true, because he fully intended to eventually end up in Faerie, in Celeste's little house where Jericho had moved about a month after his rescue.

He seemed to like it there, with her; Tristan suspected some sort of relationship between them, but he'd never asked.

Alexander hadn't been fooled, but he'd only said, "Be careful," and "How long will you stay?"

"I'll be back before dark," Tristan had told him. "I'll take the phone to make you happy--" Here, Minerva had made a noise, probably exasperation, "And no one will see me anyway, so it's useless to worry."

"I disagree," Alexander had said. "About worrying. But it should be safe enough, as long as you don't stray too far towards last night's events."

But of course that's exactly what Tristan intended to do, and Alexander knew this but made no protest. It was likely he was just as curious, and since they were--somewhat indirectly--involved now, Tristan wanted to see for himself what had happened.

He honestly hadn't expected to meet anyone out in the forest. The Morgan household wouldn't use humans to search for the runaways anyway, and he had no intention of straying near the Hunt's home, although that was tempting, too. But since the Richmond household lay farther to the east of the Morgan household, and Tristan was on foot, it was still afternoon by the time he stopped at the edge of the forest and saw the destruction.

The Morgan household, like many vampire households, had begun as a large mansion, but had been added on over the years until it resembled no particular design, but many of them, or all of them together. The resulting mess wasn't the prettiest of structures, but it had housed many Morgans over the years.

The wing that had fallen due to the tunnel collapse had been a newer wing, Tristan thought. And it had collapsed quite--spectacularly. It had also caught on fire, but the fire was out now, leaving only smoke behind. Tristan didn't see a single living person anywhere; the windows were heavily curtained; the rubble untouched; any bodies within had likely burned once the sun rose or lay in the rubble, dying.

Thoughtfully, he turned away from the Morgan household and set upon a roundabout course; he wanted to see the other household as well; the household of exiles, which wasn't that far away. He *really* wanted to show up on their doorstep; to see Cecilia, but that would mean questions, and he'd been told--warned--that his ability to walk in sunlight should be kept secret at all costs.

But then, halfway there, he heard voices; quiet voices; a woman and someone else. A human, and--and a *vampire?* Here?

Granted, *he* was a vampire, and he wasn't supposed to be out in the forest in the daylight hours either, but--curious, he followed them past the Veil, into safety, despite the fact that neither of them had been in danger before.

He couldn't let them pass without questioning this; he couldn't let this go. Alexander might disagree; Alexander might tell him to go and visit Jericho and leave it alone, but he *couldn't.*

Silently, he crept closer. Spotted them through the trees; an older woman and a man, he thought, wearing a jacket and a hat. The vampire, most definitely. The woman was human, and seemed almost motherly; which likely meant the vampire was younger. And since they were headed in the general direction of Erialas Morgan's house, Tristan suspected that this was either Tobias or Erialas, most probably the former, since he was rather tall, and he'd heard that Erialas was not. But that made no sense, because Tobias wouldn't have the same dispensation from the Veil that Tristan had; he would have heard of such a thing, and Nefir had not mentioned it.

And he could not let it go. Despite the fact that his presence would not be welcomed, he could not let it go.

He stepped out of hiding. Guessed at the woman's name. "Amaryllis Kirchner and Tobias Morgan." Perhaps he sounded more dangerous than he intended. Perhaps they merely didn't recognize his voice, which wasn't so much of a surprise, because he'd only met Tobias once that he remembered, and he'd never met Erialas' Aunt Amy before.

They froze, nonetheless. Tobias seemed to forget how to breathe.

"And you are--?" Aunt Amy asked, struggling for calm.

"Tristan Richmond," said a voice behind Tristan; an unexpected voice, because he hadn't realized that by following Tobias and Aunt Amy, he would be followed as well.

Interestingly enough, Tobias recognized this voice, because he relaxed. Or, perhaps, he recognized Tristan's name, which was also likely, since

Tristan had sent Cecilia a letter giving her permission to tell her housemates of his coup.

"And *you* are?" Tristan echoed, turning around to face the speaker, who ignored his question.

"How is it," the young man behind him asked, "that you can walk in sunlight?"

Tristan *had* actually expected him to give his name. Nonplussed, he stared at the speaker, noting a few inconsistencies; he wasn't human, for one, even though he *looked* like a human, and he was, very carefully, avoiding meeting Tristan's gaze. "If I answer your question, will you answer mine?"

"I'd like to know that, too," Tobias said from behind him. Quietly, unthreatening. As if he knew Tristan would take offense otherwise.

"And I would like to know the same about you," Tristan said, and looked back at him with a small smile. "Please don't lie to me; I've been following you since you passed the Morgan household."

Tobias looked ill, quite suddenly, as if he should have known; he started to speak, fell silent, then ventured, "Cecilia said you were not our enemy."

"That's true," Tristan agreed. "I am not your enemy." It was difficult to keep an eye on them both, so he stepped backwards so that he wouldn't have to keep turning around.

"Then why not answer my question?" the follower asked.

"Then why not answer mine?" Tristan shot back. He could be just as stubborn, but instead of going on the offense, the follower merely smiled.

"My name is Malachi," he said.

No surname, just Malachi. Which meant that Tristan should have recognized it, and he *did,* somewhat; he knew he'd heard that name before, but he couldn't remember where. And as he frowned at Malachi, trying to remember, Malachi said simply, "I am a Hound."

Of course he was. "And I am not fond of the 'proper channels'," Tristan said, and it was *almost* an apology. "But I will admit I didn't intend to seek you out--" this to Tobias, "I merely wanted to view the destruction for myself."

"You know what happened?" Tobias asked, surprised.

"Yes," Tristan said. "The Morgans sent a human girl to see if Fern had fled to us; she was born a Richmond, apparently. She didn't give any details, but Maya did, after I asked a fairy what had happened."

"Maya has never mentioned you," Malachi said.

"We've only just met," Tristan told him. "I've had dealings with the small folk, up until now. And I am actually on my way to visit my brother Jericho, who lives in Faerie, not to bother you, but I *saw* you, in sunlight past the Veil, and I--"

Tobias sighed. "And you couldn't resist."

"Well, yes," Tristan admitted, and waited, quite patiently, he thought, for an explanation.

"You were unharmed in sunlight past the Veil as well," Malachi pointed out.

This was true. "I've--promised that I would not share the reason for that with anyone," Tristan said carefully.

"So have I," Tobias said.

They stared at each other for a moment. In the silence, Aunt Amy pulled out a cell phone and started to dial a number.

"Who are you calling?" Tristan asked curiously.

"Someone who will know if you're telling the truth," Aunt Amy replied, and put the phone up to her ear. "Hello, Rose? This is Amaryllis Kirchner."

"Rose Duncan of the Rose Emporium?" Tristan asked. "Alexander knows her well."

"Who is Alexander?" Malachi asked.

"Probably the oldest vampire in the world," Tobias told him.

"I have no reason not to tell the truth," Tristan said to anyone who might be listening. "Why would I lie?" He watched as she walked away from them, talking quietly; he could have listened in, of course, but in a fit of petulance, he decided he didn't care what Rose Duncan told her about him. He folded his arms. Frowned.

After a few minutes of conversation, Aunt Amy pocketed her phone and said, "I apologize for our caution, but we've had to deal with quite a few threats from the Morgan household over the years, and some of them were fairly inventive."

"Oh--for Erialas," Tristan said, remembering what he'd heard about how he'd come to live with his mother's human family. And then, curious, he asked, "What did she say?"

"That she knows Alexander well, and because of him, she would deem you trustworthy," Aunt Amy said. "And that you are the head of the Richmond household."

"Did you really kill an entire nest of Hunters?" Tobias asked.

Tristan narrowed his eyes. Where had Tobias heard that story? "Did your mother really kill you and bring you back to life?"

"Yes," Tobias said. "Twice."

"Then, yes as well," Tristan said. "After they tortured me with molten silver and left me for dead." He paused. "I heard that Erialas survived a silver wound as well."

"He did," Aunt Amy confirmed.

"I was not unmarked," Tristan said quietly. "As I assume Erialas was not unmarked, either."

"He had very little use of the arm that was stabbed," Tobias said.

"I had very little use of most of my body," Tristan said. "I could barely move. The spells that aid my survival are held by the Veil, which is how I can manipulate it to allow me to walk unharmed in sunlight. That's the short version of the tale, I'm afraid." He paused. "Alexander will likely be cross because I told you, but since Malachi saw me past the Veil--" He shrugged. "As you said, we aren't enemies."

Tobias hesitated, obviously torn between sharing confidences with Tristan and keeping his word to stay silent. Eventually, he said, "It is a mobile ward that Michael created for us to wear." He held up his hand, and Tristan saw that he wore a silver ring set with a moonstone; an odd choice for a vampire. And *us* meant there were more than one of them, and also meant that they could be replicated.

"Does Michael want to be rich beyond his wildest dreams?" Tristan asked, knowing that--at the very least--Alexander would be interested in such a ring.

"Michael doesn't want to be a target," Tobias said slowly. "But if you already have the ability to walk in sunlight, who--"

"Alexander, of course," Tristan said. "And perhaps a few others, as well."

"I'm certain you could ask," Aunt Amy said dryly. "Since you're not an enemy."

Tristan smiled.

"How old is the oldest vampire in the world?" Malachi asked curiously.

Tristan considered the source of the question, and almost everything he'd ever heard about the Wild Hunt. "Your Master might be older," he allowed. "I'll have to ask. Alexander may refuse to tell me, though; he doesn't like to talk about it."

"Neither do we," Malachi said, and from this, Tristan inferred that he was likely just as old as his Master, which meant he was one of the original Hounds, and positively ancient, despite how young he looked.

Respectfully, because he wasn't stupid, he said, "I apologize for not declaring myself immediately and allaying your suspicions of my intentions."

"You weren't aware of my presence," Malachi said, which was true, so perhaps the apology was really for Tobias, since he would have had more to lose if Tristan had been a Morgan.

"If Cecilia has a ring like yours, do you think she would want to visit Jericho with me?" Tristan asked. "I can have her home by late afternoon; I expect that the Morgans will be out in force tonight, hunting, and I'd like to be home by dark." He had to wonder, though, if she would even want to come with him. She probably barely remembered Jericho, except for his punishment, and he doubted she would want to relive that.

"I expect they'll be out, too," Tobias said. "We're--Arthur and the others will be staying with us--"

"In your household; that makes sense," Tristan said, nodding.

Hesitantly, Tobias asked, "Would you acknowledge us as a household?"

"The Richmond household, you mean?" Tristan knew what he meant, of course; how could he not? "I've barely publicly declared my father dead, and I feel quite precarious doing so. But yes, I'd recognize your household. Are you to be its head?"

"I've been asked to be head of household, yes," Tobias said, but Tristan didn't get the impression that he was entirely okay with the idea. "Michael and Erialas are members of the Council, so they cannot; Cecilia refused, and Aaron--well, they all talked about it before they approached me." He paused, then seemed to remember Tristan's previous question. "If Cecilia wants to go with you, she is welcome to go, of course; I have no hold over her."

This was a potentially offensive question, but Tristan felt he had to ask it, nonetheless. "You don't intend to hold to your promised--arrangement?"

Tobias didn't even have to think about the answer to that question. Nor did he seem offended, which was a bit surprising, considering all the subtexts of what Tristan might have meant. "No," he said. "Absolutely not."

Tristan nodded. "Good, because I've declared all such arrangements null and void, although I haven't informed the Morgan household as of yet."

"That was prudent of you," Malachi said.

Tristan shrugged. "More self-preservation than anything," he admitted. "While I was fairly certain I could overthrow my father, I'm not as certain about Ichabod Morgan or Grandmother Morgan."

Tobias frowned thoughtfully, but didn't speak; after a moment, Aunt Amy said, "If you want to ask Cecilia to accompany you, you should probably come back to the house with us."

"And I'd best be on my way," Malachi said, and shifted shape into a white Hound before vanishing into the forest.

Tristan suspected he still wouldn't be far behind, or else there would be other watchers; even the small folk, but he saw no one as he followed Tobias and Aunt Amy back to the house. And while it felt very strange to step into what had once been a piece of the Morgan household, the occupants were not unwelcoming, and even Cecilia seemed pleased at his presence, even apologizing that she hadn't responded to his letter right away.

"I was on my way to visit Jericho, in Faerie," Tristan told her. "Tobias tells me you have the ability to walk in sunlight now--" To Michael, he added, "Could we talk about this at a later date?" And Michael had replied, "Of course."--"And I wondered if you would want to accompany me. I'll have you home before dark." He paused. "And if you don't trust me, feel free to ask someone to come with you; I don't mind, and neither will Jericho."

To her credit, Cecilia had only hesitated for a moment, and then she'd accepted his invitation, and if anyone had reservations, they didn't speak of them. And as Tristan followed her outside, she said, "I told them all about your letter."

"I didn't forbid you not to tell them," Tristan replied. "In fact, I expected you to tell them."

"I don't want to go back," Cecilia said. "*Ever.*" As if he would think otherwise.

"I know," Tristan told her. "Although I think Minerva might wish you were less of a stranger." He paused. "We sold some furniture; I should have brought you some of the profit. And do you need anything from the house? I should have--"

"It's okay," Cecilia said. "Really."

"We sent you off to exile without--"

"Tristan, it's okay," Cecilia insisted. "I like it there. They've all been very nice. And I don't want to leave. Maybe Minerva can come visit?"

"I think she would like that very much," Tristan said, abandoning the apologies; he thought she'd expect them, but apparently not.

"Why are you doing this?" Cecilia asked curiously.

"Doing what?" Tristan asked. And for a moment, he thought she wouldn't reply; that she'd fall silent, but then she said, "I know how you really are."

"You don't know me at all," Tristan protested.

"I know you don't *really* care about how I've been living, or if I'm happy there," Cecilia told him. "I know you would rather not be bothered by all of this; is it because of Alexander that you're still head of the Richmond household?"

"I--" He had to stop walking, then; he wasn't quite sure what to say to her. "Would it be so much of a surprise to discover that I've changed? Or that I'm trying to change?"

"It would be," she said. "A surprise."

"I'm--in love with Minerva," Tristan blurted out. It was the first time he'd admitted that to anyone other than Minerva, in truth, although everyone seemed to know.

"And is she in love with you?" Cecilia asked, sounding much older than her years.

"She says she is," Tristan told her. "How do you ever know, really? I think she is, though. If she's not, I think I'd rather not know. I would rather believe that she loves me, despite what I've done in the past."

Cecilia gave him a *look* that reminded him very much of Minerva. "But I know you don't really--"

"I can pretend, though, until I believe it myself," Tristan said. "I never intended to become head of the Richmond household, and perhaps I'm not really; it's more of a joint effort, to be honest." He paused. "I'm trying. To be--nice. Polite. Civilized. I haven't killed anyone since--since our father. I haven't really been tempted, either. Give me that much, at least."

"Okay," Cecilia said after a long few minutes in silence. They were almost to the point where Lark would notice them now; Tristan wondered if he would appear, curious about Cecilia's presence. "I'll give you that much."

"Thank you," Tristan said stiffly, and wondered why her opinion meant so much to him. Why should it? She was his half-sister, nothing more; a child, still, really, despite her apparent maturity. It made more sense to want *Alexander* to believe in him, or Miriam, or even Minerva. But he found himself strangely unable to leave her doubt of him in peace.

"Why is it so hard for you to believe that I could change?" he asked. "That I could learn to be different?"

"I'm not sure," Cecilia admitted. "Because no one else has ever tried to change? Because being seen as polite and civilized and *nice* has always been a sign of weakness in the Richmond household?"

"The same has always held true in the Morgan household," Tristan said. "And you don't seem to believe *Tobias* will murder you in your sleep."

"He--he *has* changed," Cecilia said.

"And it's so fantastical that I've changed too?" Tristan asked, although he really wasn't sure he'd actually *changed;* it was more that he'd learned to pretend well enough to fool everyone around him, except, apparently, for Cecilia.

Her mother wouldn't have been fooled, either. And he wasn't sure that Alexander was fooled; it was more that Alexander hoped he could learn these things no one had ever bothered to teach him, and eventually they would become second nature.

For the sake of argument, Tristan wasn't certain himself that he could perpetuate this lie until it became truth, or if he would snap one day and kill everyone, or likely be killed himself. Because he had to admit--privately, of course--that he liked killing. That was why he'd been so insistent in his quest to go after Jericho. He hadn't wanted to persist in the path his father had set for him, for fear of where it might lead. He wanted to be in control, not a slave to his own whims. To his own desires.

"Good afternoon," Lark said, appearing from behind a tree. "Who's this?"

"Cecilia," Tristan said. "This is Lark, the king's border guard. Cecilia is Jericho's--and mine--younger sister."

Cecilia's eyes had widened at the sight of the elf. "You were there!" she exclaimed, and stepped back, as if this were not a pleasant remembrance.

Tristan supposed it wouldn't be, just as he wouldn't ever want to see any of the Hunters who participated in his torture ever again, although in his case, at least, that would never be possible, since they were all dead.

"I was," Lark agreed. "And you look much better than you did, then. I'm sorry that I didn't have a chance to introduce myself before; we were rather--busy with Tristan's collapse."

"I don't remember any of it," Tristan said, but Cecilia did not look convinced that he was telling the truth.

"You came through Faerie?" Lark asked. "Or have you figured out a way to share your--ability with someone else?"

"Cecilia has her own protection," Tristan said, but did not go into detail.

"I see," Lark said with a question in his gaze that he did not voice. "I'm sure Jericho will be happy to see you as well as Cecilia."

And he was; twenty minutes later, Jericho's face lit up when he saw his sister. He set aside the guitar; stowed it securely in its case, and accepted a hug without a single hesitation.

"I'm so happy to see you," he said. "Would you like some tea?" To Tristan, he asked, "What brings you here?"

He seemed quite relieved at their presence; Celeste was apparently not present. Usually she was; and while Tristan didn't really mind her presence, he never--quite--felt welcome in her home.

"Where's Celeste?" Tristan asked.

"She went past the Veil to gather supplies and visit Ethan," Jericho said. "She'll be gone for another day, yet."

"You could have gone with her," Tristan said, watching as Cecilia noticed the large loom in one corner of the small living room; the room itself seemed too small to house everything it contained; the walls were lined with bookshelves, which were, in turn, filled with books. Tristan had only been in the kitchen, otherwise; he had no idea where they slept.

"No," Jericho said. "I--I can't."

"You're not bound to Faerie, and our father is dead," Tristan told him. "So you could have gone with her. I would understand if you wouldn't want to visit *me*, but--"

There was a peculiar expression on Jericho's face now. Half fearful; half frustrated. Tristan hadn't seen it before, but then again, he'd never visited while Celeste was away, either.

"What does this do?" Cecilia asked, indicating the loom.

And Tristan watched as Jericho seized the opportunity to talk about something else, as if he were drowning, and Cecilia had thrown him a life preserver. And he watched as Jericho explained the workings of the loom to his sister, who seemed interested, and he waited until Jericho had stopped talking, and then he said, "Have you left this house since you set foot in it?"

He *had* visited. At least once a month. Always inside Celeste's house; always with Celeste present. And he'd visited with Jericho in dreams, as well, and Jericho had not mentioned--not once--that he was a virtual prisoner.

Not through Celeste's machinations, he thought, but through his own.

"I need to--" Jericho began, then shook his head. Picked up the guitar case and cradled it in his arms. "I--"

"You don't have to answer his question," Cecilia said, glaring at Tristan quite unjustly.

"I do," Jericho said quietly.

"No, you don't," Tristan protested, not liking the look in his gaze. Not liking the fact that he seemed afraid of the answer to what should have been a simple question. Or an absurd one, at best.

"I can't leave," Jericho whispered. "I've tried. I need to be somewhere safe." He turned away, still holding the guitar case, as if it were the only thing that kept him anchored to the conversation.

Carefully, Tristan approached him. Cecilia moved to stop him; he shook his head and she backed off, frowning. But Tristan didn't say or do anything at all to upset his brother. *Their* brother.

"Do you feel safe here?" he asked gently. "Sit down. Cecilia will get the tea."

Jericho sat in one of the chairs in front of the fireplace. Tristan took the guitar case and set it beside the chair; Jericho stared into the flames, unable to meet his gaze.

"I would have come to stay with you," he said. "Or Alexander would have come."

"I told her I didn't want to bother you," Jericho whispered. "I told her that I would be fine."

"And she believed you?" Tristan asked, incredulous, because Celeste hadn't struck him as a particularly stupid person.

Jericho tried to smile. "Probably not," he admitted. "Muirghen has stopped by, and Nefir was here a few hours ago. It's only three days; it's not that long." He sounded as if he were trying--and failing--to convince himself of that. "I'm glad you came, though. I--I missed you."

And he said *this* as if he expected Tristan to laugh at him.

Or as if he expected Tristan to turn around and leave in disgust.

Instead, Tristan poured the tea when Cecilia brought it out to them, and pulled up a chair so that she could sit down. Handed out cups all around. "Does Alexander know about this?" he asked.

"I don't know," Jericho said. "I haven't told him." He hesitated. "Celeste thinks it will go away on its own, eventually."

Tristan wasn't so sure she believed that, or if she merely intended to ease Jericho's mind. It was obvious that she wasn't pushing him, which was both good and bad; good because he still felt safe with her, and bad because that only meant he remained effectively trapped in the house.

"What do you think?" he asked.

Jericho still wouldn't look at him. "I think that I don't want to talk about it right now," he said, and set down his cup. Stood. "I'm sorry," he said to Cecilia. "I *am* really happy to see you." And then, before Tristan could try to call him back, he picked up the guitar case and vanished down the hall.

"If you're trying, you're not trying very hard," Cecilia said crossly. "You didn't see him--"

"I saw him when he was chained to that tree," Tristan murmured, staring after him. "I *saved* him from that tree."

"You didn't see it happen," Cecilia persisted. "You only saw the aftermath. You didn't hear him screaming." She paused. "I'm surprised he's so--normal."

"It was my fault," Tristan said quietly. "I was supposed to protect him, and I failed. He'll say differently; he'll say it wasn't my fault, but it was."

Cecilia looked at him for a moment. It was a familiar look; he'd seen it on Minerva's face before. And Alexander's, as well. (And Nefir's, and Celeste's, and even Jericho's, if he wanted to be truthful.) "You were captured by *Hunters*," she said slowly.

"Yes, I know," Tristan said. "I remember. I wasn't there to hear him screaming; you're right. I'm surprised he's as--functional as he is, even now. Because he wasn't supposed to survive."

"Neither were you," Cecilia pointed out. "And he's probably listening to us right now--" She glanced towards the hall, but Jericho did not appear. "Did you *have* to ask him if he ever left this place?"

"I was supposed to protect him," Tristan reminded her. "And I failed. But my vow is still in place; even now--" He stood. "I'll be right back."

"Maybe you should leave him alone for a bit," Cecilia said quietly.

"I can't," Tristan told her. "He wouldn't leave *me* alone, if our roles were reversed."

"Then I'm coming with you," Cecilia said, and no amount of argument would dissuade her.

"I'm not quite sure where I'm going, but this house isn't very large," Tristan admitted. "We'll find him eventually." And they *did* find him, lying full length on a bed in a room that was obviously a bedroom, staring up at the ceiling with the guitar case beside him. Tristan did not remark on his tears.

In fact, this room seemed to be the *only* bedroom in the house, which raised an interesting question as to where both Celeste and Jericho slept. Not that Tristan truly cared; it was obvious that Celeste cared for Jericho and vice versa, but he thought, perhaps, that since Jericho hadn't mentioned a lover at all, he expected Tristan not to approve.

And it wasn't as if Jericho had any experience at all with having a lover.

"Say the word and we'll be on our way," Tristan said. "And I will leave you with your lady, and you can be happy."

"I want to stay here," Jericho whispered.

"I have no intention of forcing you to leave," Tristan told him. "I'll swear it--if you need me to, but I'm telling the truth. I want you to be happy."

Jericho looked at him. "I don't want you to leave. Not like this."

Tristan sat down on the edge of the bed. "Then I won't leave."

After a moment of silence, Jericho said, cautiously, "I want to stay here--with Celeste."

"You're in love with her," Tristan said.

"I--" Jericho sat up. "Yes."

"And does she love you?" Tristan asked. He was on shaky ground here, considering Minerva and his own inexperience.

"She says she does--" Jericho said, and Tristan heard the doubt in his voice.

"Then believe her," Cecilia said, unexpectedly. "I'll stay with you until she gets back, if you want me to." She paused. "Maybe you could show me how the loom works? I mean, if you don't mind--if you don't think Celeste would mind--"

"She wouldn't mind," Jericho said, almost too quickly.

"I promised to have you back in a few hours," Tristan said, but it wasn't really a protest; Cecilia could do as she wished, after all.

"I'll call them," Cecilia told him. "I promise."

"And you won't go back by yourself?" Tristan asked. "I don't think that would be a good idea."

"I won't go back by myself," Cecilia said. She pulled a cellphone from her pocket and glanced down at it. "I have service here--somehow--"

"Nefir arranged it," Jericho said.

"I'll call them right now," Cecilia offered, as if Tristan would doubt her word.

"I have no reason not to trust you," Tristan told her. "Call them after I leave. I'm sorry I upset you," he said to Jericho, who looked guilty. And then, "What about a mirror? If we--if someone--could arrange a portal to and from somewhere else, would that help?"

"I--I don't know," Jericho said, but he didn't sound very hopeful. "Maybe."

"Until then, he'll be safe here," Cecilia said loyally.

Awkwardly, Tristan said, "I should probably leave."

As if he'd just now realized it, Jericho said, "I thought you were living with a group of Morgans, Cecilia."

"I am," Cecilia said. "Two Morgans, at least; Tobias and Erialas. Aaron Kirschner, Erialas' cousin, and Michael Elliott, a human not related to either household, and a member of the Council. Erialas is also a member of the Council." She paused. "Tristan ran into Tobias and Erialas' Aunt Amy--Aaron's mother--this afternoon, and invited me to join him."

"That was nice of you," Jericho said, with a glance at Tristan that he could not easily interpret.

"I had no intention of seeking them out, but I wanted to see what had happened at the Morgan household last night--" Here, he realized that Jericho wouldn't know about what had happened at the Morgan household, and hesitated before continuing. "Do you want to know what happened?"

"Tell me," Jericho said simply, so Tristan did. When he was finished, he said, to Cecilia, "I didn't ask, before; I was too happy to see you. But you have your own protection against the sunlight?"

"Michael created mobile wards for all of us," Cecilia said. "We've tried to keep it under wraps, for fear of the Morgan household finding out." She hesitated. "I think Tristan intends to talk to Michael about making rings for some of the Richmonds; perhaps he can make one for you as well."

That would, of course, mean that Jericho would have to go outside, and even as far as the Veil, but Tristan didn't mention that.

Jericho glanced at the nearest window. "I'm not so sure that would be a good idea," he said.

"We can talk about it later," Tristan told him. "Will you be okay here with Cecilia?"

"Yes," Jericho said. And then, "Be careful."

"I'm not afraid of anyone in the Morgan household," Tristan said, which was only a small stretch of the truth. "I'll talk to you later."

Jericho did not look convinced, but he didn't protest when Tristan left the room, and then, the house. He felt odd, leaving Cecilia behind, but he didn't think she would be harmed; not by Jericho or Celeste or anyone else who lived nearby. He wasn't so certain that Tobias and the others would agree, but he knew she would be safe. And that left him free to return to the Richmond household without making a detour back to deliver Cecilia home.

As he walked back towards the Veil, Lark fell into step beside him. "Do you have time for a visit?" he asked.

Tristan had long since stopped trying to guess when Lark would appear. He had a knack for hiding himself, even from vampires, and while in a normal situation he'd never encourage anyone to perfect hiding themselves from vampires, Lark's ability had come in handy more than once, and Tristan trusted him implicitly.

"I assume you know what happened last night?" Tristan asked. "Or are you wanting for gossip?"

"I heard that half the Morgan household collapsed," Lark said. "I'm assuming that's a bit of an exaggeration?"

"It is," Tristan said. "And yes, I have time for a visit." He followed Lark to the treehouse, then up the winding stairs, where the tea kettle had just started to whistle. Lark poured the tea and joined Tristan at a tiny table that only sat two, one of the few pieces of furniture in the little house, and told him what had happened at the Morgan household, and also his own part in what might end up a potential war.

Tristan sometimes envied Lark's solitude, especially when Miriam was on the warpath. But he also knew the reason for the elf's solitude, and knew it would end as soon as he found his lady--or found what had happened to her. Thinking of Lark's missing wife made him wonder if anyone had bothered to ask Tobias, or even Arthur, since Helena had been a Morgan by birth.

"I doubt we'll get any searchers this far, but if anyone shows up, I'll let you know," Lark said after Tristan was finished.

"I wouldn't attempt to ascertain their intentions on your own," Tristan told him. "They're likely to be compelled to return to their Master, and he'd not likely to want witnesses to what has happened."

"I'll be discreet," Lark promised. "What will you do if they show up on your doorstep?"

"One already did; albeit a human girl," Tristan said. "Who tried to force me to drink her blood, no less. I didn't; I think Miriam would have killed me if I had." He wasn't really exaggerating. "That's how I found out about what happened; when I asked a fairy, she sent Maya with the explanation."

"I've met Maya," Lark said. "She was very interested in you the last time I spoke to her. I told her you had no intention of mistreating the small folk--"

"And I do not," Tristan said smoothly. "Why is that so surprising to so many people?"

"Your reputation precedes you," Lark said, and smiled to take the sting from his words.

"Mmm," Tristan said. "I should be on my way. I told Alexander I'd be back before dark, and I'll be cutting it close."

"I'll walk with you as far as the Veil," Lark said.

"You could come with me," Tristan offered, although he fully expected Lark to refuse. "You'd be welcome."

"I think it would be best if I stayed here, at least for now," Lark said. "Just in case there are searchers who venture past the Veil. Don't you think?"

It was better than an outright refusal. "Then later," Tristan said. "When this all settles down."

"Agreed," Lark said. "I'll still walk you to the edge, however. There are some--things I'd like to check out before the sun sets."

Tristan assumed those 'things' were vampire-related, or at least, alarm-related, although he had a suspicion that the small folk were the real alarms. And because of Maya's involvement, he knew the small folk would be watching.

Lark accompanied him to the edge of the Veil, and Tristan stepped across alone and continued on his way.

He was almost halfway home when he realized that he *wasn't* alone, but this time, he heard the Hound's approach. He turned. "Hello."

"Hello," Malachi said.

"Cecilia wanted to stay with Jericho," Tristan explained before he could ask. "She said she would call them--"

"She did," Malachi confirmed. "That's not why I'm here." He held out an envelope that bore Tristan's name. "This is from Lucas Lane. He asked me to try to catch you."

Of course. Tristan accepted the envelope and raised an eyebrow at Malachi. "Am I supposed to open it in your presence?"

"If you wish," Malachi said. "I believe it's in response to your letter." He smiled, which took some of the foreboding out of his bearing. "I don't think it's bad news."

"I asked him to visit," Tristan said. "To show him our good intentions."

"And he asked if I would accompany him on his visit," Malachi said.

"You would be welcome, too," Tristan said, and opened the envelope.

"Thank you," Malachi said.

The reply was short and to the point. Tristan, or, the Richmond household, would not need Lucas' permission to send anyone to Darkbrook, but if he wanted Lucas' permission, then he would have it. And also, Lucas agreed to visit, and promised to call to discuss times and dates as soon as possible. Lucas included a phone number if Tristan desired to call him, and he also 'welcomed the alliance between the Richmond household and the Council', which was more than Tristan would have ever hoped for.

"Did you read this?" he asked Malachi, who shook his head. "He wrote the word 'alliance'. Between us--the Richmond household--and the Council."

"Isn't that what you want?" Malachi asked curiously.

Again, Tristan noticed that he avoided meeting his gaze, and wondered if that were a Hound quirk and nothing more. When he hesitated to ask, he realized that Alexander's influence had rubbed off more than he'd expected, since he wouldn't have hesitated at all, before. He would have likely demanded to know why Malachi wouldn't meet his gaze, and he would have expected an answer.

"Yes," he said. "That is what I want. I--didn't expect it to be so easy to achieve."

"I think Lucas is willing to give anyone the benefit of his doubt," Malachi said, and fell into step beside him as Tristan started walking again.

"Are you to see me home?" Tristan asked. And then, just in case, he added, "Forgive me for any offense, but it's unlikely I could influence you at all, since you are a Hound."

Malachi smiled slightly. "I think that is unlikely, too," he said, and for a moment, Tristan thought he would not explain, but then he added, "I possess a special sort of sight. I see secrets, and I don't want to see any you might be hiding without your leave."

"Oh!" Tristan said thoughtfully. "*All* of my secrets?"

"I'm afraid so," Malachi said.

They walked in silence for a few minutes, then Tristan asked, "And if my secret is that I feel like an imposter?"

"Do you?" Malachi asked after a moment. "Feel like an imposter?"

Tristan folded the letter and tucked it back into its envelope. "I'm not a nice person," he said. "Not someone who plays by the rules; not someone who joins in alliances with the Council; not someone who--who *cares*."

He was walking much too fast for a human to follow, but Malachi had no trouble keeping up.

"Would you be able to tell if that were true?" Tristan asked. "If I am really an imposter?"

"So you don't have to try?" Malachi asked softly.

Tristan stopped walking. Now, *he* couldn't meet Malachi's gaze. "Yes, I suppose so," he said. "That's what Minerva said, too. Although Alexander would be disappointed if I didn't try. Or keep trying." He paused. "But I would like to know the truth, if you don't mind to look. I'd like to know if I really have changed, or if I'm still pretending, because I can't tell."

"What would you like me to say?" Malachi asked. "Do you trust me to tell you the truth?"

"Yes," Tristan said. "To both questions. I think." Although what if Malachi took him at his word and told him that he really hadn't changed?

That his love--professed love, since he had no true idea what that meant and no experience otherwise--for Minerva was also a pretense? What if Malachi told him that he was *incapable* of changing? That he would always feel like an imposter; that everyone would always expect him to react badly to simple things; that he would never feel compassion and empathy as second nature. That he would always wonder if his entire life was a lie, and that one day--one day, he would snap and kill everyone.

Or, try to, until Alexander stopped him, which would likely mean his death.

Alexander--and Minerva--had claimed he'd never killed out of spite. Merely self-defense. This was not quite true, but--

"You don't have to do this," Malachi said, pulling him from his thoughts so thoroughly that Tristan gasped aloud. "I can leave you in peace, if you'd like."

"I--no," Tristan managed to whisper. "Please--I want Alexander to be right in his assumption that I am able to change. That I *have* changed."

"You do realize that just by caring you *have* changed?" Malachi asked gently. "And it's clear you care very much about Alexander's opinion of you."

"But what he does--how he acts--is second nature to him," Tristan said. "It is not, to me."

"Kindness was not in our Master's nature, until he learned to care for us and for his lady and then, his daughters," Malachi said. "And our Master learned, as did we." He paused. "I don't have to look into your gaze to know that you're not an imposter."

"But you barely *know* me," Tristan protested, then wondered why he was protesting, when Malachi had told him exactly what he wanted to know.

"I don't have to," Malachi said. "You're trying. And that's what counts." But before Tristan could beg him, he met his gaze, squarely and unafraid of what he might see. And then, he said, "You are very fond of Minerva. Some might say you've fallen in love with her. But the person you think you are would never allow himself to fall in love with anyone."

This was true. Tristan knew this, deep down inside.

"And you also care very much about Jericho," Malachi continued. "Not merely as someone you must protect, but as your brother."

Again, true.

"You want others to see you as your own person, not just your father's son."

"Yes," Tristan said.

"And you don't want what happened to the Hunters--or to your father--to happen again," Malachi said softly. "Because you lost control."

"I've never killed an innocent person," Tristan said. "Well, I take that back; I have *likely* killed an innocent person, but I didn't set out to kill them. I wasn't supposed to kill them. But they died by my hand, nonetheless."

"How old were you at the time?" Malachi asked.

"Sixteen? Seventeen? It was right after Jericho left." Stubbornly, Tristan said, "That's no excuse, however."

"You feel as if you're missing something; something that others seem to have," Malachi said. "Compassion. Empathy. You're not the only vampire to feel this way."

"Who else?" Tristan asked in surprise, but then, he knew, without a doubt. "Tobias."

"You're more alike than you realize," Malachi said. "And to set your mind at ease, you're not an imposter. I see nothing false inside your--your soul, for want of a better word. You are making your way in this world as well as you can, with what help you have received, and you're doing as well as anyone would in the same circumstances."

"I have a lot yet to learn," Tristan said.

Malachi smiled. "And because you can admit that, without embarrassment, you've learned much more than many others in this world we live in." He paused. "And I know, you're not perfect. No one is. We all make mistakes, and we all strive not to repeat them."

"I *enjoy* killing," Tristan said. "I enjoyed my role as Jericho's protector. I enjoyed dispatching those our father sent after us." He paused. "I think that's where Tobias and I differ. I could see myself turning into my father without a single qualm of conscience. But I don't *want* to turn into my father. I would rather turn into Alexander, who has probably never killed a single person in his life."

Although, to be honest, it was doubtful that Alexander had never killed a single person in his long and varied life. Tristan really didn't see how that would be possible, but it was nice--or naive--to think that he was perfect instead of just as flawed as everyone else.

And somehow, they'd walked within sight of the Richmond household. Just catching sight of that familiar house--however grotesque--through the trees made something--some emotion--lurch inside Tristan's chest; it was a mixture of happiness and longing and something else he could not define.

"You would, of course, be welcome to stop for a visit," he said.

"I will, but not today," Malachi told him. "I should get back as well; I have a feeling we'll be dealing with a lot of Morgans, come sunset."

"And you'll let me know if you need aid?" Tristan asked.

"Yes," Malachi said, and left him there, standing in the forest, until he turned his sights towards home.

Minerva met him at the door. "And how is your brother?" she asked, as if that had been his only reason for venturing out.

"He's--fine," Tristan said. "And so is Cecilia, and she's visiting with him at the moment."

"That was a very circuitous route," Alexander said from the parlor doorway.

"I'm actually glad I went that way," Tristan said. "Since I met with Tobias as well, and met the others, and also a Hound." He paused. "And saw the destruction of the Morgan household firsthand, and heard a bit of that story, as well."

A child appeared behind Alexander; one of his students, although Tristan couldn't remember her name. She ducked her head when she spotted Tristan and hurried from the room and down the hall, clutching a violin case to her chest.

The parlor, despite its stuffiness, had wonderful acoustics for practicing. Sometimes, Tristan listened from the hidden room, although he'd always suspected Alexander knew of his presence.

"How is our guest?" he asked, because the human's girl's hair was the same shade as Alexander's student.

"Asleep, I believe," Minerva said with a glance at Alexander.

"There was no magical compulsion to offer herself to you," Alexander said. "She believed that she was chosen for the sacrifice, and she accepted her role most wholeheartedly." He paused. "It would have been easier if it had been a magical compulsion. Trying to convince her otherwise won't be easy without damaging her mind even more. And since she is fixated on you at the moment, I wouldn't recommend visiting her."

Tristan nodded. "I won't, then, if she is in good hands."

Alexander, as always, looked inscrutable, but for some reason, Minerva looked relieved, as if she'd expected him to insist to visit the girl. He raised an eyebrow at her, wanting an explanation, but she did not give him one. Instead, she asked, "Can the story wait for a little while?"

"Of course," Alexander said.

"I would like to speak with Tristan alone," Minerva said in a tone of voice so terrible that Tristan thought he'd inadvertently done something horrible.

"Of course," Alexander said, and disappeared down the hall.

Minerva took Tristan's hand and pulled him into the parlor. Someone had cleaned up the blood, but Tristan could still smell it; faintly overshadowing whatever cleaner they had used.

"What have I done?" he asked, because she'd never quite looked at him like this before.

"Sit down," Minerva said quietly. "Please." She paused. "I wanted to tell you this earlier, but I--" Another pause. "To be honest, I wasn't certain how to tell you. Alexander said I should come right out with it and not beat around the bush."

"You spoke to Alexander?" Tristan asked. "About me? About--about *us*?" He knew he'd guessed correctly when she flinched, slightly; and realized, with a sinking heart, what she intended to say. He stood up. "I understand. You don't have to explain. I can't be the easiest person to live with, but I hope you realize that I'm really *honestly* trying--"

"You're going to be a father," Minerva said.

"I mean, I've been trying very hard, and I'm sorry if I didn't try hard enough," Tristan continued, turning away from her now, because he wasn't sure he could meet her gaze without begging her not to leave him. "I'm--wait, what?" He gaped at her, suddenly speechless.

"You're going to be a father," Minerva said again. And then, just in case he hadn't understood, she added, "I'm pregnant."

His mouth opened, then closed, but nothing came out.

Minerva took his arm. "Sit down."

He had no choice but to sit; the alternative was to fall over in shock.

She sat down beside him. Clasped his hand in hers. Worriedly said, "I'm not leaving you, nor am I planning to leave you. I *love* you. And I want to stay with you forever." And then, softer, she added, "I know you're trying. Everyone can see that you're trying." She paused. "Sometimes, I worry that you're trying too hard."

Still, he could not speak. Could not force words past his lips. He stared down at their hands, joined, but he couldn't feel her touch.

"Tristan, look at me."

He couldn't raise his head to look at her. Couldn't seem to draw a deep enough breath, either; he felt light-headed, all of a sudden; his breath caught in his throat, and then, he said, in a rush, "Today, I told a Hound that I loved you, but I realize I've never actually said it aloud to anyone other than you."

He tightened his grasp on her hand. Brought her hand to his lips, and kissed it. "Are you really--?"

"Yes," she said. "I wouldn't lie."

"That's not what I meant," Tristan said. "I didn't think you would lie." And then, because he had to ask, "Does Miriam know?"

"Yes," Minerva said. "She's happy for us both."

"Are *you*?" Tristan asked. "We haven't discussed this--"

"I am," Minerva said. "Even though it was a bit of a surprise." She placed his hand on her stomach. "Are *you*?"

"I--I don't know," Tristan said, wanting to be honest. Not wanting to lie. "I think I will be. Right now, though, I'm more--numb." He tried to smile. Failed miserably. "Are you certain you want to have a child with me? My parentage--"

"You seem to have turned out okay," Minerva said with a completely straight face. And then, gently, "I know it's a shock. I know we didn't plan this."

"I don't want my child to grow up how I grew up," Tristan said abruptly. "I want my child to be loved."

"He--or she--will be," Minerva said.

"I don't know how to do that," Tristan told her. He turned to face her, wanting her to understand his fear. "I don't know how."

She put her arm around his shoulders and drew him close. "We'll learn together," she said. "I promise."

Tristan snaked his arm behind her and held her, and they remained there, curled up together on the couch, until they fell asleep.

Malachi

With a few hours until dusk, Malachi decided to return to Sennet's house to sit with Ben and Riala for a bit before he would be called to help guide Arthur and the others through the forest. It wasn't that he wanted to avoid them, or any of his family; not now, at least, because it seemed--from both Tristan and Tobias' reaction to his sight--that perhaps the protector's gift wouldn't be so much of a curse after all.

Sennet met him at the door. "Come in," she said, and just by the look on her face, Malachi knew there was news. "It's not Ben or Riala, but the boy Arthur rescued awoke." She paused. "For a few minutes, at least." And then, she asked, "Do you know the name Carroll?"

"I do," Malachi said. "But the boy isn't Carroll, unless there are two Carroll Morgans." He stepped inside her familiar kitchen.

"The boy's name is Walter," Sennet said. "But Carroll is--apparently--a vampire."

"He's Fern's missing husband," Malachi said. "Iris' father. Supposedly, he died in a Hunter attack before Fern and her mother moved back into the Morgan household. Fern didn't believe Ichabod's claim that Carroll was dead, so she tried to find him inside the house, but she did not get very far."

"According to Walter, Carroll is alive--or was alive--before he was taken away," Sennet said softly. "Walter doesn't know how long he was unconscious, and he's not very clear on timelines at all. But he says he's ten years old, and he says his mother is still in the household. Her name is Margaret."

"He told you a lot more than I expected," Malachi admitted.

"He was still talking when he fell asleep again," Sennet said. "And he may wake up soon and tell us some more."

"Fern will want to know about Carroll," Malachi said, and wondered how she would react. The fact of his disappearance had been in the forefront of her mind; guilt and fear, as well. Guilt because she hadn't been able to find him; fear that he would turn up, even now, perhaps dead, perhaps a prisoner.

Although, Malachi doubted that he'd been a prisoner, considering Arthur and the others had full access of the cells in the basement. But then again, if Ichabod wanted to hide his brother, or leave him to die, there had to be other places that Arthur and the others did not know about.

"I think we should speak with Walter again before you tell her," Sennet suggested. "Perhaps get a little more information? Don't you agree?"

"Is there any way to find him if he *is* alive?" Malachi asked.

"Not blindly," Sennet said. "Healers go where they are needed, but we need to *know* where we are needed, first."

"But you *are* needed there," Malachi said, not quite sure why he wanted to argue with her. It wasn't as if she could slip inside the Morgan household and rescue everyone on her own. Healers were powerful, but Sennet was only one person, after all.

Patiently, Sennet said, "If I randomly opened a portal into the Morgan household, not knowing who it was I intended to rescue, or where they were housed, how well do you think that would work out? What if the portal led directly to Ichabod Morgan or Grandmother Morgan? I don't think they'd uphold the rule of neutrality. I rather think they'd kill me first and ask questions later."

"Oh," Malachi said, "I see your point."

"If I had a lock of Carroll's hair, or even a drop of his blood, or even something from Walter's mother, I could open a portal directly to either of them and find them that way. It's still quite a risk, however. And I wouldn't want to do it at night, for fear of pursuit."

"Of course," Malachi said. "I apologize if I--"

"Don't apologize," Sennet told him. "I feel just as helpless as you do right now. I *want* to help them. I really do. But that's not as easy as it would seem." She led the way down the hall to where she'd left the boy--Walter. "I would--if you don't mind--like for you to look at him. To see if there's something he can't tell us that might help."

"Can you use his blood to find his mother?" Malachi asked, not quite certain how he felt about using his sight deliberately. "Or Carroll with a drop of Iris' blood?"

"Unfortunately, it doesn't work that way," Sennet said. "Will you look at him? Please? He doesn't have a lot of strength, and I'd like him to rest as much as possible."

"Yes," Malachi decided. "I will."

To Malachi's eyes, Walter looked no better--and no worse, really--than before. Perhaps he slept less deeply, because he stirred at their arrival, and opened his eyes. Licked dry lips, then whispered, "I'm safe here."

Sennet sat beside him on the bed. "Yes, you are. Do you remember my name?"

He focused on her face. "Sennet. You're a Healer."

"Yes." Sennet smiled at him. "I'm glad you remembered."

Walter frowned. "I--I told you about Carroll? And my mother?"

"You did," Sennet said.

"Did you save them too?" Walter asked.

Gently, Sennet said, "It's not quite that simple."

Walter nodded. His eyes slipped shut, then opened again. "Carroll drank my blood. He didn't want to do it, but he had to."

Sennet glanced at Malachi. "I might be able to work with *that*," she said, then frowned. "Maybe."

"Carroll wasn't the only one who drank your blood," Malachi said quietly. "Was he?"

"No," Walter whispered. He reached up and touched the bandage on his throat. "No."

To Sennet, Malachi said, "Maya might be able to help. Some of the small folk have been inside. They might be able to find something you can use."

"That won't solve the problem," Sennet said. "We can't sneak inside and save them all."

"We can if Grandmother Morgan and Ichabod Morgan are dead," Malachi said, and saw Walter's eyes widen at his words, although he made no protest.

"*That's* not something you can do alone, either," Sennet pointed out.

"I have no intention of trying," Malachi told her, which was the truth.

"Are you a wizard?" Walter asked. "Grandmother Morgan and Ichabod are wizards."

"No," Malachi told him. "I'm not a wizard. I'm a Hound."

It was--interesting--that Walter showed no fear. No concern, either, just acceptance; nor did he seem surprised. Malachi met his gaze, and saw no hidden secrets, just memories of panic and fear. Walter sucked in a breath. Coughed.

"You can read my thoughts," he whispered, unafraid.

"Not your thoughts," Malachi said, and took Sennet's spot beside him on the bed. "More your secrets. I can see what happened to you." He paused. "And why you're not afraid. They told you not to be afraid, didn't they?"

"Yes," Walter whispered. And then, "It worked. I'm not afraid of you."

"But I'm of the mind that you should make your own decision whether or not to be afraid," Malachi said. "Will you allow me to break the compulsion they put on you so that you can make your own decision?"

Walter held out his hand. Malachi glanced at Sennet, who nodded. "He should be free," she said. "But be cautious; there may be traps inside of his mind."

Malachi nodded. "I know," he said. "And I will." He took Walter's hand, and concentrated on the compulsion. It wasn't difficult to see--and even less difficult to break, and there were no traps. No surprises at all, as if the vampire who had placed the compulsion had not expected Walter to live through what had been done to him.

And perhaps he wouldn't have lived, except that Arthur had found him, and had not left him behind.

"Carroll did that to you," he said aloud. In Walter's mind, Carroll was someone to look up to, despite his injuries; despite the fact that he could not speak. To Sennet, he said, "Carroll has been badly injured. I don't think he placed the compulsion on Walter for ill; I think he placed it to help him, because he expected him to die."

"Yes," Walter said. And then, "I'm still not afraid of you."

Malachi smiled. "Good. Can you tell us about Carroll?"

"He didn't want me to suffer," Walter whispered. A tear leaked down the side of his face. "He couldn't save me, so he did the next best thing."

"He made it so you wouldn't mind," Sennet said quietly.

"It was the only thing he could have done," Walter said.

He was probably correct. By placing the compulsion on Walter, Carroll had allowed him to sidestep what had happened to him; ignore the pain and suffering and just--let go.

"He did that for the others, too," Walter continued. "Sarah, and--Barnaby. Sarah was sent to the Richmond household. I liked her. I'm sad she's dead."

"She's not dead," Malachi told him, remembering his conversation with Tristan. "She's alive and well in the Richmond household."

Water blinked at him. "They didn't kill her?"

"No," Malachi said. "They didn't kill her. I give you my word that she's alive."

Sennet gave him a *look*. Not for the first time, Malachi wished that others had access to the bond, if only so that he could tell Sennet what he knew about Sarah--although Tristan hadn't mentioned her name--and how he'd come by that information. He hadn't mentioned anything to her about meeting Tristan in the forest, and he realized now that he should have told her everything that had happened.

"Walter, Malachi and I are going to check on the others who are here," Sennet said. "We'll be right back. Would you like to rest for a little while?"

"Yes," Walter said, and obediently closed his eyes. It didn't take him long to fall asleep; Malachi could only hope that he did not dream.

He followed Sennet out of the room and back to the kitchen. "Talk to me," she said. It was almost an order. "Sit down. We'll have some tea while we talk."

"I ran into Tristan Richmond in the forest," Malachi said. "Well, he followed Tobias and Erialas' Aunt Amy when they left our house. He said he wanted to see what happened to the Morgan household, and ran into them on their way back. Not the whole way, but far enough to know that Tobias had protection against the sunlight."

"I imagine Tobias wasn't happy about that," Sennet commented as she filled the tea kettle.

"He wasn't, but as Tristan pointed out, he's not their enemy, either," Malachi said, and sat down at the table, since Sennet seemed to have everything in hand. "Although I imagine he's rather interested in the rings. Not for himself--"

"Which was my second comment," Sennet said. "Or question, I guess. Tristan has protection too? He would have to, if he followed them even part of the way. The Richmond household isn't anywhere near the Veil."

"His protection is tied to the Veil," Malachi said. "And the Veil holds the spells that keep him mobile, apparently. He was captured by Hunters less than a year ago, from what I've heard. They used silver, but he did not die."

"I've heard some of that story," Sennet said. "From the elf Tristan's brother lives with--her name is Celeste--and from Muirghen, who is a Healer in Faerie." She paused. "Celeste has a healing talent as well, but she is also a weaver."

"A weaver?" Malachi asked, intrigued. He remembered seeing a loom once, a very long time ago, in an old house far away, but that was a memory best left to the past.

"She has ties to the Walker household," Sennet said. "And I've met Tristan's brother Jericho, but not Tristan."

"He mentioned a vampire named Alexander Ross," Malachi said. "Who is apparently the oldest vampire in the world." He paused. "Maybe even older than our Master."

"Or you," Sennet pointed out, but that wasn't something Malachi liked to think about either. "I haven't met Alexander, but from what I hear, he's a very nice person. He restores musical instruments, and has been a bit of a recluse, up until he got involved with Tristan and Jericho."

"And the entire Richmond household," Malachi said.

"I'd rather have them as allies rather than enemies," Sennet told him, and carried the tea things over to the table. "Cream? Sugar? Did you eat today? You've been rather busy."

"Yes," Malachi said. "I ate lunch. I'm fine, but thank you for asking. And I'll take mine plain."

There was a noise in the hallway then; a faint, furtive noise that made Malachi wonder if Walter had somehow managed to get out of bed. Sennet paused at the sound, then took out two more mugs from the cupboard. Gave Malachi a meaningful look. "I'm glad you're here for this," she said, then, louder, "You can come into the kitchen, Ben; no one will harm you here. My name is Sennet, if you remember me. I'm a Healer, and you are safe."

Malachi started to stand, then sat back down, not wanting to seem a threat, since Ben would likely remember him from his time as the protector's other, and he wasn't quite sure of his reception to the fact that he was now free.

Before he could speak, Sennet said, "Malachi is here with me. You remember Malachi?"

Benjamin Dawson appeared in the doorway, wary and unhappy. He hesitated, then slowly stepped inside the room, holding onto the doorway, then a chair, for support. "Yes." His voice cracked. "I remember Malachi."

"Please, sit down and we'll talk," Sennet suggested, and he sat across from Malachi, staring down at his clasped hands.

"I haven't aged," he said. "But I know a lot of time has passed."

"More than fifty years," Sennet said.

"I should be old," Ben said, and frowned down at his hands.

"I'm six times older than you, and I've not aged," Malachi pointed out, although he wasn't really certain of the actual span of years he'd been alive. It wasn't as if they'd counted each day or each year as they passed.

Ben finally glanced his way, surprised. "*Will* I age?"

"I don't know," Sennet said. "I don't see why not, but it remains to be seen if you are merely a vampire now, or if you've been changed."

"Changed in what way?" Ben asked.

"You were seen in sunlight," Malachi said.

"The protector--changed my talent so that it could also protect me from sunlight," Ben said. "Before--before I became the protector's other. I have no reason to believe that has changed."

"It would be quite a risk to find out," Malachi said.

Ben stood up, walked over to the kitchen door, and opened it. He only hesitated for a second before he stepped outside into the sunlight and did not burn. Then he turned and walked back into the kitchen and closed the door. Leaned against it with his arms folded. "I'm still alive."

"That you are," Sennet said. She hadn't moved. Hadn't expressed any alarm at all, although Malachi found he'd risen from his chair without even realizing he had moved.

Ben met Malachi's gaze. Malachi had not intended to meet his gaze for fear of what he might see; the protector's other had been fierce, after all. But instead of a secret, Malachi saw--knowledge.

"You know what the protector did for me," he said aloud.

"Yes," Ben said. He started to say something else, then hesitated. "I'm sorry. I don't think the protector realized--what would happen."

"I'm not so sure," Malachi said. "But what's done is done now; the protector isn't here to take it back."

Ben looked at him closely. "I don't think it *could* take it back," he said. "You've changed it, somehow--" And then, his eyes widened and he said, "I can--Oh. I couldn't do that before. See things. You were right. I'm not the same." He sounded more relieved about this than Malachi had expected.

"Would you like some tea?" Sennet asked, and Ben sat down again. Accepted a cup, and drank from it slowly, as if he'd forgotten how to drink from a cup. Or, more likely, as if he'd forgotten what tea tasted like in the first place.

"How--how long have we been here?" Ben asked that question cautiously, bracing himself for an answer he wouldn't like.

"A little over a week," Sennet said. "Riala's parents were here, but they've gone back home."

Ben flinched slightly. "They--weren't happy, I'd guess. Did they want to take her away?"

"They did," Sennet confirmed. "I convinced them that wasn't a good idea."

"And what will happen now?"

"Do you have any contact at all with the protector and its other?" Sennet asked.

"About Riala?" Ben guessed. "No. But I can't feel her anymore. I'm--I'm alone in my head." He sighed. "I guess I'll have to get used to that now."

Malachi could sympathize, especially if they'd been connected for the past fifty-odd years.

"Do you have contact with them otherwise?" Sennet asked gently.

Ben froze. "I--ah--when I was asleep. I dreamt of them. But I don't know if it was really a dream." His tone of voice; the look on his face; said that it was not. "The protectors--there are two of them now--told me about the bargain you--Malachi--made with it. And how you saved us. And that I shouldn't be angry." He quickly added, "I'm not. Thank you for saving us."

"You're welcome," Malachi said gravely. That Ben knew there were two protectors meant his dream was true communication; he wouldn't have known, otherwise.

Ben tried to laugh. "Although I'm not certain we were worth saving. Am I remembering correctly that the Dawson household is gone?"

"Yes," Sennet said. "The household was destroyed in a Hunter attack about twenty-five years ago, from what we've been able to determine."

"I never hated my aunt," Ben said quietly, staring down at his hands again. "She took me in--she didn't have to do that."

"A lot has changed since you've been gone," Malachi told him.

"Yes--you're a person now, for one," Ben said, then flushed. "I'm sorry, I didn't mean--"

"It's okay," Malachi said. "And I think that instead of trying to learn everything that has happened, you should learn it as you need it, to be honest."

"That sounds like a good plan," Sennet agreed.

"It won't be quite as overwhelming that way," Ben murmured. "Because right now, even *this* is overwhelming." When he glanced up, his eyes were bright with tears. "I need to know what will happen now, though. To me. And Riala. They're going to want her to come home--her parents, I mean."

"Yes, they likely are," Sennet said. "When she wakes up."

"But she's not--*we're* not children anymore. Not really." Ben's breath hitched in his throat. "We've lived together--" He hesitated. "I don't think they would let me see her again, if they took her home."

"I think Riala might have something to say about that, if they don't listen to you," Sennet said. "Neither of you are truly children anymore."

"I don't think Riala's parents will agree," Ben said pragmatically.

He was likely correct. Even though Riala wasn't awake yet, it was only a matter of time before Riala's parents discovered that Ben was, and they were likely to try again to take her away, despite Sennet's efforts to the contrary.

"I would like your promise that you won't try to flee from here," Sennet said. "Especially into the mists. *Especially* with Riala, before or after she wakes up."

Ben bit his lip. Shot a glance at Malachi, then said, "I don't know how to go into the mists on my own." He took a deep breath. "And I have no intention of fleeing. You have my word."

Sennet nodded. "Thank you."

"But I can't sit here all day long and worry," Ben said. "Is there anything I can do while I'm waiting?"

"You can help me," Sennet told him. "Feed Riala when it's time. Don't be surprised if Tobias Morgan shows up later on--"

"Tobias Morgan," Ben said. "Did we meet?"

"I'm not sure," Malachi said. To Sennet, he asked, "Was Tobias there before you took Ben back into the Mists?"

"No," Sennet said. "He was already *in* the Mists by then."

"I remember--your Master, and your Master's daughter," Ben said slowly. "And Lucas, and Sennet, of course. Who is Tobias, please? I assume since he is a Morgan, then he's a vampire. I--don't remember any *good* stories about the Morgan household at all."

"That's because there aren't any," Malachi said, and told him a little about Tobias and what he had done. "They are forming their own household, and Tobias is to be its head. I'm sure they would welcome both you and Riala, if you end up wanting a place to call home."

"A household of exiles." Ben looked thoughtful. "We would fit right in." And then, curiously, he asked, "Who is the human boy in the room down from ours?"

"His name is Walter, and he was rescued from the Morgan household yesterday evening," Sennet said. "Along with four others--all Morgans, although they're not here." She explained about that as well, and Ben listened without interrupting, his eyes wide.

"Even when I--even back when I came to live with my aunt, the Morgans weren't known for their kindness," Ben said. "How did they manage to hide for so long?"

"With spells, and a lot of luck," Malachi said. "But they're far away from that now, and they'll be safe with Tobias and the others once the sun sets." He glanced at the window; it wasn't quite dusk yet. "They're at our house for now." He paused. "You could come with me if you'd like, and meet them."

"And leave Riala alone?" Ben shook his head. "I don't think that's a good idea. What if she wakes up? What if she thinks I've--" His head snapped up suddenly; his mouth opened in surprise.

"Or maybe you both could come," Malachi said quietly, because it was obvious that Riala was awake now, and also that their bond had not vanished once the protector and its other set them free.

Ben vanished. One moment he was sitting in the chair, the next, it fell backwards onto the floor and he was gone. Sennet followed him; Malachi wasn't far behind.

In the room they'd shared, Riala no longer lay on the bed. She stood in the middle of the room, her arms wrapped around Ben, whose arms, in turn, held her tightly. They didn't speak, but Malachi had no doubt they were communicating.

Sennet stopped at the door. Malachi stood beside her. After a few minutes, Riala raised her head from Ben's shoulder, her gaze fierce, and said, "You brought us back."

"I made a bargain with the protector to save your lives, yes," Malachi said.

"And what happens now?" Riala asked.

"I think that's up to you," Malachi said.

"My parents might disagree with you," Riala said.

""You should be allowed to make your own way in life," Sennet said.

"They'll want me to go back," Riala said, and tightened her grip around Ben. "Without Ben."

"They also lost both their children," Sennet said, and the fierceness faded from Riala's gaze. She looked guilty now, and worried. "And only recently found you again."

"I'm sorry," Riala whispered, stricken.

"They *did* want to take you away," Sennet said. "I convinced them otherwise. I think that if you explained the situation, they might understand. If not, well, I'm not inclined to let them take you back without Ben. You've been together for too long."

"Thank you," Riala said, then added, "Ben told me everything you've told him. I remember Tobias." She loosened her grasp and Ben stepped away, still touching her, but not quite as closely. He looked less unsure of himself now that Riala was awake. "You want us to accompany you? Why?"

"To meet them," Malachi said. "And to show you that there are other options, now that you're awake."

"Are you expecting trouble?" Ben asked.

"Nothing we can't handle," Malachi said honestly. "The Morgans are unused to the forest, and to Faerie. We are very much at home in the forest and in Faerie. And we have the small folk on our side to distract and lead any hunters astray."

Riala glanced at Sennet. "And this would be okay with you? If we went with Malachi?" And then, to Malachi, "Are you certain they would want us there? Maybe it would be best if we waited."

"That is your decision," Malachi said. "And no one will fault you, either way."

"And no, I wouldn't mind," Sennet said. "You were brought here because you needed a place to recover. You are not prisoners. You've done nothing wrong."

Riala looked doubtful. "I'm not sure my parents will agree."

"You are no longer a child, despite your appearance," Malachi said.

"I think there's something you don't understand," Riala said. "Well, I don't *think;* I know it. I'm not like you. I'm a dragon. It's different for us." She hesitated, not looking at Ben now, as if she knew he would disagree. Or disapprove. "I would have to petition the King to live on my own. It's not something we do. They'll say there's safety in numbers, living amongst my own kind. They'll say you can't be trusted, because you are a Hound." To Sennet, she added, "And you are a human. And what do humans know about dragons?"

"And I am a vampire," Ben spoke the words she didn't want to say. He said them simply, without emotion, as if they'd spoken of this before.

Perhaps they had.

"When you last lived here, things were different," Sennet said. "Do you know about Solomon?"

"No," Riala said. "Who is Solomon?"

"Your King," Sennet said.

Riala waited for a moment, as if waiting for Sennet to explain.

"A lot of time has passed since you've been gone," Sennet said. "A lot of things have changed. Would it help if you spoke to him before you speak to your parents?"

"You can just *do* that? Summon the king?" Riala seemed doubtful.

Sennet smiled. "I can," she said. "And he will come here if I ask."

"For *me*?" Riala asked, then, "For us?"

"Yes," Sennet said.

"Will you be here too?" Ben asked Malachi. "When he comes?"

"I'm expected to accompany Arthur and the others to safety," Malachi said. "But I could return here, afterwards."

"Would you mind?" Ben asked, and Riala looked at him curiously, as if she did not understand why he would want Malachi present.

"Things *have* changed," Malachi said. "Before, the king of the dragons wouldn't even *speak* to a vampire. Or a Hound."

"That's true," Riala said slowly.

"And I would not mind," Malachi said.

"Because you feel responsible for us," Riala said.

"Because I made a bargain with the protector for your lives," Malachi told her. "Without considering what that would mean. I only meant to save you."

Riala's eyes were wet with tears. "Thank you," she said after a moment of silence. She tried to smile. Almost succeeded. "I didn't want to die. Not there. Not like that."

"You're welcome," Malachi said quietly, surprised that she could bring herself to say it. He'd expected anger; perhaps resentment. Clearly, he'd misjudged them both. "But for now, I should be going. It's almost dark."

"Be careful," Riala said.

"I will," Malachi promised. "And I'll return here afterwards. And then we can see about your future."

He left them, then, in Sennet's expert care, and walked, unmolested, back home, trying not to think of the night ahead.

Arthur

And then, the sun set. Arthur watched it with more trepidation than joy, because the various preparations for their journey only heightened the possibility that they would run into trouble in the forest, even though everyone assured them--over and over again--that the possibility was faint; impossible, even, and they would have enough protection for even discovery not to matter.

Soon after sunset, Tobias arrived, with Aunt Amy again, and Erialas, whom Arthur had never met. Erialas, who was a cousin as well as a member of the Council; Arthur didn't quite know how to treat him, but he seemed nice enough.

They were to leave through Faerie. The small folk would be watching, and the Hunt would accompany them. Not the *entire* Hunt, but Malachi and Josiah, which was close enough.

And then, Maya arrived, and Arthur felt himself relax. He wanted very badly to trust in the Hunt, and the Council, and even Tobias, but he didn't know them well enough. Maya, on the other hand, had already proven herself to be trustworthy. *And* she had trolls at her disposal, among other creatures of the forest, *and* she would not allow them to die, or be captured. Arthur knew--and believed this--from the very bottom of his heart. He suspected it was rather irrational, since the Hunt and Tobias and the others would also not let them be captured or killed, but he couldn't help but feel the way he felt. He *knew* Maya. He didn't know the others as well--yet.

They had no bags to pack; no possessions to gather.

"Thank you for your hospitality," Arthur said to Emle, who smiled.

"Come to visit anytime," she said, and meant it; and even Chloe ran up to Arthur and wrapped her chubby arms around his legs in her interpretation of an enthusiastic hug.

Iris' mother hugged Emle; Arthur couldn't bring himself to do that in front of everyone, so he made do with words, instead. And then, after goodbyes and be carefuls, they were off. Tobias led the way; Arthur found himself beside him. The Hounds had melted into the forest, but Maya had stayed, and she walked beside Arthur. This--interestingly enough--seemed to unsettle Tobias, or maybe he was merely uneasy about the silence in the forest. Despite his words to the contrary, maybe he'd secretly *expected* an attack.

But Arthur's father was smarter than that. More cunning, perhaps, was the word. Because he did not send out dozens of searchers. He sent out two.

Malachi appeared out of the forest; a hound one second, and then in his more familiar shape. "Come this way," he said, and led them to the right. "We'd rather the searchers not meet up with you at all."

Arthur let out a breath. "So there *are* searchers," he said.

"Two," Malachi told him. "Two that we've seen, at least. A woman and a younger man; the woman is older, and not happy, the young man's name is apparently Nicholas."

"Nicholas is a cousin," Tobias said with a glance at Arthur. "Highly placed, now that we're gone. He's--what, twenty?"

"Yes," Arthur said, and wondered if he should tell them what he knew about Nicholas, and the secret he'd stumbled across.

"The woman would be my mother, of course," Liam said from the back of the group. Iris' mother put her arm around his shoulders; he did not pull away.

"There are others, closer to the household; I think they're really not certain if you died in the collapse or not," Malachi said. "Continue on this way; we won't let them get close to you."

"Thank you," Tobias said formally.

"You're not--planning to hurt anyone?" Arthur asked Malachi, who shook his head.

"Not unless they try to hurt us first," he said. "With luck, they'll never see us."

"Nicholas is--" Arthur began, then fell silent, not wanting to break his cousin's trust. At everyone's sudden interest, he said, lamely, "I don't think he'll be a problem."

"Is he--" Tobias began, then, more cautiously, asked, "Would he want to join us?"

"I think his intention is to flee, yes," Arthur said. "If he can get away from Liam's mother, he might just walk into the forest and never go back."

"I didn't know that," Iris said, surprised. "When did you find out? Did you tell him we could have helped him?"

They'd discussed rescuing cousins before they needed rescue from the basement cells before, and decided it was too risky. Arthur's discovery of

Nicholas' secret, however, had changed things a bit, though, because before, he hadn't really expected to find anyone willing to flee. "It was right before Liam was imprisoned," he said, which wasn't exactly true, but it was close enough. "And I didn't tell him anything; he doesn't know that I know." He paused. "And I would rather not talk about it here."

"We won't hurt him," Malachi said. "But if the woman *is* your mother?" This to Liam, who bit his bottom lip.

"She's with *him*," he said. "Uncle Ichabod."

"She is," Iris' mother confirmed. "And she'll either want to take Liam back or kill him."

"Then we won't allow her to come near you," Malachi told Liam, who nodded, his eyes bright with tears.

"We're nearly there," Tobias said. "If they're the only searchers, then we'll be fine." He sounded more as if he were trying to convince himself than anyone else, but Arthur didn't comment on it. "If Nicholas shows up at our door, though--"

"He'll be safe to let in," Arthur said. "I'll vouch for him, if my opinion counts."

"It does," Tobias said. "Okay. Let's go, and quickly now. The others are waiting."

Since they'd come through Faerie, anyone watching the road would be disappointed; they arrived via the backyard, so Arthur's first sight of the house--smaller than his father's house, but still quite large--was from the back. There was a patio, and a set of French doors, and some metal furniture that looked rather old and worn. There were two people waiting on the patio--Michael and Uncle Mark. Erialas' Aunt Amy had already told them about their Aunt and Uncle preferences; and Tobias had told them that Cecilia was visiting her brother Jericho, who lived in Faerie.

"This is where I'll be leaving you again," Maya said to Arthur, who had stopped at the edge of the forest, staring at what was to be their new home. She put her arm around his shoulders. To his surprise, he discovered that he was now a little taller than her. "You'll be fine with your cousins."

"I hope so," Arthur said.

"I know so," Maya responded. "Now go." She hugged him. "Join them."

And they were waiting for him, standing awkwardly in the middle of the lawn, Iris, her mother, Liam, Aunt Amy, and Erialas. In full view of all of them, Arthur hugged Maya, then left her to join them. And when he glanced back, she was gone.

Not gone forever, though, and he spied Blossom perched in a small tree not that far from the patio, watching over them, which made him feel more secure. And as they walked near that tree, she flew down to perch on his shoulder and whispered in his ear, "Can I come in with you?"

"Of course," Tobias said without even looking to see who had spoken. "There's a brownie who lives here; her name is Rebecca. And sugar cubes in the kitchen."

Arthur smiled, and followed the others inside.

Later, after they'd been shown their rooms, which were together down a short little hallway, and Tobias had explained that they could decorate their rooms however they wanted, or swap them, even, because there were plenty of unused bedrooms in the house and Michael had explained how Tobias had visited the Hunt's home during the daylight hours (at that point, Iris' mother had quietly excused herself, because it was all too much; Aunt Amy had followed her, and Arthur heard the low murmur of their voices as they stood in the hallway and listened to Michael explain how the rings worked.) Iris had stayed, fascinated, especially after Michael offered to show them his workroom, Tobias had said, "I would like to speak with you alone, if you don't mind."

And Arthur, knowing that this had to be about what they had done, perhaps even about his father, said, "Okay," and followed him into the library. Liam and Iris stayed with Michael. They didn't protest, but Arthur knew they wanted to.

The library was where, Tobias had explained, they gathered for house meetings, and where Erialas had found the spell he'd traded for Michael's spell to restore his mother to life. And now, Aaron's father--Uncle Mark to everyone else--waited, with someone Arthur didn't recognize.

"This is Sennet," Tobias said. "She's a Healer."

"The Healer who took the human boy?" Arthur asked, feeling guilty.

"Yes," Sennet said. "He's spoken to me twice. His name is Walter."

Arthur tucked that name away.

"I think he'll be fine, with plenty of food and rest. Once he's up to eating food, of course."

"Of course," Arthur echoed, then felt he had to add, "I didn't know, if that's what you intended to ask me. I didn't know."

"Nor did I," Tobias said, his tone of voice gently letting Arthur off the hook.

"Healers go where they are needed," Sennet said. "I'm sorry I couldn't take all of you with me, but Walter would have died if I hadn't brought him back to my house." She paused. "I don't want any others to die. The humans who live in the Morgan household do not deserve this. The *vampires* don't, either."

"My father--and my grandmother--will not agree," Arthur said. Despite Tobias' tone, he felt almost on trial, as if they, by standing there in front of him, had already judged him for his ignorance and merely wished to pass their judgment. "They'll *never* agree." But then, he remembered what he'd said to Iris and Liam and Iris' mother, back in the room in the basement, and he wondered if Blossom had passed along his intent. "I had hoped that by saving him, someone would be willing to fight for the rest of them," he said. "But I--that's not something I can do on my own. Or even with Liam and Iris."

"I agree," Uncle Mark said. "From what I've heard about your father and grandmother, and from what your family tried to do to get to Erialas, I don't think they'll go quietly."

"They won't *go* at all," Arthur said.

There was an awkward silence.

"Please don't ask me to go back," Arthur said quietly.

Tobias looked surprised. "Oh, no, I had no intention of asking you to go back," he said. "And neither did Sennet. Or anyone else."

For some reason, Arthur did not feel relieved. "Then what do you intend?" he asked. He hesitated. "I can't--"

"No," Uncle Mark said immediately. "You can't. And we wouldn't ask that of you."

"Then what?" Arthur asked. "Do you have a plan of some sort to--depose my father and my grandmother?"

"Not yet," Tobias said. "But I'm hoping we can come up with a plan." He paused. "What I hoped you could help with was a way inside, and perhaps the whereabouts of the humans who reside there."

"I could help you get inside," Arthur said, "I can draw you a map of most of the household. But I don't have any idea how the humans live; that's not something we were ever permitted to see. Iris might know; she's good with locks, or Liam--" And then, he realized that this was not likely to be a simple rescue. Sennet couldn't slip inside and spirit the humans away, or she would have done that already. This was something else, something more permanent.

And Tobias wasn't a wizard. Which meant-- Carefully, Arthur asked, "Are you planning to attack the Morgan household? Because most of the vampires who live there aren't like my father and grandmother. Some of them are, but most of them just can't disobey. They're not strong enough."

"I--have a thought about that," Tobias said. "Because you *know* I'm no wizard--"

"Yes," Arthur said. "I know. But you have the Council on your side--"

"If the Council decides to involve itself in the vampire households, what do you think will happen?" Uncle Mark asked.

"Please, sit down," Sennet told him, and Arthur obeyed, but only because he couldn't think of anything else to do.

"I think the other vampire households might feel a bit--threatened," he finally said. But then, maybe not. The only households nearby were the Richmonds and the Walkers, and the Richmonds weren't under Connor Richmond's will anymore.

Could the Morgan household be--different? Arthur felt his throat tighten at the thought. At the mere *thought* of such--betrayal. He wanted to stand up and walk away; to forget he'd even thought of such a thing.

"We would only need a map, and locations," Sennet said. "Nothing more. You wouldn't have to be involved."

"But *you're* not a wizard, either," Arthur pointed out. "And my father won't care that you are a Healer. Neither will my grandmother." He knew *this* for a fact; they would not hesitate to kill her. "I'm sorry."

"You don't need to apologize for your father or your grandmother," Sennet said quietly.

"I feel like I should," Arthur whispered, and felt himself stiffen under their regard. To Tobias, he asked, "What do you have in mind?"

"I don't think the Council should be--openly involved," Tobias said. "And I have a few ideas, but I need to speak with Tristan Richmond first." He paused. "I spoke to him in the forest, on our way back from the Hunt's house this afternoon."

This didn't seem to be news to anyone other than Arthur. "Why was he so far away from his household?"

"Cecilia's brother Jericho lives in Faerie," Tobias said. "Tristan took the long way around to visit him, since he wanted to see the destruction of the Morgan household firsthand. Aunt Amy told *me* it wouldn't be a good idea to get too close, but Tristan had no qualms, apparently." He hesitated. "And Tristan has the help of quite possibly the oldest vampire in the world. I'm hoping they might be willing to lend their aid, if all goes well."

"You're talking about launching an attack on the Morgan household," Arthur said, just to be clear. He knew why Tobias didn't want to come right out any say it, because it sounded entirely too ridiculous, knowing how much power their grandmother and Arthur's father held. To expect that Tristan Richmond and the oldest vampire in the world would be willing to what, exactly? Swoop in, kill them both, and leave the rest of the household for the Council to clean up?

But then, if they succeeded, Arthur's father and grandmother would never be able to hurt anyone else. The rooms in the basement would be emptied. No other human children--or adults, for that matter, if there *were* any adults--would ever be left to die; there wouldn't be any stupid rules about Tobias or anyone else; no executions; no fear--

No fear.

Arthur, and Iris, and Liam, and everyone else could start afresh.

"My father has lieutenants," he said aloud. "Two of them used to be vampire hunters. They're--very adept at their jobs. They'll need to be dealt with quickly." He knew his tone of voice had changed, but he couldn't help that; he thought Tobias would understand. "And I--I'm pretty sure both Iris and Liam--and I--would have to be involved. Especially if you don't want anyone else to get hurt."

"We wouldn't want that, yes," Sennet said.

"They won't know you, and they won't trust you, Tobias," Arthur said. "And they certainly don't know Tristan, if he agrees to help. They'll think the worst, and try to defend themselves, and it won't go well at all." He hesitated. "If you met Tristan in the forest on your way back from the Hunt's house, then does he have protection as well?"

"He does," Tobias confirmed. "But it's tied to the Veil, and has something to do with the wounds he received while captive."

"And if he is wounded, you think he can help defeat my father and our grandmother?" Arthur asked doubtfully.

"We'll see," Tobias said.

"Who is the oldest vampire in the world?" Arthur asked.

"His name is Alexander Ross," Uncle Mark said. "I've never met him, but I've heard the name before. He repairs musical instruments."

"I've heard his name before, too," Arthur said. "I'm not sure where, though. The Morgans were never a very musical family, but I've heard some of the Richmonds are."

"I intended to call Tristan right after talking to you," Tobias said. "If you'd like to join me, feel free."

"I think I should talk to Iris and Liam," Arthur said. "But then again, if Tristan refuses to help, you're not going to pursue it, are you?"

"No," Tobias told him, and it sounded like the truth. "I won't pursue it if Tristan can't help."

"Then maybe we should ask him for help before I speak with Iris and Liam," Arthur said. "And if it never happens, then they don't need to know."

"I--ah--don't think they'd be pleased if they found out you kept something like this from them, whether it happens or not," Sennet pointed out, which was likely true.

"She's right," Tobias said unexpectedly. "That's not the way this household is supposed to work. We're supposed to work together, and not keep secrets from each other. It's not going to be easy--"

No, it wouldn't be. The Morgan household existed on secrets. But still, it would be interesting to find out if it worked. "Then I'll tell them," Arthur said. "Or they can join us when you call Tristan."

"I think that's the best idea," Uncle Mark said.

"Then I'll go and get them," Arthur said, and waited to see if Tobias had anything else to add.

Surprisingly, he said, "I'm sorry about this. I don't believe this will help you feel more secure here at all."

"On the contrary," Arthur said, surprising himself. "I think that might make us feel more secure." He smiled. "And maybe we'll have a better chance at a future."

"Yes," Tobias said, and said nothing more, so Arthur took his leave and thoughtfully walked back to where he'd left Iris and Liam.

They were waiting for him, Iris and Liam, at least, in the room Liam had chosen. When Arthur let himself inside, he found them seated on Liam's bed, talking quietly. They fell silent when he appeared.

Arthur didn't want to disturb their peace, but he felt he had no choice. "I've been talking to Tobias," he said. "And a Healer named Sennet--the one who took the human boy--his name is Walter--and Uncle Mark." He hesitated, then told them Tobias' plan.

Iris was the first one to speak. "Why would the Richmonds want to do this?" she asked.

"Because they don't want the Morgans to attack them," Liam responded. "They had all sorts of arrangements in place; if Uncle Ichabod finds out that they're null and void, what do you think he'll do?"

"I think he'll start by murdering every Richmond in the household," Arthur said quietly. "And there are a lot of Richmonds."

"Like my mother," Iris said quietly. "Are you sure this is a good idea?"

"No," Arthur said. "But I think it might be for the best, if they--if *we*--succeed. Otherwise, we'll spend the rest of our lives looking over our shoulders and wondering when my father will strike." He paused. "*We're* safe here. But no one else is, and it's just going to get worse. You know that."

Iris nodded. "I know. And I agree with you. But what if Tristan refuses to help?"

"Then Tobias won't pursue it," Arthur said, but he didn't really like that thought, either; it felt too much like giving up. *They* were safe, after all...and then what? Should they forget everything and move on with their lives? Or, if they had a chance to help those who remained, should they pursue it regardless of Tristan's help?

Would Tristan *want* to help?

"What do we know about Tristan Richmond?" Iris asked, as if she'd come to the same conclusion.

"Not a lot," Liam said. "He killed an entire nest of Hunters while horribly wounded."

"My mother might know something," Iris said. "She's lying down, in her room. But we could ask her, later."

"Tobias intends to call Tristan soon," Arthur told them. "If not in the next few minutes. I told him we'd want to be there to listen."

"And Tobias didn't protest?" Iris asked in surprise.

"No," Arthur said. "He apologized, actually." He hesitated. "Because he wanted us to feel safe here."

Iris smiled, as if Arthur were joking, but then she asked, "That's really what he said?"

"Yes," Arthur told her.

Liam nodded, unsurprised. Hesitantly, Iris said, "My mother made me promise I wouldn't be alone with him." And then, quickly, "I don't believe he'd do anything at all. I believe he has changed."

"You won't be alone, either way," Arthur said, because he couldn't reply to whether or not Tobias had changed, since they'd only just arrived. He suspected, however, that Iris was correct, because surely there would have been clues, even now.

Iris nodded. "My mother's not happy about this," she said. "I think she'll be okay, but I really think she expected to find my father, somehow, and run away with him--and me--"

And now that wouldn't happen. "I understand," Arthur said. "I'm sorry."

"This isn't *your* fault," Liam protested. "It's mine. *I'm* the one who should be sorry." He paused. "I didn't think things through. I didn't think I'd be caught."

"I know," Arthur said. "I'm not angry with you anymore."

Liam smiled hesitantly. "I'm glad. I'm not angry with you, either. Anymore."

"Why would you be angry with Arthur?" Iris asked, then added, "I'm not angry with either of you. I'm just glad we're all here, and safe."

"I didn't tell Liam that the arrow wasn't silver," Arthur said. "He didn't know."

"Oh." Iris looked at Liam, who flushed and glanced down at his hands.

"I thought he was dying," he explained. "And that it was *my* fault, since I was the one who got caught."

"No more secrets, then, okay?" Iris asked, not mentioning the fact that she hadn't known about the weapons either. "We're here together. And in this together. Okay?"

"Okay," Liam said, and Arthur echoed his words, remembering what he'd said to Tobias and the others, and how Sennet had responded. Maybe, just maybe, Tobias was right. That wasn't the way this household was supposed to work.

And maybe it wouldn't work that way.

"We should go, right?" Iris asked, and slipped off the bed. "Where is Tobias making this call?"

"I don't know," Arthur told her. "But I left him--them--in the library, downstairs, so I'm assuming we should meet back there." He was curiously reluctant to leave, although Iris didn't seem to share his qualms. For a moment, he couldn't understand why he would feel so...nervous, but then he realized that everything rather hinged on Tristan's reaction to Tobias' request. If Tristan refused to help, Arthur knew no one that he'd met so far could overcome his father and grandmother to free the Morgan household from their influence.

Overcome was a nicer word than what they would be proposing, since Arthur knew they both would have to die. Neither would surrender. Arthur knew that for a fact. And that--that distressed him more than he cared to admit.

He wondered if Tristan had felt the same way before killing his father. Or Tobias with his mother. He suspected they had not.

But he made no protest when Iris led them to the door, and made no protest as he followed her down the hall to where Tobias waited for them to arrive, because he knew they had no other choice, truly, if they wanted to do anything at all to help those who remained inside the Morgan household.

No other choice at all.

Tristan

"Why," Tristan asked, looking around at the now-familiar hotel room, "do we always meet here?"

"I don't know," Jericho said from where he sat on the now-familiar chair. "It's a neutral place, perhaps."

"You should have told me that you were afraid to leave her house," Tristan said, completely destroying any neutrality in their conversation.

Jericho avoided his gaze. "I don't want to talk about it here." The guitar was out of its case and in his lap; he busied himself by rubbing a small cloth across the gleaming wood.

Tristan sat down. "Okay."

Jericho looked at him narrowly, suspecting a trap. But when Tristan didn't continue, he said, "Cecilia tells me that she doesn't believe you are different."

"She told me the same thing," Tristan said.

"I believe you," Jericho told him.

"Thank you," Tristan said. And then, "Cecilia can believe what she wants to believe. I'm not going to try to force her to believe I have changed. I think that would rather prove her point, if I did."

Jericho smiled.

"You still should have told me. If only--if only so that I could help you." It cost a lot to say this; to offer help when Jericho had not asked. But he didn't seem to be offended.

"Perhaps," he allowed, and picked up the cloth again.

"I have something to tell you," Tristan said quietly. "I'm not sure how I feel about it yet. I know how I *should* feel--"

"What is it?" Jericho asked. "And how *do* you feel?"

"Frightened," Tristan admitted. He could admit that, at least, to Jericho. "Minerva--Minerva told me we are going to have a child."

Said like that, stilted and formal, it didn't sound nearly as frightening.

"Oh," Jericho said. "I see." And then, "Does Alexander know?"

"Yes," Tristan said. "I haven't spoken to him about it. I just found out, myself." Almost to himself, he added, "I guess that means I'll have to make a decision now, won't I?"

"About what?" Jericho asked.

Tristan hadn't realized he'd spoken aloud. "Oh. The Morgans."

"What *about* the Morgans?" Jericho asked when he didn't continue.

"I don't know," Tristan admitted. "That's part of the problem. I want to be able to defend my household against them, if they decide to attack us for what I've done. But I also realize that by attacking them outright, it would not go over well with the Council. And I doubt I could do it on my own. I'm not certain how Alexander feels about any of this. Whatever plan I might put into place is amorphous, at least for the moment."

"Did you talk about this with Tobias?" Jericho asked.

"No," Tristan said, then smiled. "But if I can get his cooperation, at the very least I could pretend to want to cash in on the bounty to get inside--" He stopped talking, because the plan had formed in his mind, just like that.

Jericho frowned, clearly not liking Tristan's line of thought. "I doubt Tobias would trust you enough to allow you to take him back in there as a prisoner," he pointed out. "Especially since you said the Richmond household was very low on money, so it would even make sense if you decided to cash in on the bounty."

"I know," Tristan said, and smiled broadly. "It's a perfect plan, don't you think?"

"A perfect plan that hinges on Tobias' cooperation and your ability to kill the head of the Morgan household," Jericho said. "And *Grandmother Morgan, who I've heard might be more powerful than her son."*

"More powerful than me?" Tristan asked.

"You're probably more stubborn," Jericho allowed. "I haven't met them, so I don't know if you are more powerful. If you intend to do this, though--I hope you are."

"So do I," Tristan said thoughtfully. "So do I."

He awoke on the loveseat with Minerva beside him. She was awake; Alexander sat on the couch across from them, and they were talking, predictably about him.

He made a show of yawning. Kissed Minerva, then asked, "Do you think Tobias Morgan will agree to pretend to be my prisoner so that I can get inside the Morgan household to liberate it from Ichabod and Grandmother Morgan?"

"What?" Minerva asked, twisting out of his embrace to stare at him.

"I haven't met Tobias," Alexander said. "So I can't comment. But he called, and awaits your reply. I told him you were asleep." He didn't say anything about Tristan's plan, which was rather worrying.

"I wouldn't be able to do this on my own," Tristan said, and wondered if Alexander would make him beg. "I wouldn't be able to do it without your help." And then, because he felt he had to say it aloud, "If Tobias is willing and trusts me enough to do this, will you help me liberate the Morgan household? Please?" He glanced at Minerva. "So that our child can grow up in a peaceful, loving--"

"Don't push it," Minerva advised wryly, but she was smiling now, at least, and no longer looked as if he'd lost his mind.

"What, exactly, do you propose?" Alexander asked, and Tristan told him. "It's plausible that I would be interested in the bounty, after all," he said into the silence. "And with Tobias in tow, they'd let me inside."

"They likely would," Alexander said.

"Or, you could go inside and subdue them both--" Tristan suggested. "Without any bloodshed at all."

He hadn't intended to say that; he knew how Alexander felt about showing his power. Subduing the girl had probably broken some sort of self-imposed edict about not harming humans; Tristan would not have been surprised at all if that were true.

"I could," Alexander told him, unoffended. "But then what? Who would I turn the household over to afterwards? Because I certainly have no interest in becoming head of the Morgan household."

That was a good and valid question. Tristan didn't truly have an answer. "Perhaps the Council?" he asked, knowing Tobias wouldn't be interested, either.

"I think we would have to talk to the Council first," Minerva said, perhaps interpreting the look on Alexander's face as anger instead of amusement.

"Then perhaps that is what we should do," Alexander said slowly, as if trying the idea on for size.

"I think a meeting--a face-to-face meeting--would be prudent," Tristan said.

"I agree," Alexander said. "And since you need to call Tobias back, perhaps you could suggest a meeting? Somewhere neutral, or somewhere they feel safe?"

"Since you and Minerva cannot walk in daylight, it would have to be this evening," Tristan said.

"You would want *me* to join you?" Minerva asked, surprised.

"Of course," Tristan told her. "Why wouldn't you join us?" He didn't stop to wait for her reply. "I would want Maya to join us as well. And Lucas Lane, and any of the Council." He paused. "And the Hunt."

"I think Miriam should be here to hear of your plan," Minerva said abruptly.

"It's not a plan yet, without cooperation," Tristan pointed out, but she ignored this, and summoned her sister. Miriam took one look at Tristan's face and asked, simply, "You've come up with a plan?"

Sighing, Tristan told her of his plan.

"And you haven't talked to Tobias yet," Miriam said, as if to make sure.

"No, not yet," Tristan told her, and waited for her judgment.

"And you think Tobias will agree to this?" Miriam asked, but she was looking at Alexander now, as if she expected him to--

"I'm certainly not going to compel him to agree to this," Alexander said.

Miriam nodded, as if it had really been a question. "Good. I think anyone who participates in this plan of yours must go into it with all of their facilities intact. If only to prevent problems later, if you fail."

Tristan couldn't resist. "You have no objections?"

Miriam looked at him steadily. "Would it matter if I did?"

"Yes," Tristan said, deciding to be honest. "I value your judgment."

"I see a million ways this could go very horribly wrong," Miriam said after a moment of silence. "But I also see a few ways it could go *right*. And if you get Tobias' cooperation; if he agrees to this, then I think you're right. They'll let you in. And what happens after that will be up to you."

"And if I fail, you will keep care of the household?" Tristan asked. "Because if I fail, I'll be dead." He knew she would; she likely cared about the household more than he did, after all. But he wanted to be certain.

"Of course," Miriam said.

"Then I should call Tobias and see what he has to say."

Wordlessly, Alexander held out his phone. Tristan took it, then hesitated, not really wanting to have an audience, even though he knew he had their support. But he dialed the number instead of asking to be alone *because* he had their support, and listened to the phone ring.

Tobias picked up. "Hello?"

"Hello," Tristan said. "I heard you called, so I thought I would call you back." That sounded horribly awkward, so before Tobias could reply, he added, "I would like to propose a meeting. Face to face. It can be somewhere neutral, if you'd like."

Cautiously, Tobias said, "I called to ask you to a meeting as well."

"Oh," Tristan said. "Well, then. You first." And then, because he had a hunch, "Perhaps our meetings have the same agendas?"

"Perhaps they do," Tobias said, but went no further. "I agree a neutral location would be ideal, but I'm not certain there *is* one that will fit everyone."

"I would want the Council to hear what I have to propose, and the Hunt as well," Tristan said. "And anyone you might wish to attend." He paused. "We could come to you, since our--contingent would likely be three of us and no more."

"You, Alexander, and Minerva?" Tobias asked.

"Yes," Tristan said. "Unless Miriam wants to come--" But she was, of course, already shaking her head. "Three of us, then, yes. And more than a dozen of you, so you would definitely have the advantage. We could pick up Cecilia on our way, if you'd like." Or, perhaps, Lark could accompany her to the meeting. The idea had some merit, considering the likelihood of the small folk's involvement as well.

For a moment, the sheer audacity of what he intended to suggest overwhelmed him. It was one thing entirely to return to the Richmond household intent on murdering his own father in revenge for what he had done to Jericho. And yet another thing entirely to put the Morgan household in his sights and decide to attempt to liberate *them* as well.

It was sheer insanity, and also why it just might actually work.

He realized, then, that Tobias had said something, and he hadn't been paying attention. "I'm sorry; what did you say?" he asked.

"I asked when will you be coming?" Tobias repeated patiently.

"Soon?" Tristan asked. "Is tonight too soon? Do you need to speak with the others first?"

"No, they're here with me," Tobias said. "Tonight is fine; Arthur and the others are here as well. You may run into searchers in the forest, so I'd avoid the Morgan household entirely."

"We will," Tristan said, a bit surprised that Tobias had agreed so readily to a meeting. But then again, the Richmond cohort would be traveling to Tobias' home ground, a distinct disadvantage. Although, with Alexander, there were really very few disadvantages at all.

"And yes, if Cecilia is ready to come home, please fetch her," Tobias continued. "She is part of this--household, so she should be here, too."

He'd stumbled over the word 'household', which wasn't really surprising. What they were doing; forming their own household under the protection of the Council--and the Hunt as well--was so much more than their betrayal of living outside their own households in the first place. It took a lot of courage to do what they intended, and Tristan liked them all the more because of it.

"Now that I think of it, there's someone else I'd like to invite," Tristan said. "And he can bring Cecilia, because he lives near Jericho and Celeste. He's an elf--will that be a problem?"

"No," Tobias said, then, curious, "Why would it be a problem?"

"He is searching for his missing wife," Tristan said. "Although not having much luck in Faerie. Her name is Helena. She was born a Morgan."

"An elf married to a vampire?" Tobias asked in surprise. "And a Morgan? I don't remember a Helena, but that doesn't mean anything at all. Arthur might know of her. I can ask--"

"Please do," Tristan said. "I'll call him. We could be there within the hour or a little later, if you can gather everyone on your end by then."

"I think we can, yes," Tobias said. "We'll see you then."

When Tristan disconnected the call, Alexander said, "Unless we're walking, we can be there in less than fifteen minutes."

"I still have to call Lark," Tristan said, and dialed his number. "He might take a little convincing." Truthfully, though, he'd forgotten about Alexander's car. He was so used to walking that he'd just assumed they'd do the same. After all, it was much easier to defend oneself while not trapped in a moving piece of machinery.

Lark, however, took no time at all to convince. "I can check in with Cecilia to see if she's ready to return; Celeste may be back by now. I think Nefir called her to come home a bit early."

Because of Jericho, Tristan said, but did not say it aloud. "Minerva and I could walk," he suggested. "And meet you. Alexander could take the car."

"That seems needlessly complicated," Alexander said. "We could *all* walk, together."

"Okay," Tristan said. "We'll all walk together."

Minerva sighed, but did not protest. Puzzled, Tristan looked at her, waiting for an explanation.

"Cars seem a bit safer, to me," she said.

"Not to me," Tristan told her. "But we can go by car if you prefer. I think we're less likely to be noticed if we walk."

"Very well," Minerva said. "We'll walk. But we'll need to leave soon, especially if we'll have to avoid searchers in the forest." She narrowed her eyes. "You're not thinking of *doing* anything to anyone we might encounter?"

"*Doing* what?" Tristan asked. "I would defend, not attack. I don't want word to get back to Ichabod Morgan or Grandmother Morgan, after all. I would *hope* to pass unnoticed."

Minerva didn't seem quite convinced, but she didn't press the issue. Tristan wondered if she really should come at all, considering her condition, but he knew--without asking--that if he brought it up, she would never forgive him, so he remained silent. And anyway, with Alexander accompanying them, there was very little likelihood of discovery.

And in truth, once they were on their way; once Minerva decided what was appropriate for Tristan--and herself--to wear for a visit to their new allies. Tristan hadn't really thought about what to wear, but apparently, it was an important decision. He didn't argue with her; it was pointless anyway, because he really didn't have very many clothes to choose *from.*

They ran into Maya, or she appeared, at least, on the outskirts of the Morgans' territory.

"Hello again," she said from where she leaned against a tree, apparently waiting for them to arrive. "I believe Lark and Cecilia should be here shortly, if you'd like to wait."

"We can wait," Tristan said. "Are you coming to our meeting?"

Maya raised an eyebrow. "Am I invited?"

"Of course," Tristan said, as if there would really be any question.

"And what is it you are meeting *about*?" Maya asked, then, when Tristan didn't reply, added, "There's no one nearby. Ask Alexander if you don't believe me."

"We are quite alone," Alexander said, even though Tristan had decided not to ask him.

"The liberation of the Morgan household," Tristan told her. "A joint effort. I'm certain we'll need your help."

"A *joint* effort?" Maya inquired, although Tristan rather suspected she already knew, and just wanted to hear it from him.

"The Council will be at this meeting, and so will the Hunt," he said. "And Tobias' household as well, and the recently rescued cousins." He shrugged. "And likely others."

"You've put yourself at a disadvantage, meeting them in their own territory," Maya said.

"Have we?" Alexander's voice was mild, but Tristan *almost* heard a threat. Or a warning.

"Well," Maya allowed, not responding to the warning, but to Alexander's presence. "Perhaps not." She smiled. "But you have yet to meet the Master of the Wild Hunt, and he'll likely be in attendance."

"I'm looking forward to meeting him," Alexander said. His tone did not change. "We aren't here to challenge anyone."

"Except for the Morgans," Maya said. "And it's not as if I intend to disagree with *that*." She paused, then, because Lark and Cecilia had arrived, the latter looking a bit out of her depth.

"Did you have a nice visit?" Tristan asked, but she ignored him in favor of Minerva, who had stepped forward to greet her.

"I did," she said later as they continued their journey. Not with Maya; she'd promised to come a bit later, and Tristan hadn't argued. "What kind of a meeting is this?" She stole a glance at Alexander. "Are you planning something?"

"Yes," Tristan said. "And without sounding trite, all will be revealed at the meeting. And truthfully, nothing may happen. We might return home without planning anything at all."

"Because you need Tobias' cooperation for this, and you're not certain he'll agree," Cecilia said shrewdly. And then, a moment later, "Oh. This has to do with the Morgan household, doesn't it?"

"It does," Tristan said.

They walked in silence for a moment. Tristan knew Cecilia was trying to figure it out; he could tell from the look on her face. And since she was a Richmond, she was likely to guess without much trouble, considering what he had told her already, and what she knew about the Morgans.

Only a moment later, she asked, "Do you really believe he'll agree to this?"

"To what?" Tristan said, which earned him an elbow in the side from Minerva, who frowned at him fiercely.

"Hmm," Cecilia said with a speculative glance at Minerva. "You said you've changed, but you're still very stubborn."

Alexander laughed aloud. It was such an unexpected sound that Tristan wasn't sure how to respond.

"We like him stubborn," Minerva said. "Most of the time."

"We're here, anyway," Tristan told them both, thus saving himself from defending his idea from Cecilia's wrath.

"So we are," Alexander said.

They'd come out of the forest at the back of the house, near to where Tristan had been before. There were lights on, downstairs, but no visible movement, at least from here. The wards hid the occupants from prying eyes, although the forest itself was quiet; almost serene.

For a moment, they paused at the edge of the forest, just standing there, as if waiting for a signal to approach. But then Cecilia stepped forward, over the wards, and said, "Let's not keep them waiting," and with that thought in mind, Tristan and the others followed her inside.

Chapter Ten

Tobias

It was times like these that Tobias missed Cecilia's presence. Not because she would have comforted him, but she would have understood how he really felt about this meeting, and the potential results of it, and she would have found a way to wrest his mind away from worrying. But without Cecilia, he had Michael and Erialas and Aunt Amy and Uncle Mark, and then Lucas, and Gabriel, and Malachi and Josiah and Eri; and Aunt Amy had said something about where to put everyone, and that sent them all into a panicked clean-up of the unused formal dining room, which held a table that spanned the room, and more than twenty chairs.

They couldn't find enough in the way of lightbulbs for the chandelier, so Aunt Amy had gathered up every candle she could find. The result was--a bit overpowering.

"I feel--underdressed," Tobias murmured as he hesitated in the doorway.

"Is it too much?" Aunt Amy asked, standing back to view the results of her work. "It's very--"

"Haunted," Erialas interjected when she couldn't find the word she wanted. "Surreal. Mysterious."

"Ridiculous," Aunt Amy decided. "But it's the best we can do right now, without lightbulbs or magic, and I'd rather use candles than magic."

No one else seemed to think it strange, or overwhelming, although the Hounds were hard to read at the best of times, and neither Lucas nor Gabriel would ever admit they were uncomfortable. Lucas even managed to not look disapproving, but Tobias suspected that was more for show than anything else, because how could Lucas *approve* of something like this?

Although, truthfully, Tobias had no idea what Tristan intended to propose, and no idea how he would respond to it. Or, rather, he hadn't allowed himself to consider what someone like Tristan would propose, and what it might mean to his sanity, or even his life.

But there was no time for speculation, because Cecilia appeared from the back door, spotted Tobias, and said, "I told them they could come inside. They said--well, *Tristan* said--they would wait until you're ready."

"We're as ready as we're going to be," Tobias said honestly, and moved past her towards the door.

Cecilia caught his arm. "Tristan has a plan," she said, "And one that requires *your* cooperation. But you don't have to agree. Okay? You're under no obligation to agree."

"I thought you said you would vouch for him," Tobias told her, wondering what had changed.

Cecilia bit her lip. "I did. And I would. But this--"

It didn't take long for Tobias to realize what Tristan intended to propose. After all, how *else* could he gain entrance into the Morgan household? "Oh," he said. "Oh, I see." And then, because he couldn't keep them waiting, he opened the door.

"Come inside, please, and be welcome," he said simply, and stepped aside.

Tristan entered first, then Minerva, then Lark, then Alexander, who seemed too unassuming to be the Alexander Tobias had heard about; quite possibly the oldest vampire in the world.

Tristan took one look at Tobias' face and started to round on Cecilia, but Tobias said, "She didn't tell me. I guessed." And perhaps the numbness; the disinterest in his voice gave Tristan pause, because he hesitated, then said, "I didn't think it would be a good subject to talk about over the phone."

"No, it wouldn't have been," Tobias told him. "Please, follow me."

The dining room was only a short walk down the hall. Before they reached the doorway, though, Alexander spoke. "Have you named your household yet?"

If Tobias agreed to Tristan's proposal and they failed, there would *be* no household. "No," he said. "Not yet. We haven't had time."

"We mean you no harm," Tristan said. "Truly. If you don't agree to do this, we'll return to our home and leave you in peace."

Tobias had no real reason to believe him, other than his word, and he supposed that would have to be good enough, because he *did* believe that Tristan and his entourage would leave without argument if Tobias refused to allow him to--

He stopped in the doorway. Everyone else had already taken their seats, including Cecilia, who sat next to his empty seat. Sennet had arrived, too; she'd taken the seat beside Iris' mother, and whispered something to her that had left her stunned and weeping. The Hunt sat next to each other. Lucas sat beside Gabriel. There were seats on the other side of the table for Tristan and his entourage, which put Alexander directly across from the Master of the Hunt, which, in retrospect, was probably not the best idea in the world.

"I believe," Gabriel said, "Introductions are in order?"

He spoke softly, but no one in the room had any trouble hearing him.

Tobias waited until Tristan and the others had taken their seats, then said, "That's a good idea."

So they went around the table, and everyone introduced themselves, and then the room fell silent, and Tobias realized that they were waiting for him to speak. "Tristan has a proposition that involves my cooperation. I haven't heard it yet, but I'm pretty sure I know what it entails."

Into the silence, Tristan said, "As you know, I--inherited the Richmond household from my father. And please forgive me if I seem a bit awkward; I've never actually done this before, and I'm not entirely certain how to go about proposing what I'm about to propose."

"Just say it," Malachi suggested. "No one will recoil from you in shock or horror."

"I intended to ask Tobias if he would allow me to claim the bounty on his head so that I could gain access to Ichabod Morgan, Grandmother Morgan, and their lieutenants," Tristan said baldly. "My father left the Richmond household in dire straits financially, so my claiming the bounty would be a logical chain of events. The Richmond household is known for its--partnership with the Morgans, so even that would make sense. I had thought to propose that while we are busy, a second attack could be made to liberate the innocents in the Morgan household away from their abusers, and once Ichabod and Grandmother Morgan and the lieutenants are dead, perhaps the Morgan household could become a safe place instead of a house of horrors."

"And how, exactly, did you intend to claim the bounty?" Lucas asked into the sudden silence. "I believe it involves the price on Tobias' *head,* not his entire body."

"Well, obviously I have no intention of killing him," Tristan said with a glance at Tobias, likely to see how his words had been received. Out in the open, spoken aloud; Tobias felt as if nearly everyone expected him to outright refuse. And, perhaps, storm from the room.

"You intend to kill my father, my grandmother, and all five lieutenants on your own?" Arthur asked, not mincing his words. He spoke plainly, unafraid but cautious, meeting Tristan's gaze with a slightly skeptical gaze of his own. "Because if you show up with Tobias in tow, they'll let you inside. My father wants Tobias dead more than anything, except maybe me. Or Liam or Iris. And I've heard how you killed a whole nest of Hunters, but they weren't vampires." He took a deep breath. "And my grandmother is another story entirely."

"I will take care of Grandmother Morgan," Alexander said, breaking his silence.

This was surprising enough for Tristan to forget himself and stare at him in surprise. Apparently, he hadn't expected Alexander to offer to do anything at all, and Tobias wondered why. From the little he'd heard about Alexander, he hadn't involved himself in the households up until his relationship with Tristan and Jericho.

"No," Maya said from the shadows. "Grandmother Morgan is mine." She stepped into view right behind Arthur's chair, and placed both her hands on the back of it.

Arthur briefly closed his eyes.

"This is, of course, your father and grandmother we're plotting to destroy," Tristan said gently. "And I apologize for it. But I see no other way around their deaths. They will not listen to reason, and they will not step down. And under their rule, more innocents will suffer."

"I know," Arthur said. "I know."

Iris' mother spoke. "The boy you rescued," she said to Arthur. "He--he woke up. And told Sennet that Carroll was--that my husband; Iris' father was--" She covered her face with her hands and turned away, unable to finish.

"Alive," Sennet said. "Carroll was alive as of a day or so ago."

"Then it's all the more important that we act now," Tristan said. And then, to Tobias, he added, "But you would have to trust me. And you would have to agree. Because without your cooperation, there is no plan." He smiled, briefly. "And I know you're going to feel as if you have no choice. But I want you to feel as if you have a choice."

"Even if you do kill them, what then?" Iris asked. "No one there will trust the Council or the Hunt--no offense."

"None taken," Lucas said.

"They'll need to see familiar faces," Iris' mother said levelly. "*You're* not--"

"No," Iris said, interrupting her. "Don't say it." She glared at her mother. "We've risked our lives for almost four years. We know what could happen."

"What almost happened," Liam pointed out.

"And if my father is there, and a prisoner, and I never found him, then I want to know where he was," Iris continued hotly. "I've opened nearly every door in that house, and I--"

"He's with the humans," Malachi said before she could work herself up to a full-blown fury. "I could find him, from Walter's perspective, at least. I doubt he knows the entire household, however."

"Oh," Iris said, suddenly subdued. "I--I couldn't open that door." Her mother put her arm around Iris' shoulders and hugged her closely. Iris did not pull away.

Almost sighing, as if he thought they'd expect him to speak, Arthur said, "I know where my father keeps the key, but I've never been past the door."

"Walter is *not* well enough to show us the way," Sennet said. "But he will recover."

"I didn't get you out of that place to turn around and send you right back," Maya said. "Surely this can be done without your participation." She glanced at Gabriel, then at Alexander, as if waiting for them to volunteer.

"Perhaps you could draw us a map?" Uncle Mark asked. "Of the household?"

"Can you withstand vampires?" Tristan asked bluntly. "Because I think that if you can't--and that would go for anyone here at this table--you should refrain from attending. I can protect Minerva and Tobias--and maybe one more."

"How dangerous are these lieutenants?" Lucas asked.

"Two of them were once Hunters," Tobias said.

"And they wouldn't hesitate to murder anyone they catch," Liam said.

"I could protect all of you," Alexander said slowly, as if trying on those words for size. "But that would mean I would need both your trust and your complete surrender, and I'm not certain I want to have that power over any of you."

Even Tristan looked uncomfortable at this declaration, however reluctant.

"I don't believe we would ask you to do that unless it is an emergency," Gabriel said, and met Alexander's gaze. "I believe you would be better off--and more useful--with Tristan and Tobias, if Tobias agrees to this. You hide your power behind the persona you project; would Ichabod be able to see past it?"

"No," Alexander said. "But it's likely that my name would not be unknown to him."

"I think that you should go with them, nonetheless," Gabriel said. "For Tobias' protection, if nothing else."

"From *me*?" Tristan asked. "Or from his uncle?"

"I would expect Alexander to be strong enough to stop you if you--forgot yourself and try to kill anyone other than your targets," Gabriel said, his voice completely neutral. "I've heard stories, about you."

"I've heard stories about *you*," Tristan said, sounding a bit offended, although Gabriel didn't seem to care.

"Either that, or we dispense with the subterfuge and you and I take care of Ichabod Morgan, Grandmother Morgan, and their lieutenants, and everyone else can concentrate on the lives you wish you save," Gabriel's gaze was fixed on Alexander now, even as his Hounds--and his daughter--gasped in shock at his words.

"No," Tristan said, almost plaintively.

"Why not?" Gabriel asked, his voice soft.

"Because--" Tristan and Tobias spoke at the same time. After a moment, Tristan nodded for Tobias to continue.

"Because this is not your fight," Tobias said. "This fight belongs to the Morgans and the Richmonds." Although a large part of his mind was of the opinion that he should step aside and allow Gabriel and Alexander to deal with his uncle and grandmother, he knew that wouldn't be the right response.

And then he realized he'd agreed to Tristan's proposal, without actually saying anything aloud.

"We would need your aid," Tristan said, almost as if they'd rehearsed this. "To help those of our cousins who cannot help themselves. To bring them to safety. We would need *everyone's* help. I swear to you; I will not hurt Tobias. I will not forget myself. But I would ask that someone accompany us into Ichabod Morgan's den, as it were." He paused. "If Tobias agrees. If we do this, I believe Alexander would be of better use helping to protect those of you who cannot withstand us."

"If I understand correctly, that would mean we would surrender ourselves to Alexander," Lucas said. "I'm not sure I like that idea."

"Having been on the other end of a vampire's suggestion--" Aunt Amy looked at Erialas, who flushed. "However noble the sentiment, it felt as if I had no control over my actions. It wasn't something I would willingly submit to again."

"There may be another way," Michael said.

And of course it would be Michael. Tobias knew he'd been working on something other than the taste of bottled blood, but he'd kept fairly quiet about it. He wasn't entirely surprised that it would have something to do with vampires, considering Michael's treatment at the hands of Stefan and Tobias' mother. And the twins.

"A spell?" Alexander asked, breaking his silence.

"More of a ward," Michael said.

"I heard that you've created something else, as well," Alexander said.

"Rings, yes," Michael told him. "To protect vampires from sunlight."

"What?" Minerva asked, horrified.

"And the wards I've created will need to be tested," Michael said. "But I have no reason to believe they won't work."

Quizzically, Alexander asked, "You've already created them?"

"Would you be willing to test them?" Michael asked.

"Of course," Alexander said. "But *wards*? Against vampires?"

"Against vampire influence," Michael told him.

Under her breath, Cecilia whispered, "You've no idea."

"Michael--" Tobias began, then stopped, because he didn't really know what to say.

Michael looked at Lucas, who sighed, then nodded. "If you wait a few minutes--Tristan already knows about the rings, but doesn't need one because he had his own protection--and are willing to trust me, I can give you--Alexander and Minerva--rings that will protect you against the sunlight if you find yourself out past dawn."

It was obvious that Tristan had not told Minerva or Alexander about the rings. Perhaps he hadn't had time. But only Minerva seemed uncertain; Alexander took it all in stride.

"The rest of us need to make our own plans," Gabriel said. "And I don't think you should know them, just in case."

It was assumed, then, that Tobias had agreed to Tristan's plan. Tobias wasn't certain how he felt about that assumption, but he felt he had to say *something,* so he whispered, "I am under no compulsion to agree to this, but it seems this is the best--if only--way to free ourselves and the rest of our cousins." He paused. "I'm sorry, Arthur."

Arthur nodded, but did not speak. He seemed to be busy with a piece of paper--Liam had a similar one--drawing a map of the household, Tobias supposed. *Would* they come as well? Iris seemed determined to do so, despite the danger.

Tobias met Maya's gaze. She nodded at him, then said to the room at large, "I will be responsible for Grandmother Morgan." As if she expected Alexander, perhaps, to protest.

He didn't protest. No one did. Satisfied, Maya gave Arthur's shoulder a quick squeeze, bent to whisper something into his ear, and vanished.

Michael walked up to where Alexander sat. "If you would come with me?" he asked. "All of you and Tobias, first."

"You knew about this?" Alexander asked Tristan, who nodded.

"I did intend to tell you, but because of Minerva's news, it slipped my mind."

Alexander seemed satisfied with this explanation. "You do realize that by creating these rings you've opened yourself up to some powerful enemies?" he asked Michael, who countered with, "And powerful allies."

"Yes, true," Alexander allowed. "How did you test these rings?"

"I volunteered," Tobias said.

"Without my knowledge," Michael said. "I couldn't ask someone to volunteer--"

"So you took it upon yourself to do so?" Minerva asked incredulously. "Not knowing if they would work? You walked *outside*?"

"At dawn, at noon, and at sunset," Tobias said. "Although after noon, I was pretty sure it worked."

"What kind of deathwish did you *have*?" Tristan asked. "You couldn't have captured someone and just--"

"No," Tobias said, turning when he heard Cecilia call his name. Erialas and Aaron were with her.

"I didn't want you to leave without saying goodbye," she said, and hugged him.

"I'm planning to come back," he said, or tried to, but his voice caught in his throat and he felt tears prick his eyes.

"I'll never forgive Tristan if you don't," she said.

Tristan thankfully did not reply to that; he'd gone ahead with Michael, Alexander, and Minerva.

"Be careful," Erialas told him.

"I intend to," Tobias said. "But if--"

"No," Aaron said firmly. "No 'but ifs'. It's your job to stay alive, okay? Let Tristan do what needs to be done. You just stay alive. Okay?"

Tobias did not trust his voice. He nodded instead. Turned away from them. He was only two steps down the hall when he heard Maya say, "Water. Or anything wet, for that matter. Not just water."

"What?" Tobias asked, and turned towards the sound of her voice, even though he couldn't see her at all.

"To summon me," Maya told him. "If you need to, while you're in there." She paused. He still couldn't see her. "Even blood." When he did not reply, she added, "And I *will* take care of Grandmother Morgan."

"Thank you," Tobias said, and he was alone again, He walked down the basement steps into Michael's lair a moment later. There was a warren of rooms down here, most of them empty. Michael had claimed two of them. The first room was fairly safe. Tobias had been there before. But the second's door was always locked, because that was where Michael fashioned the jewelry he formed into wards. The rings first, and then others awaiting owners. The anti-compulsion wards were necklaces. Pendants, oblong, with no set design. They were almost scraps of silver, formed into flattened, polished shapes. And there were two dozen of them.

"If these work, it's a fairly simple spell," Michael said. "But first, the rings. I've--tuned them, for lack of a better word, to their respective owners. Mostly for safety's sake; if someone pulls yours off your finger, they won't be able to use it." He picked out two rings. Murmured something over them, then handed one first to Alexander, then to Minerva.

Somehow, they fit perfectly. Tobias still wasn't sure how Michael had managed to do that, but he supposed it could be something like Aunt Amy's talent for finding clothes that fit perfectly without ever knowing sizes.

"Will we need to give these back afterwards?" Minerva asked curiously.

"Allies get to keep them," Michael said.

"But of course you could remove the ward at any time," Alexander commented, inspecting his ring closely.

Michael blinked. "That never actually occurred to me, but yes. I could remove them. But no one else can."

"No one else?" Minerva asked doubtfully.

"Maybe, with time," Michael admitted. "But there are a lot of safeguards built-in."

Tobias hadn't asked *any* questions when he'd secretly volunteered to test the rings. He'd just slipped it on his finger, taken a deep breath, and stepped outside.

"I would like very much for us to be allies," Tristan said, and took Minerva's hand. Smiled down at her ring. "This means you can come with me now, when I go visit Jericho."

"That's true," Minerva said thoughtfully.

Alexander had yet to put on his ring. He held it in his hand, staring down at it, then said, "You made these for your friends. To protect them."

"Yes," Michael said.

Alexander nodded, slipped the ring on his finger, then asked, "How would you like to test your wards?"

"I thought I would wear one and you could try to--" Michael began.

"Have you ever been under a vampire's influence before?" Alexander asked curiously.

"While under a truthspell," Michael said. "Tobias' mother. And I was wounded at the time."

"Then I will attempt to be gentle," Alexander said. "Would the rest of you please wait outside?"

"I would rather not," Tristan said as Tobias and Minerva turned to obey.

Tobias stopped. Should *he* insist on staying? For Michael's protection, if nothing more?

"On second thought, I would like Tobias to stay," Alexander said, ignoring Tristan's protest. "Have *you* ever been under the influence of another vampire?" He paused. "*Not* your mother?"

Tobias swallowed hard. "No," he said. "Just my mother."

"Your uncle will likely attempt to control you," Alexander said. "Fear will make it harder for him to hold you."

"That won't be a problem," Tobias said. "I'm rather terrified."

"But if he cannot hold you, he might force himself into your mind," Alexander said. "He might not want you dead if he thinks he can break you--and have you as a living example of what will happen to anyone who dares to disobey."

Tobias hadn't thought of that. He'd assumed that once they'd reached the Morgan household and were admitted into Ichabod's presence, his uncle would demand that someone kill Tobias, and Tristan would attack, and then--he had no idea what would happen after that.

He realized two things right then: Tristan had followed Minerva out of the room without further comment, and that both Michael and Alexander knew exactly what he was thinking. The latter he almost expected; the former was almost as frightening as talking to Malachi--and knowing that every word he spoke; every thought he had; held potential judgment.

Of course, that could apply to anyone, really.

"If my wards work, I want you to wear one of them," Michael said.

"And I would like to place safeguards in your mind," Alexander said. "With your permission, of course."

Tobias had to clear his throat before he could speak. "Safeguards?"

"If your uncle tries to force himself into your mind, you can retreat behind the safeguards I'll put into place, and you won't lose nearly as much of yourself as if we send you in there without any protections at all." Alexander hesitated. "Do you have talent of your own?"

"No," Tobias said. "Not really."

"Then with your permission, I will be extra cautious," Alexander said. "And nothing I will do will hold you bound or beholden to me."

"You have my permission, then," Tobias said hoarsely.

Michael handed him one of the necklaces. "Put this on," he said, and slipped one over his head.

And Alexander removed his glasses. Folded them up, and slipped them into his shirt pocket. When he met Tobias' gaze, all of his masks were gone.

Tobias physically *felt* Michael's wards snap into place. And, dimly, he realized the wards were the only things that kept him from fleeing; the only thing that kept him from debasing himself at Alexander's feet and swearing loyalty to him for the rest of eternity. His reaction, however tempered by Michael's ward, was so strong and so disturbing that he stood there, gaping like an idiot, until Alexander nodded and looked away.

Looked at Michael this time, who calmly--*how could he be so calm?*--stared back.

"I see what Tristan meant now," he said. "Why you did not agree to Gabriel's proposal, I mean."

"I couldn't," Alexander said. "Not without--complications. Tobias, the ward did not work?"

"It's not that it didn't work," Tobias said thoughtfully, surprised that his voice didn't shake. "I didn't run away. I felt it take hold. But it only muted what I felt when you looked at me." And he noticed Alexander was very careful not to do so again. "Will you--will you try again?"

"If you wish," Alexander said. "But your uncle will give you no warning; you do realize that?" This time, he pushed harder, and Tobias found himself responding, despite his efforts. Not to obey; the ward seemed to have worked on that piece completely. But, oddly enough, Tobias found himself wanting to struggle past the fear and push *back*.

Which would have been utter suicide, if Alexander had been his uncle.

"It works," he managed to say. "If I can get past my fear of you, it works."

"What if I tell you not to be afraid?" Alexander asked, and Tobias let out a breath.

"That's almost worse," he admitted. "And I think part of my reaction is my own fault."

"Your mother's fault," Alexander clarified. "I think she did you a great misservice in keeping you beholden to her." He held out his hand. "May I?" And, just like that, the terrible power vanished, even without putting his glasses back on.

Tobias let out a breath. "Yes, you may," he said, then realized, perhaps from the speculative look in Alexander's eyes, that something wasn't quite right.

"You're not afraid anymore; why?" Alexander asked.

"Because you--" Tobias began.

"No, I did not," Alexander interrupted him. "Not yet, at least. Michael?"

"Wards should be adaptable," Michael said simply.

"But they usually aren't," Alexander said. "*All* wards?"

"I'm working on that," Michael said. "Did it work?"

"I--I feel like I could carry on a conversation with you without cringing," Tobias said. "It's--as if we're equals."

"When this is over, may I speak with you privately about fashioning something similar for *me*?" Alexander asked Michael, who nodded.

"Of course," he said, and Tobias thought Michael was not surprised by this request.

Alexander's hands weren't quite steady when he replaced his glasses, but even with his masks back in place, Tobias could see no difference, and that was a staggering thought.

"You'll still need protection," he said. "If I may?" He held out his hand again. This time, Tobias did not hesitate to take it.

The actual setting of protections took less time than he expected. Tobias heard a strange echo inside of his mind; Alexander muttering under his breath--"This far, no more"--"Here, no farther"--and felt something settle over his shoulders; an invisible cape, perhaps, protecting him. As far as he could tell, Alexander did not pry into his mind or his memories. He merely placed his protections, then stepped back.

"No heroics," he said. "Concentrate on staying alive. Let Tristan handle your uncle and his lieutenants."

"Okay," Tobias said, his voice suspiciously hoarse again, and then he realized there were no other reasons to delay. It was time to leave, and suddenly, Tobias could not force his feet to move.

"Good luck," Michael said gravely.

"You too," Tobias managed to reply; forcing himself to remember; to *believe* that his life was not the only one on the line here. And that thought helped him walk out of Michael's room and to the staircase where Tristan and Minerva waited.

"Let's go," he said. "Before I lose my nerve."

"Very well," Tristan said. And then, "We'll need a car."

"Do you even know how to drive?" Minerva asked, which wasn't a good indication of the success of their plan at all.

Tobias followed them outside. "I'm *not* driving myself to my own funeral," he said.

"Not even at knifepoint?" Tristan asked. "Even if it's silver?" He sighed. "No, I suppose not."

There were three cars parked in the driveway--Aaron's in its usual spot, Lucas' little grey sedan, and Uncle Mark and Aunt Amy's car, which Tobias had tried to destroy once before.

"So my thought was that I would restrain you, probably knock you out, steal a car, and drive as fast as I could to the Morgan household to claim the bounty," Tristan mused aloud. "But Minerva's right; I've never actually driven a car."

There was a jangle of keys behind them. A *deliberate* jangle, to alert them of Alexander's presence.

"I'll drive," he said. "And then make my own way inside."

"Like Lark?" Tristan asked, and glanced around, as if he expected the elf to appear.

"Aaron's only request was that we not get any blood on the seats," Alexander said with a glance at Tobias. "So any restraining or wounding will have to be done right outside of their wards."

Tobias nodded.

"It is unlikely their wards will allow a car down the driveway, but you will be able to walk," Alexander said. "And the wards will not notice the car."

"You sound very certain of that," Minerva ventured.

"I am," Alexander said.

Without a word, Tristan climbed into the backseat. Minerva joined him, leaving the front seat for Tobias, an odd place for a prisoner, even a supposed one. But he did not complain, and no one spoke until Alexander started the car and pulled away from the house.

Tobias did not look back. He couldn't look back, because if he did, he knew he wouldn't be able to go through with this. "You realize," he said, "That if this were true; if you really wanted the bounty, you've put yourself in a perfect position to claim it. You've gained our trust; you told a good story--"

Tristan laughed. "And the household will be overrun with the Wild Hunt and members of the Council in less than an hour, which would make getting away a bit tricky."

He had a good point, although Tobias had to wonder that with Alexander's help, Tristan likely would be able to flee, but to where? Would the Hunt avenge his life if he were to die? Would the Council? Or were their protections in name only, meant to look like something they were not?

In the car, the Morgan household was five minutes away. Five long, but very short minutes, and then Alexander slowed the car. "Here's where you get out," he said.

Surprisingly, Tobias did not have to force himself to exit the car. He stood on the side of the road with Tristan and Minerva beside him, and watched as Alexander drove away.

"Do it now," he said hoarsely. "Whatever you're going to do; do it now. I don't think I can--" A blinding pain exploded through his head. All at once, he found himself lying flat on the ground, staring up at Tristan who stood over him with a rock in his hand. When he brought his makeshift weapon down again, Tobias tried to raise his arms to fend him off, but they had turned to lead.

He only caught snippets of the next few minutes. Knew they'd tried to force him to stand; knew that he'd fallen again, dizzy and sick, unable to stop the ringing in his ears. They tied his arms behind his back with something that looked like clothesline--probably from the clothesline back at the house; it wasn't as if anyone actually *used* it, just that it was there--so that when he fell again, he couldn't break his fall and landed face first in the gravel of the driveway.

They dragged him the rest of the way. Deposited him on the front stoop of the house--no porch here; no wish to be welcoming, not here--and Tristan used the hilt of his dagger to pound on the door.

And then, voices. First, normal voices; obviously someone not very high in ranking; someone who would have been dead immediately if this was an attack. Tobias suspected Tristan pushed his way inside; he felt carpet under his cheek now; managed to crack open one eye, although he really didn't want to see the look on his cousins' faces.

Someone even dared to kick Tobias as he lay there; he curled around that new pain, unable to stop the moan that escaped from his lips.

And then Tristan, haughtily, "No. Leave him be. I've come to claim the bounty. I want to speak to Ichabod. *Right now.*"

"You--bastard," Tobias managed to croak, and this seemed to convince them of Tristan's intentions, because no one else approached them after that.

And then, somehow, Tristan and Minerva managed to pull Tobias to his feet. And somehow, they marched him down the hall. And only when they approached a room Tobias remembered; only when they stopped outside of the tall, carved doors that would open into a large room with faraway windows--a part of Tobias' mind realized this was a childhood memory now; obviously he'd been punished here before--did he try to wrest away from them, shouting incoherently, struggling free of Minerva's grasp even as she tried to hold onto him--

Tristan had kept the rock. And he had no qualms about using it again. And Tobias lost himself to darkness, which was probably for the best.

Tristan

If he wanted to be honest, Tristan thought it would have been more difficult to gain an audience with Ichabod Morgan. Perhaps Tobias' pitiful groaning helped; it was so obviously not a setup that no one had really argued past that first, shocked minute when Tristan had appeared at their front door.

He'd truly expected Tobias to struggle, but he hadn't expected his desperate attempt to break free; he'd nearly knocked Minerva over in his haste and Tristan had been forced to hit him with the rock again, then once more for good measure. Even so, he was semi-conscious by the time the doors opened to allow them entrance into Ichabod's presence.

There were--two lieutenants. One obvious Morgan, who had to be Ichabod. Grandmother Morgan was not in attendance, but Tristan couldn't worry about her, because Ichabod and the lieutenants would be difficult enough to subdue without issue.

Minerva held Tobias upright. He couldn't stand on his own; his face was a mask of blood. Not that blood would matter much, in this place; the floor was sticky with it, and other things, dried and rotten and stuck to the floor. It was almost hard to breathe through the stink of it, but then the entire household smelled of death. Its occupants were probably used to it by now.

"I've come to claim the bounty," Tristan said into the sudden silence as they all stared at him and his prisoner.

"And who are you?" Ichabod Morgan asked.

"Tristan Richmond," Tristan said. "After my father's untimely death, I am also head of the Richmond household. As I'm sure you can imagine, my father left the household nearly penniless; I thought the easiest way to gain some income was to claim your bounty."

"The--*easiest* way?" Ichabod asked, and climbed down from his chair, which was set up on a dais and almost a throne. He stopped a few feet away. Motioned to one of the lieutenants, who pulled a chair out of the shadows that lurked along the walls. The chair had arms--and restraints. "Sit him down."

Minerva obeyed only after a glance from Tristan. Tobias sat slumped, his head nearly touching his chest, unmindful of anything now. He didn't even move when the lieutenant secured him to the chair with thick leather straps.

"Wake him up," Ichabod ordered, and the lieutenant dumped a bucket of bloody water over Tobias' head. He jerked awake, spluttering; fighting weakly against the restraints until he realized it was no use.

"The bounty only specified his head. I'll give you nothing extra for bringing him to me alive."

"Well," Tristan pretended to consider this. "I *had* hoped you would be able to get more use out of him alive." He sighed. "I could, I suppose, see if the Council is willing to give me more for his safe return."

Ichabod Morgan smiled. "And you believe I would let you leave here alive?"

Tristan met his gaze, unsmiling. Interestingly enough, Ichabod made a show of glancing away, as if he no longer mattered. He walked over to where Tobias sat. Reached out to touch him, then let his hand drop, which was even *more* interesting, because Tobias wasn't at all powerful. Ichabod shouldn't have hesitated to try to break him. Had something happened?

"Where is my mother?" Ichabod asked, and one of the lieutenants immediately left, presumably to find her. To the other, he said, "Go fetch the bounty, plus an extra ten percent." To Tristan, "My final offer. Take it and leave, but Tobias will be staying here."

"You drive a hard bargain," Tristan said as the second lieutenant left the room. He held out his hand. "Agreed."

After a moment of silence, while Ichabod stared down at Tristan's hand as if it were a deadly snake, Ichabod said, "My household and yours are not allies. You've done me a service, and you will receive your reward. But that is *all* you will receive from me." He turned to walk back up the dais steps to his chair. Perhaps he would have ignored them all until the lieutenant returned with the bounty, but then Tobias raised his head. Spat out a mouthful of blood, and croaked, "It's too late, uncle."

"Too late for what?" Ichabod snapped and turned towards him. Half-delirious, barely able to open his right eye from the swelling; even Tobias had enough self-preservation left to shrink back at his approach. "Your mother should have left you *dead*." He raised his hand to strike Tobias down--interestingly enough, he did not attempt to compel him or use magic in any way--but Tristan neatly inserted himself between them.

"Not until I get the bounty," he said sharply. "He lives until then. After that, I don't care what you do to him."

"You dare!" Ichabod hissed, spittle flecking his lips. His eyes narrowed to slits. He made a motion with one hand, but no one appeared to help him; he'd sent the lieutenants away.

For a second; a moment, really, he didn't quite seem to know what to do. And Tristan read the weakness in his gaze, and knew without a doubt that Grandmother Morgan was dead, and that Ichabod had no idea what had happened.

Perhaps she had bound him to her. Perhaps it was a compulsion. But their connection was broken, and that had left him vulnerable.

And dangerous, of course, but especially vulnerable.

And in Tristan's mind, vulnerable meant he was already dead.

Which was, in hindsight, an error in judgment, because Ichabod was not stupid. Nor was he unarmed.

Tristan felt a kiss of pain across his side, then a deeper numbness as the dagger found its mark. They were standing close enough for their movements to be mistaken for an embrace; he doubted Minerva had realized what had happened. Tristan's hand found the hilt; he pushed himself forward; made the wound worse--it wasn't silver, at least; it wouldn't kill him--and smelled the fetid stink of Ichabod's breath. Saw the madness in his gaze.

And the fear when he realized he was alone in his mind, perhaps for the first time in his life.

It was almost too easy to overpower him, even wounded. To push him backwards and delve into a mind so twisted and horrible and *wrong* that Tristan felt soiled just from touching him.

What he had done to those he was supposed to protect was far worse than what Tristan's father had done. Tristan's father had allowed--*encouraged*--terrible things to happen under his watch, and had done terrible things as well. Ichabod Morgan had a standing order to drain the blood from newborn babies because he thought their blood was sweeter than any other. Ichabod

Morgan expected the female human members of his household to bear children over and over again with very little in the way of medical care just to serve his own twisted needs.

Ichabod Morgan had kept his own brother prisoner; kept him starved so that his wounds would not heal properly; blinded him; tried to break him--this was Iris' missing father, Tristan realized, and wondered if they would want him back if he were that damaged.

If he were still alive, since Ichabod had apparently taken out his fury at losing Arthur and the others on his brother, and had left him lying in a pool of his own blood, deep in the depths of this hateful house.

And now, *now,* as if finally realizing that Tristan's intentions were not merely to collect the bounty, Ichabod tried to defend himself; tried to fight back, but without his mother's presence, he had nothing to fall back on, and Tristan's disgust and horror were so great that Ichabod's attempts at defense crumbled before any of his hooks could sink into Tristan's mind. It wasn't that he fought him off; it was more that he dismissed them; ground them under his feet until they were broken and useless and until Ichabod cried out a wordless curse and tried to use magic instead.

Angry now; furious, even, Tristan batted his efforts away as if they were snowflakes. He thought he heard someone speaking; felt a hand on his arm that was *not* Minerva's--he hoped it wasn't Tobias, either, because he struck without thinking, and then struck again for good measure and then he saw the lieutenant who had gone to fetch Grandmother Morgan lying dead at his feet, and Ichabod gaped down at him and Tristan said, "*My* dagger is silver."

He was still inside of Ichabod's mind, even now. Still there, almost trapped now, by the horror that flew past his mind's eye, and yet he saw the spell right before Ichabod readied its release, and knew what would happen if he released it, because Connor Richmond had held a similar spell, tied to the members of his household, and Tristan's mind had almost buckled under the weight of it.

And now, again. With only a second to prepare.

"They will all die," Ichabod spat blood in Tristan's face. Dimly, Tristan realized he'd already used his dagger; he didn't remember that part at all.

"Hopefully not," Tristan said, and watched as the life drained out of Ichabod's gaze.

The spell hit him like a blow. Like being run over by a truck, perhaps, only with more pain; with more fury; he very nearly lost it as he fell to his knees in front of Ichabod's body. Very nearly let his mind buckle under the onslaught and let it go.

And for a moment, he didn't think he *could* hold it. That he would lose the entire Morgan household in one fell swoop; that he would watch Tobias die first, and then hear the others, screaming--

He didn't realize that he was the one screaming until he felt hands on his arm again; Minerva's hands; he would not mistake *Minerva* for an enemy, despite Tobias' hoarse warnings; he managed to tell her about the spell, his eyes squeezed shut against the pain, and that silenced Tobias very quickly after that. For a moment, he teetered between failure and success, and then he realized that he heard another voice, a voice from someone who was--most definitely--not in the room.

"I'm here."

Jericho.

"Play for me," Tristan whispered.

"What did he say?" he heard Tobias' voice, as if from very far away.

"It's a long story," Minerva replied. "I'll tell you it, but--can that door be locked?"

"I don't know."

"Sit down," Jericho said, his voice echoing inside Tristan's mind. Calming the maelstrom, just enough for him to function. "I will play for you."

Tristan opened his eyes. He sat in the familiar chair, in the familiar motel room. Jericho sat across from him, as usual, with the guitar in his lap. "I can't stay here."

From very far away, he heard Minerva speak his name. Felt the briefest touch of a hand on his shoulder.

"I know," Jericho said. "What happened? Is there anything I can do to help?"

"I don't know," Tristan admitted. "I can't think. This is much worse than before--I don't think I can hold it by myself." It hurt to admit that he would fail. He'd failed before, and look what had happened to Jericho. Now, an entire household of vampires and humans would die by his hand. Now--

Someone knocked on the door. Mystified, Tristan stood up and opened it as Jericho started to play behind him.

"I thought I'd find you here," Alexander said, and stepped inside the room. "Give me your hand. You're wounded."

Tristan touched the front of his shirt. It was wet with blood. He hadn't noticed. "Yes. But I won't die from this. Are you--where are *you?"*

"Kneeling beside you," Alexander said. "Or, beside your apparently dead body."

"Oh," Tristan said. "I don't feel *dead--"*

"I'm glad," Alexander said. "Because you're definitely not breathing. Please take my hand. Jericho, keep playing for as long as you can."

"I will," Jericho said as the room faded from Tristan's view; the only constants now were the sound of music and the strength of Alexander's grasp, pulling him forward, back into the light.

Back into the maelstrom.

In his mind's eye, he saw a door. And Grandmother Morgan, walking down a hallway. It had to be Grandmother Morgan, although Tristan had never met her; he'd seen her enough in Ichabod's memories to know her face. She'd passed the door, and something had thumped *against the wood, alerting her.*

Tristan felt a surge of fury towards Arthur and his damned trophies. And how Ichabod had allowed the child to venture out into the forest without escorts. And how he'd betrayed the entire household with his lies and his spells and his friends.

Something hit the other side of the door again. For a moment, only a passing thought, really, Grandmother Morgan had hesitated to open the door. To peek inside. She knew what lay within; a bunch of dead small folk and fairies, expertly mounted by her grandson. She'd ordered Ichabod to seal the room, or burn its contents, but he had refused; he had actually refused--

She opened the door. Stepped inside. It swung shut behind her. It never opened again.

And then, he found himself in a dark, dank room. Heard something scurrying along the walls; heard a faint whisper, which he followed until he found a human girl, dressed in rags, and a vampire, lying on the floor against the wall where Ichabod had left him. A sputtering candle was the only light in the room, but even in that dimness, Tristan could see clearly, and did not like what he saw. Where was Sennet? Where were the others? Why hadn't someone found them yet?

And then a door creaked open. Someone whispered a question. The girl, Tristan thought. The vampire lying against the wall reached out to grab her arm; tried to speak--

"You promised me--"

"No," Tristan whispered. "Don't do it." He had no idea if either of them could hear him, but he knew what the girl had promised, and he knew what the vampire intended to do, if Ichabod were to return. "Ichabod is dead, and so is your mother. Your wife is here, trying to find you, along with your daughter. They know you're alive. Don't do it."

And the vampire released the girl's arm, and she stood up, shakily ready to defend him, even if it meant her death.

And Tristan was swept away again.

Malachi

Iris and her mother had, predictably, insisted that they accompany Sennet and Aunt Amy and Eri so that they could search for Carroll while Sennet and the others concentrated on the humans.

Malachi thought Gabriel would have preferred to have a Hound with each group of rescuers, but there weren't that many Hounds to go around. Malachi ended up in the basement with Josiah, Arthur, Liam and Uncle Mark at first; Erialas and Michael had elected to watch the front of the house for any stragglers; Aaron and Cecilia were in the back. Lucas was with Gabriel (Gabriel had insisted); and Malachi had no idea where Alexander had gone off to; after spotting him once, he'd vanished, along with Lark.

But the basement cells were nearly empty, so Malachi left Arthur and Uncle Mark alone and followed Liam when he slipped--guiltily--away.

Of course, since Liam was a vampire, Malachi couldn't sneak up on him; outside, in the hall, Liam turned to him and said, "I should do this alone, I think."

"No one does anything alone until we know it's safe," Malachi said, and told Uncle Mark that he and Liam had a separate errand to run. Arthur had not protested, but Liam wouldn't look at him; after a moment, Arthur had said, "I hope you know what you're doing," and Liam had walked away.

"Where are we going?" Malachi asked as they walked down the deserted hallways. It was early enough from a vampire's point of view to be early morning, so Malachi wasn't that surprised they'd met no resistance.

Yet.

Liam murmured something to the floor. Malachi waited for a moment, then guessed, "Your mother? I'm not sure that's a good idea."

"Not my mother," Liam said, and stopped walking. "I--There's something I wanted to get from my--from her--room."

"And if she's *in* her room?" Malachi asked.

"She won't be," Liam said, and he spoke the truth. When they arrived at his mother's room, it was empty; stripped bare, except for a stained mattress on the floor. But under a loose floorboard, where no one had thought to look, Liam liberated a small, rusty candy tin and shoved it into his pocket without checking its contents. "I didn't have time to get it, before. When they--when they came for me." In a whisper, he added, "I had a sister, once. Her name was Fiona. She died a long time ago."

"I'm sorry to hear that," Malachi said.

"She was only a baby," Liam said. "But she was--" He stopped then, frozen, as someone appeared at the door.

"What's this?" And then, to Malachi, "Who are *you*?"

And then, this vampire, who had no constraints of civility attached to his actions; who was used to immediate response from those he terrorized in the household--Malachi suspected he was a lieutenant, and quite possibly one of the former vampire hunters Ichabod had turned--dispensed with questions and attacked.

First Liam, although he merely tossed him aside as if he meant nothing. But then he closed the door behind him, and went after Malachi with a dagger in his hand, and Malachi--in hindsight, he'd never actually faced an enraged vampire before in his life, and even Hounds had their limits--could not withstand him.

He fought; of course, he fought. He had no other choice *but* to fight. But he fell, and as he fell back across the mattress, as he saw Liam crumpled in the corner; as he felt the blade sink into flesh despite his efforts; despite everything, he thought he saw Tristan standing in the doorway. Watching. But then, he faded away, and Malachi faded with him, until blackness was the only thing that remained.

Tristan

Tristan sat bolt upright, then scrambled to his feet before anyone could react. He was almost to the door before anyone thought to question his miraculous recovery, although he would have preferred to stay dead for a little while longer, especially if he could have figured out a way to help Malachi survive what he had seen.

Survive. Was he dead?

"Wait," Alexander said. "Where are you going?"

Tristan had no doubt he looked deranged when he glanced back at them. Tobias gaped at him; Minerva looked shocked; even Lark seemed surprised. Alexander was the only one who had remained calm.

"I have to go," he said. "I saw--"

"Go, then," Minerva told him. "Go with him," she said to Alexander, who needed no additional encouragement.

They raced down the hall; the silent hall, now, because Alexander had solved the problem of the maelstrom by coaxing most of the household to sleep. Not all of them; there were still two lieutenants (Gabriel had apparently killed one of them earlier, although Tristan hadn't seen *that)* and one of them had found Malachi and Liam, and even now, since only--maybe--half a minute had passed--

They burst into the room. The lieutenant had left Malachi where he lay in a widening pool of blood, and now crouched over Liam, whose eyes were closed. Since he was a lieutenant, he reacted immediately, but he was no match for Tristan's blind fury. And when it was over, and he was dead, Tristan heard Malachi whisper, "I saw you--"

And he turned, and watched, numb, as the life drained from the Hound's gaze, as the severity of his wounds were too much, even for a Hound.

If Ichabod Morgan had not already been dead, Tristan would have killed him without a single thought. As it was, when the fourth lieutenant arrived, no doubt alerted by the death of the other, he had only stepped inside the room before he, too, was dead.

By then, Liam had awakened. By then, Tobias, Minerva, and Lark had arrived. By then, Josiah, on some awful hunch, had left Arthur and Mark in the basement and ventured upstairs to see after Malachi and Liam, and had walked right into the carnage.

Tristan spoke into the silence. "I saw it happen," he whispered. "While I was dead. I came as soon as I could. He was still alive--"

And he was babbling now, so he shut up.

Tobias glanced at Josiah, who stood frozen in the doorway. And something passed between them, but Tristan couldn't tell what it was. "Could you all please step outside?" Tobias asked, and touched Josiah's arm. Led him into the room. "And someone find Liam a Healer?"

Liam had started crying as soon as he realized what had happened. Minerva put her arms around him and led him from the room; Tristan followed first, then Lark, then Alexander, last.

"Sennet's in with the humans," Alexander said.

"Perhaps I can help," a new voice said, and Celeste appeared from around a corner. To Tristan, she said, "Jericho insisted I come."

"I'm fine," Tristan said, although he wasn't so sure, now that the adrenalin had started to drain away. "But Malachi--"

Celeste vanished inside the room. After a moment, she reappeared, her face grave and still. "Josiah has asked that you not tell anyone else what happened here. Not yet."

"Okay," Tristan said. "But--"

"Please," Celeste said quietly, and knelt in front of Liam. "Where are you hurt?"

"There's one lieutenant left," Tristan said to Alexander. "And I really need to kill him."

"Then let's find him and do so," Alexander said, and walked with Tristan down the hall.

And they *did* find the last lieutenant, and they *did* kill him, but for some strange reason, it didn't make Tristan feel any better at all.

Tobias

And then Josiah and Tobias were alone. Tobias had sent the others outside, to wait in the hall, because he'd seen the look in Josiah's gaze, and knew, without a doubt, what had crossed his mind at the very moment he realized Malachi was dead.

Josiah had dropped to his knees beside Malachi. Gently touched the wounds he could see. After the silence became unbearable, Tobias asked, "Are you--"

"When Seth and Zechariah died, Lucas offered our Mater the use of Michael's spell to bring them back," Josiah whispered, gently closing Malachi's eyes. "He refused. He said that if he started; if that was an option, then when would it ever end? I never questioned his decision." He paused. "Do you remember when you died?"

"Every single time," Tobias said. "I try not to think about it."

"Then he would know," Josiah said. "I couldn't do it in secret, because he would know." He took Malachi's limp hand. Squeezed it. "I can't imagine life without him."

"Do you know the spell?" Tobias asked, although he already knew the answer to that question.

"I memorized it," Josiah admitted. "Lucas doesn't know."

"Does Gabriel?" Tobias asked.

"No," Josiah said. "He doesn't pry anymore. I told myself I memorized it just in case."

"Well, this is a good indication of 'just in case'," Tobias said.

Celeste had arrived, then; a Healer, although there was nothing she could do at that point. And after Josiah asked her to tell the others not to share the news of Malachi's death, Tobias knew what he had decided to do.

"I know what he meant now," Josiah murmured. "How can *anyone* make that decision?"

"It took a lot of strength to make the decision not to use that spell," Tobias said.

Josiah looked up at him. "I'm not as strong as our Master," he whispered, and what seemed to be only a moment later, Malachi blinked. Drew in a breath. His eyes closed; this time, when he opened them, they were clearer. And wholly cognizant of what Josiah had done.

He opened his mouth to speak. Coughed, instead, then whispered, "I can--I can *see* you, Josiah."

And Josiah had burst into tears.

After that, the liberation of the Morgan household proceeded quite smoothly. With Alexander's help, Tristan deactivated the spell that would have killed the entire household, and when they awoke from their unnatural slumber, they found that their situation in life had changed, quite dramatically. Iris and her mother found Carroll lying where Tristan had seen him, and despite his injuries, had not succumbed to suicide before they found him. Later, he would say that a voice had told him to wait, and he had trusted that voice. Tristan never admitted to anyone but Minerva and Alexander what had happened while he'd been unresponsive; he suspected no one but Malachi would believe him, and that was likely true.

If anyone seemed surprised by Malachi's return from the dead, they hid it well, although Liam wrapped his arms around Malachi's waist and wouldn't let go until Arthur arrived to pry him away.

If Malachi himself seemed a bit off-balance, everyone thought that was because of the attack, nothing more; that part was common knowledge quickly, being the safest truth of what had actually happened in that little room.

And when Eri abandoned her post, panicked because she'd felt something she couldn't explain through the bond, neither Josiah nor Malachi had admitted the truth.

Tobias had to respect their decision to stay silent. Sometimes, silence really *was* the best option.

By dawn, the Healers had largely commandeered the Morgan household. There were so many who needed help--human and vampire--that Sennet called in reinforcements. Carroll and his family were spirited away to her house, however; the rest of the Morgans stayed behind.

Right before dawn, Sennet ordered everyone to their respective homes. Tristan tried to argue with Alexander about this, but in the end, Alexander was the one who volunteered to stay behind to ensure the Healers' safety.

Arthur and Liam returned to the household with Tobias and the others. Much later, Cecilia found Tobias in the library, sitting silently, staring blankly at the books that lined the walls.

"You should be asleep," she said.

Tobias had offered Tristan and Minerva a room for the night, but they'd opted to return home. Lark, ever-hopeful of news of Helena, had stayed behind, just in case. The Hunt had left; Lucas had gone back to his house, and Tobias had no doubt that Uncle Mark and Aunt Amy were asleep by now, along with Erialas and Michael as well.

"I'm not sure I *can* sleep," he admitted. "Not yet, at least." Not until he stopped seeing Malachi's lifeless form every time he closed his eyes.

"Do you want to talk about it?" Cecilia asked, and slowly, Tobias began to tell her what happened. Not about Malachi; that wasn't his story to tell. But everything else? In this case, silence was the *worst* option.

Malachi

And still, much later, Malachi lay awake in his bed, listening to Josiah's breathing on the other side of their shared room. It wasn't that he could see *in* the dark now, with his sight restored; it was more that he could see *through* the dark. And he knew that Josiah wasn't asleep, no matter how he wanted to pretend it was so.

"I didn't say thank you," he whispered into the darkness, and felt Josiah's eyes snap open.

"I didn't do it for your thanks," Josiah finally whispered back. "I did it because I don't want to live in a world without you."

They had been through so much together, from the very beginning when the Wild Hunt had stumbled across Josiah dying in the snow.

"Thank you anyway," Malachi said, although privately, he thought that there should have been a stronger word he could have used. "I'm glad I'm alive, Josiah. Never doubt that."

"But if he--"

Malachi knew his argument already. It was the same one that had haunted him since their Master had made the decision not to bring Seth and Zechariah back to life. "I know," he said, wondering if Gabriel already knew. Apparently, no one had missed him from the bond, but he had to wonder about Eri's feeling, and what that might mean in the future.

"Go to sleep," he finally said, and then, "You can sleep in my bed if you'd like." And he waited until Josiah crawled into bed beside him before closing his eyes and surrendering to sleep.

Gabriel

And then, long past the liberation of the Morgan household, after the events therein were no longer so vivid in their minds, Gabriel found Josiah napping beside the petrified troll in the garden. And he sat down beside his youngest Hound and he leaned back against the moss-covered troll, and he said, very quietly, "I know what you did, Josiah." And then, before Josiah could digest this distressing news, he added, "And I wanted you to know that I know. I felt him die, just like the others. And I hoped against hope that it wasn't true, because he has vanished from the bond before. But when I saw the look on Liam's face and the surprise on Tristan's face--and Tobias still cannot look me in the eye--"

"I'm sorry, my lord," Josiah whispered, his voice thick with tears. "I couldn't--I'm not as strong as you."

Gabriel laughed. "There is no strength in the decision I made. I made that decision for fear I would misuse what Lucas offered. That I would never allow myself to let any of you go, if or when that time came." He paused. "However much of a family we are now, I forced you to become my Hounds. I cannot control both life and death; that power is too easily misused."

Josiah contemplated this in silence. "Did you know--he can see again?" he asked. "And not only with the Protector's gift?"

"I had my suspicions," Gabriel said gravely.

"What now?" Josiah asked.

"Now, we--all of us--continue on with our lives," Gabriel said. "And if you ever have to make a decision like that again, I trust you'll choose wisely."

"Thank you, my--" Josiah stopped. Glanced down at his hands. "Thank you, Gabriel."

Gabriel smiled. It was a start.

You can find ALL our books up on our website at:

http://www.writers-exchange.com

all our fantasy novels:

http://www.writers-exchange.com/category/genres/fantasy/

Jennifer St. Clair grew up in Southern Ohio and spent most of her childhood in the woods around her home. She wrote her first novel when she was thirteen, and hasn't stopped since. She lives with her ball python, Fester, and two cats, Ash and Rowan.

In her spare time, she crochets, makes cloth dolls, collects antiques, books, and vintage clothing, and takes digital photographs with varying degrees of success.

Her *Beth-Hill series* is set in the area in America that contains many supernatural creatures: Wild Hunt, Vampires, Dragons, Faery and more.

It is part of the Universe that her *Jacob Lane Series*, *Karen Montgomery Series* and vampire trilogy, *The Shadow Series* are set in.

Follow all her books on her author page:
http://www.writers-exchange.com/Jennifer-St-Clair/

If you want to read more about other books by this author, they are listed on the following pages...

A Beth-Hill Novel (Stand Alone Novels)

Are creatures of the night and all manner of extramundane beings drawn to certain locations in the natural world? In the Midwestern village of Beth-Hill located in southern Ohio, the population is made up of its fair share of common citizens...and much more than its share of supernatural residents. Take a walk on the wild side in this unusual place where imagination meets reality.

Blood of the Innocents

Ten years ago, Orien, crown prince of the Seleighe, was captured by his mortal enemies, locked in a dungeon and turned into a vampire. Six years into Orien's sentence, the Healer's brother Cullen disobeyed his mistress's orders to kill him and turned him into a vampire instead, thus sealing both their fates for all eternity.

Now both Orien and Cullen are set free. But a secret only Cullen knows lies locked inside his mind, threatening to drive him mad before he can uncover the identity of a traitor--the very elf who betrayed Orien and left them both to die in darkness.

Publisher: http://www.writers-exchange.com/Blood-of-the-Innocents/

Full Moon

Werewolves change into wolves when the moon is full. But Edward's curse only allows him to be *human* when the moon is full.

Alone and despairing, Edward hides himself away from the world. He's scraped out a meager existence for himself for almost a century in the forest he's grown to love and call home. But in the depths of a terrible winter, he stumbles across clues from the life his mother left behind in Faerie. The truth may give him the answers he needs about the source of his birthright... and the curse that holds him captive.

Publisher: http://www.writers-exchange.com/Full-Moon/

A Beth-Hill Novel: Jacob Lane Series

Are creatures of the night and all manner of extramundane beings drawn to certain locations in the natural world? In the Midwestern village of Beth-Hill located in southern Ohio, the population is made up of its fair share of common citizens...and much more than its share of supernatural residents.

Jacob Lane is a ten-year-old girl who's spent her life unaware of her magical heritage. After being sent to Darkbrook, a school of magic, supernatural mysteries seem to spring to life all around her and her new friends.

Book 1: The Tenth Ghost

After Jacob Lane's parents mysteriously vanish, she's sent to Darkbrook, the only school of magic in the United States. While there, she and her new friends stumble upon a series of mysterious deaths in the nine ghosts that haunt the halls of Darkbrook. These ghosts were students who died at the school over the past hundred years. Will Jacob become the tenth ghost, or can she stop a witch's reign of terror?

Publisher: http://www.writers-exchange.com/The-Tenth-Ghost/

Book 2: The Ninth Guest

When Jacob's friend Ophelia's family decides to open up their castle for guests, amateur paranormal sleuth Jacob Lane is invited to join in on the fun. "Spend the night in a vampire's castle and live to tell the tale!" is supposed to be a fundraiser to help Ophelia's family pay the bills. Heating a castle costs quite a bit, after all. But, after the truth of an old secret is uncovered, what began as an innocent business venture soon turns deadly when vampire hunters get involved.

For years, the vampire hunters have had only one goal: To destroy all vampires. With the help of a new friend, Jacob and Ophelia must work together to save the entire VonBriggle family from extinction.

Publisher: http://www.writers-exchange.com/The-Ninth-Guest/

Book 3: The Eighth Room

For two hundred years, the Selkies have kept themselves separate from those who live on land. But now the Selkies need allies or they'll be crushed by their ancient enemies, the Finfolk.

Jacob and Ophelia, students at the only school of magic in the United States, uncover a mystery that dates back to Darkbrook's beginnings. While helping clean out old storage rooms for classroom expansion, they find something that might save the Selkies from extinction. With the help of the youngest member of the Wild Hunt who are no longer so wild or terrifying, they must foil the Finfolk who desire the Selkie's destruction...or die trying.

Publisher: http://www.writers-exchange.com/The-Eighth-Room/

Book 4: The Seventh Secret

After a picture of Niklas, the dragons' liaison to the only school of magic in the United States, shows up in too many newspapers to count, Darkbrook is forced to go on the defensive. The secret of Darkbrook's existence has been discovered. But there are more than dragonhunters in the forest, and, as Jacob Lane, supernatural sleuth and student at Darkbrook, learns how to use her newly discovered talent of healing, she helps to right an old wrong and must battle a teenaged wizard intent on proving--once and for all--that magic is real.

Publisher: http://www.writers-exchange.com/The-Seventh-Secret/

Book 5: The Sixth Stone

Jacob Lane, supernatural sleuth, and Danny, her werewolf friend, stumble across an alternate world where the Wild Hunt was never bound, and Darkbrook, the school of magic they attend, was abandoned a hundred years ago.

But when the Hounds of the Hunt wish to surrender, the two students are swept up in a whirlwind of heartbreak, betrayal, and the discovery of a lost treasure.

Publisher: http://www.writers-exchange.com/The-Sixth-Stone/

A Beth-Hill Novella: Karen Montgomery Series

Are creatures of the night and all manner of extramundane beings drawn to certain locations in the natural world? In the Midwestern village of Beth-Hill located in southern Ohio, the population is made up of its fair share of common citizens...and much more than its share of supernatural residents. Take a walk on the wild side in this unusual place where imagination meets reality.

Karen Montgomery was an ordinary woman until she stumbled into the extraordinary... A bargain with elves worth its weight in gold. A plague of sinister ladybugs. Rogue vampire hunters, including one who tries to turn over a new leaf--with disastrous consequences. A ghostly huntsmen of the Wild Hunt wishing for redemption. Karen's life will never be the same again.

Book 1: Budget Cuts

Karen Montgomery is used to taking care of the unpleasant jobs no one else wants to deal with. When a shortage of funds forces her to fire fifteen employees from the library, she isn't happy, but the nasty task has to be done and she is, after all, the boss. But Karen finds finishing her task impossible when she can't seem to track down Ivy Bedinghaus, a night clerk she's never actually met. Once she finally does confront Ivy, she's thrust into a centuries-old conflict that makes her previous troubles radically pale in comparison.

Publisher: http: //www.writers-exchange.com/Budget-Cuts/

Book 2: The Secret of Redemption

Karen Montgomery, librarian, finds herself embroiled in another otherworldly adventure...

A member of the Wild Hunt--ghostly myths that aren't so ghostly (or myth-like) anymore--needs help in reconciling who he once was in life and who he is now.

A little girl has gone missing. And the one most likely responsible for her disappearance is the one Karen must prove innocent.

Publisher: http: //www.writers-exchange.com/The-Secret-of-Redemption/

Book 3: Ladybug, Ladybug

An innocent attempt to rid the library of a plague of ladybugs turns sinister when a rogue vampire hunter gets the contract for pest control.

Ivy Bedinghaus, who works for Karen as a night clerk--along with all the vampires in Beth-Hill--are in danger, and their only hope for survival is with the help of Karen, a member of the Wild Hunt, and Russell Moore, a reformed vampire hunter.

Publisher: http://www.writers-exchange.com/Ladybug-Ladybug/

Book 4: Detour

One wrong turn sends Karen down a road that shouldn't exist, to the site of an old accident and an even older mystery. With reformed vampire hunter Russell Moore's help, Karen finds the key to the mystery. But Russ keeps his own secrets...some of which are deadly.

When old friends from Russ' past come to call, Karen realizes his secrets might just mean his doom. After a terrible incident three years ago, before Karen met him, Russ wants only to live the rest of his life quietly in Beth-Hill. But his secret might not allow him the new lease on life Russ longs for.

Publisher: http://www.writers-exchange.com/Detour/

Companion Story: Russ' Story: Capture

Long before Russell Moore ever met supernatural sleuth Karen Montgomery or set foot in Beth-Hill, he was a vampire hunter, possibly the best vampire hunter of all. He brought down whole nests of vampires, caring little about the consequences of his actions. Anyone who lived with or helped the vampires became enemies to be slaughtered.

So what kind of an idiot would capture a ruthless vampire hunter without a conscience and try to reform him?

Ethan Walker was that idiot. Wanting to protect his family, Ethan set out to prove to Russ that vampires weren't all evil, soulless creatures. If Russ would allow himself to witness their lives, see their humanity, surely he and other vampire hunters like him would let them live in peace. *Surely?*

Publisher: http://www.writers-exchange.com/Capture/

Secrets When in Shadow Lie

Twelve years ago, Ryan Grey was cursed by a witch to hide a secret. He's lived with the curse of being unable to die permanently, and, over the years he's slowly losing the memory of his past until almost nothing remains.

But now, after a chance meeting with an elf named Zipporah, he discovers the key to unlocking the secret and breaking the curse once and for all...if he can survive the breaking.
Publisher: http: //www.writers-exchange.com/Secrets-When-in-Shadow-Lie/

The Dead Who Do Not Sleep

Will Spark only wants a good night's sleep after a night of drinking. Instead, two thugs bang on his door, demanding answers to questions he can't understand. And then they killed him...
Publisher: http: //www.writers-exchange.com/The-Dead-Who-Do-Not-Sleep/

A Beth-Hill Novel: The Abby Duncan Series

Are creatures of the night and all manner of extramundane beings drawn to certain locations in the natural world? In the Midwestern village of Beth-Hill located in southern Ohio, the population is made up of its fair share of common citizens...and much more than its share of supernatural residents. Take a walk on the wild side in this unusual place where imagination meets reality.

Situated in Beth-Hill, where imagination meets reality, is The Rose Emporium, owned by elderly and not-a-little-odd Rose Duncan. The large Victorian house smackdab in the middle of nowhere is a cross between a pawn shop and an antique store that caters to supernatural creatures needing to barter. Rose's twenty-something niece, Abby Duncan, discovers that the world isn't made up of just run-of-the-mill, ordinary humans but an entire spectrum of unusual beings. With her preconceptions about what's normal and what's not turned upside-down, Abby is in for a whole lot of startling truths, mysteries--about herself and the people and places around her--and danger.

Novella 1: By Any Other Name

Woodturner Abby Duncan decides to sell her spindles at a local Renaissance Festival with only some success. After all, no one really spins their own yarn anymore, do they? While there, she discovers that one of her newfound friends is not what he appears--and his secret is about to get him killed!

Publisher: http://www.writers-exchange.com/By-Any-Other-Name/

Book 2: The Uncrowned Queen

Abby Duncan's elderly Aunt Rose has always been a bit odd. And now she's off on a mysterious trip, leaving Abby behind to run the Rose Emporium, an unusual sort of antique shop. Such an extraordinary store would have been a perfect place for Seth and the others, her friends from the Renaissance Festival, to take a break from traveling between Faires. But when tragedy strikes and Abby and the others discover the true nature of the Rose Emporium, they'll have to travel into Faerie itself before their tightknit group is whole again.

Abby doesn't know much about her family history, but she's about to find out the truth...whether she likes it or not.
Publisher: http: //www.writers-exchange.com/The-Uncrowned-Queen/

A Beth-Hill Novel: The Shadows Trilogy

Are creatures of the night and all manner of extramundane beings drawn to certain locations in the natural world? In the Midwestern village of Beth-Hill located in southern Ohio, the population is made up of its fair share of common citizens...and much more than its share of supernatural residents. Take a walk on the wild side in this unusual place where imagination meets reality.

A Dreamer dreams the future when the past is not yet laid to rest. Ten years ago, a plague swept across the Seven Kingdoms. Ten years ago, the Queen of Iomar's son was exiled and named the author of the magical plague. Now, in the present, Terrin works to complete his ultimate goal: Control of the Seven Kingdoms using his son's power to supplement his own. But his attempt at dominion meets resistance and the fate of the world rests in the unlikely hands of an exiled prince, a Dreamer, and a vampire...

Book 1: The Prince of Shadows

When Alban's father Terrin appeared at the castle door with a vampire in tow and apologies on his lips, Alban fell under his spell just like everyone else and welcomed him home. But Terrin didn't return to live quietly in his brother's kingdom. He had other plans and, with Alban's untrained powers at his disposal, he begins his ruthless plan to destroy the Seven Kingdoms and rule them all, beginning with his brother's death.

Terrin engineers events to cast the blame on his nephew, Teluride, intending to see the boy executed for his father's murder. But there are those who would thwart Terrin in his mad plan for power, and Alban forms an unlikely alliance with Skade, the reclusive Queen of Iomar, and Terrin's slave, a young vampire with no memory of his name or origins.

Although the future looks grim, Alban and the vampire attempt to stop Terrin...and they almost succeed.

A darker history lies at the heart of Terrin's treachery, and only Skade knows the true reason why Terrin would murder his own brother and attempt to destroy both Alban and the vampire to achieve his goals. The Ghost who resides in Skade's mirror--her servant and thrall--holds one of the keys to Terrin's madness. Unfortunately, more than one person wishes for the past to remain the past and the future to hold no shadows of what might have been...

Publisher: http: //www.writers-exchange.com/The-Prince-of-Shadows/

Book 2: Lost In Shadows

Events set in motion ten years ago come to a head as Skade, the reclusive Queen of Iomar, and Nicodemus, who is imprisoned by Skade, struggle to free Alban and the vampire from Terrin's grasp. Old secrets come to light when Skade's exiled son is forced to face his past--or die trying to redeem himself once and for all. Can the crimes of the past truly be forgiven? Only time will tell...and time is running out.

Publisher: http: //www.writers-exchange.com/Lost-In-Shadows/

Book 3: Bound In Shadows

With his power crushed, brother to the king and father to Alban, Terrin is forced to take drastic measures to regain his sons after they are freed and harness the power they possess. But he has an ally inside the healer's house where they are recovering who works to further his plans. The Queen of Iomar, Skade's son, courts redemption to try to save his mother's life, and the vampire who no longer remembers his own name dreams a dream that might save them all...or damn them if success is thwarted.

Publisher: http: //www.writers-exchange.com/Bound-In-Shadows/

A Beth-Hill Novel: Wild Hunt Series

Are creatures of the night and all manner of extramundane beings drawn to certain locations in the natural world? In the Midwestern village of Beth-Hill located in southern Ohio, the population is made up of its fair share of common citizens...and much more than its share of supernatural residents. Take a walk on the wild side in this unusual place where imagination meets reality.

The Wild Hunt roamed the forest outside of Beth-Hill until the Council bound them for a hundred years. Nevertheless, a century of existence has made an indelible mark not easily forgotten for these ghostly myths that are no longer so ghostly or myth-like...

Book 1: Heart's Desire

The Wild Hunt roamed the forest outside of Beth-Hill until the Council bound them for a hundred years--a lifetime for a human but only a passing thought to one such as Gabriel, Master of the Wild Hunt. As the Council's binding draws to a close, old enemies reappear to ensure that the Wild Hunt is bound once more--to a creature much worse than the Council has been.

Publisher: http://www.writers-exchange.com/Hearts-Desire/

Book 2: Fire and Water

As a young vampire, Erialas Morgan brought his mother back to life with a spell that shouldn't exist, shouldn't have worked...perhaps shouldn't have been performed at all. Desperation and love are his only excuses for doing the unthinkable.

There are others who wish to use that same spell for their own gain--and to destroy the Wild Hunt once and for all. Caught in the middle of a war between the Morgan clan of vampires and their human kin, Erialas turns to the Hunt for help. But even Gabriel, the Master of the Wild Hunt, may not be able to stop the tide of death and destruction once it turns.

Publisher: http://www.writers-exchange.com/Fire-and-Water/

Book 3: The Lost

Almost sixty years ago, Darkbrook, the only school of magic in the United States, opened its doors to students of decidedly different natures, sending out letters of invitation to the elves, the dragons, and the vampires. The three who responded to the invitation banded together despite their differences but vanished only weeks later along with an entire classroom full of students and their teacher after a field trip gone horribly wrong.

The Wild Hunt has healed and the Hounds have grown closer together, keeping Darkbrook's forest safe and secure for those who live there. Malachi, one of the eldest members of the Wild Hunt, has adapted to Josiah's spell to help him see, but when a demon boy trapped in the body of a human body for sixty years inside the school disrupts the newfound calm, the Hunt--and those they protect--are thrust into a struggle that should have ended long ago when a vampire, an elf, and a dragon vanished into the Mists.

Publisher: http: //www.writers-exchange.com/The-Lost/

Book 4: A Glint of Silver

Jericho is a vampire who wants is to live away from the Richmond household of vampires led by his ruthless father Connor. When Jericho tries to escape, Connor punishes him and leaves him to die. Tristan is determined to be the one to bring Jericho back, but he can't see him suffer for wanting a normal life. As long as Connor lives, Jericho will never be safe or free. As long as Connor *lives...*

Publisher: http: //www.writers-exchange.com/A-Glint-of-Silver/

Book 5: All That Glitters

As a member of the cruel Morgan Household of vampires, twelve-year-old Arthur Morgan has been abused all his life.

Maya, a water fairy, shows him just how horrible and twisted the household he's grown up is. With her help, and the unexpected help of an adult vampire, Arthur attempts to escape.

Can he become something more than what his father has decreed?

Publisher: http: //www.writers-exchange.com/All-That-Glitters/

The Chelsea Chronicles

Normally a quiet, serene place, Chelsea Kingdom seems like the perfect location for a centuries' old vampire to blend in and live a normal life, even escape hunters and an angry mob. Unfortunately, his timing couldn't be worse...

Book 1: So You Want to be a Vampire

Chelsea Kingdom is usually a pretty quiet place but recent murders--committed by a vampire--upset the calm. Newcomer to town, Vlad Dhalgren wants only to blend in and live a normal life. He quickly learns that isn't possible, given that other vampires have been hiding in the shadows around the castle--in plain sight--for years.

Despite her lineage, Anna Everett, the crown princess of the Kingdom of Chelsea, isn't a wizard like her father, which means she will never be Queen. She has only one friend, Valerian Moreton--Val--who has secrets he's never shared that could get him *and* Anna killed...

Publisher: http://www.writers-exchange.com/So-You-Want-to-be-a-Vampire/

Book 2: Transformation

As Anna, crown princess of Chelsea, adjusts to life as a vampire after recent events, Vlad plans for a future he has no real hope to seeing come to pass due to injuries sustained while attempting to save Anna's life. But, as life goes on for Anna and her friend Valerian "Val" Moreton, it changes for others--some of whom are not quite what they seem...

Publisher: http://www.writers-exchange.com/Transformation/

You can find ALL our books up on our website at:

http://www.writers-exchange.com

all our fantasy novels:

http://www.writers-exchange.com/category/genres/fantasy/

www.ingramcontent.com/pod-product-compliance
Ingram Content Group UK Ltd.
Pitfield, Milton Keynes, MK11 3LW, UK
UKHW021933200726
13853UKWH00010B/503